Stomping Moon Dust

Vaishali Hamlai holds a master's in human resource management and is dedicated to making reading accessible and relatable. Through her writing, she explores evolving societal norms, offering nuanced insights while dissecting assumptions and perspectives. As a columnist for *Beyond Words*, her voice resonates with readers eager for thoughtful analysis.

Vaishali's literary journey began with *Rhea@Suraksha*, a story rooted in her personal experiences, followed by *Down Under*, which addresses racism from a fresh perspective. Her other works, including *Mind Trap*, *Through the Open Window*, and *Trust Me, I Won't Leave*, explore themes of accountability, mental resilience and love's transformative power.

Stomping Moon Dust is her sixth novel.

Also by Vaishali Hamlai

Through the Open Window
Trust Me, I Won't Leave

Stomping Moon Dust

Vaishali Hamlai

Published by
Rupa Publications India Pvt. Ltd 2025
7/16, Ansari Road, Daryaganj
New Delhi 110002

Sales centres:
Bengaluru Chennai
Hyderabad Jaipur Kathmandu
Kolkata Mumbai Prayagraj

Copyright © Vaishali Hamlai 2025

This is a work of fiction. Names, characters, places and incidents
are either the product of the author's imagination or are used fictitiously,
and any resemblance to any actual person, living or dead, events
or locales is entirely coincidental.

All rights reserved.
No part of this publication may be reproduced, transmitted
or stored in a retrieval system, in any form or by any means,
electronic, mechanical, photocopying, recording or otherwise,
without the prior permission of the publisher.

P-ISBN: 978-93-6156-398-0
E-ISBN: 978-93-6156-925-8

First impression 2025

10 9 8 7 6 5 4 3 2 1

The moral right of the author has been asserted.

Printed in India

This book is sold subject to the condition that it shall not,
by way of trade or otherwise, be lent, resold, hired out, or otherwise
circulated, without the publisher's prior consent, in any form of
binding or cover other than that in which it is published.

Trigger warnings: Self-harm, drug abuse

★

PROLOGUE

Mumbai, the enchanting city of dreams, pulsates with an intensity that defies description. It is where the essence of life intertwines seamlessly with faith, belief, love, benevolence, triumph, ecstasy, mirth and desire. Yet, in the same breath, it harbours shades of sadness, viciousness, hatred, regret, darkness, loathing, prejudice and delusion.

This sprawling metropolis stands as a testament to the spirit of migration, a tapestry woven from the threads of countless souls who have journeyed from distant lands and converged here—from the misty hills of Shillong to the majestic mountains and valleys of Kashmir, from Bihar to Uttar Pradesh, and from Odisha to the heartlands of Tamil Nadu. Mumbai is a place where some have ascended the ladder of success, their names etched in the annals of fame, while others have found themselves on the fringes of fortune's favour. For the latter—labourers, bar attendants, delivery agents or even the disillusioned denizens of the night—the slums of Dharavi or Kuala Bandar provide a fragile refuge. These slums, cobbled with makeshift shanties, cling to the city's streets like tattered sentinels, vulnerable to the tempestuous storms and rains that lash Mumbai several times a year, turning it into a quagmire of stagnant, germ-infested water. Within these cramped spaces, with rooms barely measuring 20 feet by 10 feet, 15 migrants huddle together, the scarce water supply and poor sanitation facilities perpetuating their hardship. The very air hangs heavy with the stench of filth and the dawn hours witness long queues as people await their turn for the most basic morning ablutions. It is a city where even the existence of the middle class can mutate into a harrowing nightmare.

Every corner of this metropolis breathes its distinct story. Open drains wind through the labyrinthine alleys, mingling with the high weeds, ashes and piles of discarded refuse. Cellars lie submerged beneath black, fetid waters, while the walls of houses, strangers to the touch of whitewash or a scrubbing brush, exude a dampness that permeates the very fabric of their being. The denizens of these forgotten places, estranged from soap and water for months on end, loiter and slumber on street corners, evading the burden of work. Some find solace in doorways while others squat on steps, their words a vile tapestry of foul epithets hurled at unsuspecting passers-by. These foul streets and stinking alleys, their essence reeking of decay, fill the senses, embodying the essence of Mumbai's slums.

Now, here I stand on the beach, surrounded by a teeming mass of humanity, where every soul seems in a constant state of restless motion, scurrying like frenzied flies. Exhausted and gasping for air, I strive to regain my composure. I edge towards the water in a determined attempt to distance myself from the clamour that envelops me. Yet, the distance stretches farther than anticipated, and each step forward feels like a weight threatening to shackle me to the sand below. My feet sink into the soft grains, compelling me to surrender to their embrace, but my mind yearns to push forward, to seek out other human beings. I crave genuine connection, to converse with those who can understand, empathize and extend their compassion without judgement.

Words linger unspoken, emotions suppressed since childhood, imprisoned within the confines of my being. They claw at my insides, desperate for release, like a butterfly yearning to break free from its cocoon. For years, I have conversed with myself, but now, I ache for the comfort of a tangible dialogue—a conversation about myself, about others, about my loved ones and not mere musings about Mumbai's weather, the impending monsoons or the fate of the government.

As I draw nearer to the sea, the waves roar with an unrivalled intensity, the sound crashing into my ears. Perhaps I am screaming or gasping for breath, but my sounds are drowned out by the thunderous chorus of the sea. A glimpse of the beach materializes through the haze, the wet sand bearing an enigmatic name scribbled upon it. It is both familiar and elusive, its meaning hovering just beyond my grasp. The language feels foreign to my senses. The haze thickens, isolating me in my confusion, while the crowd on this daunting beach appears composed, their nonchalance a stark contrast to my faltering steps.

With trepidation, I glance down at myself; my clothes cling to my scrawny frame, the fabric worn and tattered by time. My once vibrant sari now bears a tear near the chest, as if someone had tried to forcibly snatch the cloth away. Wrinkles etched upon my skin reveal the passage of time and hardships endured—my neck sagging like that of a woman far beyond my years. My trembling hands too betray the harshness of life, their craggy skin adorned with patches of brown and needle marks etched upon my wrist.

Desperate for refuge, I attempt to call out, to seek solace within the throng of people surrounding me. But my voice, it seems, has deserted me, leaving me silent and unheard. My gaze falls upon a group of fishermen, their wares on display on the beach. As I peer into the eyes of the fish, a profound fear reflects back at me—an unspoken understanding that their fate lies in the hands of those who would consume them, their lives reduced to a mere commodity, destined to be roasted and served on dinner plates.

Driven by an unseen force, I press on towards the waves, irresistibly drawn by their call. And finally, the name scribbled upon the shifting sands becomes clear, imprinting itself upon my heart. This name, inscribed in the transient embrace of loose grains, holds the power to define my entire world.

'SHIVA.'

My cherished deity in the divine pantheon of Hindu mythology, Shiva embodies the essence of both creation and destruction. He stands alongside Brahma and Vishnu as part of the sacred trinity, a god of immeasurable significance. This divine entity assumes the role of our guardian, personifying benevolence while simultaneously being the ultimate creator and destroyer of the Universe.

He is the beloved spouse of Parvati and the proud father of Lord Ganesha, whose annual worship captivates Mumbai, bringing the bustling city to a halt.

A solitary tear descends from my eye with the gentleness of a first raindrop, as if it had patiently waited to fall from my weary gaze. My body throbs with agony; every fibre, every inch feels battered and torn. It is as though my very flesh has been stripped away, leaving me a mere skeletal figure. I nestle my aching feet within the curved confines of the letter 'S' and find solace in its embrace. The initial pangs of guilt give way to a newfound sense of security and tranquillity that begins to seep into my veins. With each repetition of his name, I exhale, releasing the burdens that have weighed on me for so long. Once, twice, thrice and onward, I chant his sacred name. The azure sea stretches before me, the darkness of heavy clouds scattering into nothingness. It is within this name that I find solace, more profoundly than ever before.

★

The waves now ebb; she is lost in a trance. Perhaps the pain has dulled her senses, disappearing as if by magic. She is in deep slumber, the waves and the winds cocooning her like blankets. She lies there, still and alone, while others go about, busy with their lives, salvaging the pleasures in their pristine forms. The words scribbled on the sand rapidly fade away, swept away by winds and waves. 'Shiva' disappears, and the sand beneath her is now a blank canvas.

How ephemeral objects are! How transient are our existences! Our lives constantly turn new pages, leaving us to brood over memories—dark memories ensconced deep inside, resurfacing to trouble us at the most awkward moments. Nightmares overshadow sweet memories, casting long shadows over fleeting joys.

Part I

1

The sun advanced gracefully through the hours, distancing itself from the lingering shadows of the night. Though the sun and the moon seem fated never to unite, they rendezvous twice daily, akin to soulmates burdened by predetermined sorrows.

The sun and the moon bestowed upon the wheel of time the precious gift of division—a fortunate offering. Yet they themselves became martyrs to time's whims. Occasionally, when the heavens open, they weep at their ill fate. Sometimes they voice their discontent through resounding thunderstorms; other times, they radiate brilliance. Nevertheless, the world relies on them to bring the sanctity and tranquillity of day and night. They exist for those fleeting moments of encounter when their paths intersect. Who are we to lament the sun's and the moon's smiles as they rise and set!

Down by the sea, she visualized herself, all of 15 years and wearing a pink frock. Her long, thick dark brown hair was neatly tied in two plaits. With every movement, her hair caught the light and twirled gracefully alongside her.

She was writing something on the sand, erasing it and then rewriting. After a few attempts, she was finally satisfied with the outcome and stood to look at it.

It once again read 'Shiv'.

She reigned upon the ocean's bed, a throne of power, awaiting the emergence of mermaids from the depths of the majestic azure sea. Their ethereal presence resonated with rainbows, adorned in shimmering scales, their tails defying mortal limitations. The knowledge of their existence had been gleaned from ancient times, but for her, it transcended words. She wielded the faith of miracles, firm in her belief that unwavering conviction could bring forth wonders. At the mere age of 15 she possessed an intellect beyond her years, intoxicated by the enchantment that surrounded her.

While others succumbed to doubt and scepticism, she stood apart, a beacon of unwavering faith. Her inner flame blazed fiercely, impervious to the whims of fate. She was destined to radiate brilliance, undeterred by the gusts of adversity. Her fire burned wildly, an unquenchable force that none could extinguish. It resided deep within her core, unyielding and inviolable. A faint voice beckoned, calling her name from a far-off realm, an echo of her extraordinary destiny.

'Maya!' she heard again, the voice now closer.

She looked around—the voice was familiar and it struck her like an epiphany—it was her brother. She clambered up abruptly, not forgetting to erase the name she had scribbled with so much care. She could hear her Bhai closer now, but she didn't respond. Deciding to be mischievous, she ran towards the palm tree to hide behind it.

Her Bhai was panting by the time he reached the shore. Squinting his eyes against the sun, he searched for her in vain. The frustrated look on his face expressed his worry and exasperation, but Maya did not budge. She stood hiding behind the palm tree, lips shut tightly, trying her best not to giggle out loud in case Bhai heard her. But her frilly frock gave her away. He spotted her and tiptoed from behind to scare her.

Bhai had protected her for 15 years and been an inspiration in her life. She swore by her brother. If Bhai said it was night, then it was night for her, notwithstanding the bright sun rays flashing from the azure blue sky. She had always trusted him blindly.

Her mind wandered off to another day in her life as a child, when she had stolen a gold necklace from her careless aunt's ornament box and pawned it to the jeweller a few kilometres away.

She hadn't known that the jeweller was close to her uncle, that they were fast friends. She was just an innocent little girl, hardly 10 years old. The grim look on her uncle's face when he entered their home that evening had been terrifying. The jeweller had guessed whose ornaments they were and informed him.

After a round of scolding, she knew the thrashings were about to begin, and they would be brutal. Her uncle was a cruel man, and he would beat her black and blue. Bhai had overheard him and rushed in. 'It is me who asked her to do this. Here is your money.' He had searched her only hideout, which he was aware of, found the cash intact, and handed it over.

The events of that night, even after so many years, sent shivers down her spine. Bhai had been lucky to come out alive.

There was just one catch.

Bhai hated Shiv.

He didn't want to startle her, so he placed his hands gently on her shoulders from behind. But he still got kicked for scaring her. After all, she had once done the same to him. She hurtled ahead as if she had spied a ghost. She faked a groan, hoping to gain his sympathy, but he was smarter. He loved her more than he loved himself, cared for her more than he cared for himself. Their love was mutual. For her, Bhai was the ultimate source of happiness.

She giggled a little, like an irrepressible bubble of joy. Nothing around her was dull; she radiated happiness to everyone around her. And she was the apple of his eye. He wouldn't let an ounce of pain trouble her. A tear from her eye would pierce him more sharply than a nail. He protected her like a flower, untouched and shielded from the cruel world. It would be apt to say that he was overly protective of her. His sharp intuition helped him pre-empt any potential harm to her, like the day she had stolen the jewellery. He ensured to keep her far away from danger.

But this was also a straightforward recipe for disaster. When Bhai wasn't around, she suffered because she was not independent enough to stave off malevolence from horrid persons, unprepared for the cruel world around her.

Once, they had been playing hide-and-seek in the fields near their house, which held countless childhood memories; the fields had witnessed them grow up. As always, Bhai was the last to be caught. He ran away from the pursuer, moving swiftly at the speed of a sprinter and jumping over a fence. However, he landed awkwardly on the uneven surface, tripping and falling headlong on to a sharp rock. He lay still for a while, and the other children stood petrified, gaping with terrified eyes as they peered over the fence.

After a few moments, Bhai scrambled up and made a face, groaning in pain. His face was splattered with blood, which streamed like the currents of a turbulent river, oozing from every gash. Maya screamed and dashed to their mother, yelling and crying. Maa immediately rushed outside; she could sense that something terrible had happened. Maya clutched her mother but could not utter a word to describe what had happened. Maa also did not wait to find out and they ran as fast as their legs could carry them to reach Bhai.

Maa's initial reaction was to scream, but she immediately composed herself. She did not wish to display panic in front of either Akaash or Maya. She took him by his arm and rushed him to the doctor. Bhai's injury was grave, causing excruciating pain that would have made anyone cry out in agony. However, Akaash possessed extraordinary resilience and managed to maintain his composure. It was a testament to his inner strength and the realization that revealing his suffering would only amplify the distress of his loved ones. He shut his eyes tightly, concealing his anguish, silently bearing the burden of protecting those around him. In that pivotal moment, his unwavering resolve and selflessness shone through, leaving an indelible impression on all who witnessed his remarkable feat of endurance.

Maa instructed Maya to keep Bhai away from mirrors for the next few days. His face was badly bruised, but his eyes and reflexes remained intact. This must have been one of the most painful days for the family, Maa's anguish apparent and unbearable.

★

Their town was breathtaking, nestled amid the snow-clad peaks of the Kumaon mountain range, adorned with blooming flowers and lush green meadows where tourists enjoyed horse riding. It was also a garrison town steeped in tales of bravery, serving as the headquarters of the Kumaon Regiment.

The legendary palace in Kumaon was mysterious and enchanting, famous for its grand architecture and intricate carvings. Built by a queen mesmerized by the region's beauty, the palace was the centre of power and conflict, hosting royal celebrations in its grand halls and surrounded by exotic gardens. It also functioned as a spiritual centre for seekers of enlightenment. Although the palace no longer stands, its ruins whisper the region's rich heritage, inspiring awe among visitors.

Ranikhet was a slice of heaven for its inhabitants. While the tourist season brought its share of stress, it remained peaceful compared to nearby hill stations like Nainital and Mussoorie. The winters were harsh, yet the beauty of the mountains and valleys—sometimes shrouded in mist, sometimes clear—captivated all. The mountains seemed alive, guarding their secrets, wary of human greed. Unlike other tourist spots, Ranikhet remained relatively untouched, which the locals appreciated, though some wondered why tourism hadn't flourished.

Despite nearby attractions like the Dunagiri Hills and Mahavatar Babaji's cave, tourists rarely stayed overnight, preferring to visit from Nainital or Mukteshwar and return by evening. While some believed that more publicity was needed, others were content without the influx of visitors. The locals led a simple, non-consumerist life, treasuring their culture and natural beauty over the luxuries of modern civilization.

However, a few families, influenced by relatives in the plains, wanted to promote tourism to bring more wealth and modern amenities. They lobbied the government for support, but Ranikhet's unpredictable weather made it a risky holiday destination. For many, this kept their peaceful existence intact, while others envied the prosperity enjoyed by the neighbouring hill stations.

Ranikhet did have interaction with city-dwellers, as some built houses to escape the summer heat of cities like Delhi. These respectful visitors blended well with the locals, creating a small tourist economy that provided livelihoods, such as caddying at the local golf course. Additionally, boarding schools in the area also brought wealthier families, but their students mostly stayed within their own exclusive circle.

For the locals, life in Ranikhet was simple and fulfilling, far removed from the luxuries of urban existence, untouched by the glamour of city life.

★

Maya always had several girls hovering around, dancing to her tune but spitting venom behind her back. They were envious of her natural charisma and ability to cast a spell on everyone she interacted with, her intelligence, precociousness, athletic prowess and her unconventional charm and beauty, which was untouched. Nonetheless, they flocked around her not because they were in awe of her talents but because of her brother.

There were girls in the village who would be only too happy to risk their married lives to rest in his arms just once, to feel the softness of his tongue. He could mesmerize and hypnotize girls, drawing them towards him like a magnet. Maya was oblivious to this; she was naïve and believed her friends were there for her sake. Bhai was aware that his sister was still too young to see through the ulterior motives that guided the other girls—they used her as a conduit to him.

Several cloth swings hung from the branches of the neem tree, the green leaves of which had yellowed around the edges with time. The magnanimous tree had a character of its own; it was like the adult protecting the young girls from the cruelty of the sun and the harshness of the rain. Maya and her friends loved to swing and sing local songs they had heard their mothers crooning to them as children, singing and humming alongside the birds and the bees. The sun, glowing with a warm saffron hue—the colour of sacrifice—began its descent below the horizon as the moon rose, ready to take on the night shift. Golden rays danced among the retreating clouds, playing one final game of hide-and-seek before bidding them goodnight. Maya waited all day to witness the sun's golden rays fall on the tree and peep through the branches. She loved to view the works of art that the shadows on the ground created. It amazed her how creative Mother Nature could be even though she was petrified of its ferocity during fierce rainstorms.

They hopscotched towards their house as the sun set on the western horizon beyond the snow-clad mountains and the birds returned to their nests, their hunger evident through their restless wings. Maya darted through the house after her usual evening games as if on roller skates. The smell of the food made her hungrier. But her mother refused to serve her until she had cleaned up.

Maa was, as usual, to be found in the tiniest room of the house—the kitchen. Maya always wondered why kitchens were the smallest spaces in every home, especially when the woman of the house, the only one who spent time there, devoted the maximum time of her life in it. According to Maya, it would make sense to have a large kitchen; it should be the most significant section of the house as it was where the food was cooked, sacred to our bodies and souls. Unfortunately, it was always the smallest area after the bathroom.

The kitchen held a magical aura for Maya since her childhood; she had always wished to help her mother cook some items but was always discouraged. 'Now is the time to play and study, not to cook. Your entire life lies ahead for cooking and preparing food,' her mother would say.

Maya was often reminded of her first experience inside the kitchen, the first day she could finally venture inside and supplement her mother's efforts. It was a rainy day; the monsoon had just commenced, but it was not raining that heavily. Her mother had turned introspective, not that it was a novelty—it happened often. She would never scream at them, but retreat into her cocoon those days. Her moods were inscrutable, lying beneath layers and layers of the subconscious.

It was on these days that Maya would insist on cooking. It would start with breakfast; after all, making *puris* and a light *sabzi* was the easiest. Like other days, Maa was gently irritated when Maya insisted she be allowed to prepare breakfast. Maya hated to cause irritation or pain to Maa; she would withdraw immediately and sit quietly outside their house, beneath the tree, indulging in poetic imagination. But that day, the unimaginable happened; she heard her mother calling out after her.

'Today, for the first time, I will allow you to try your hands; you can make the rice. Come after an hour, okay?'

They were silent during breakfast; during the days when her mother turned contemplative, both Bhai and Maya also felt miserable and, as if to commiserate with her, indulged in no banter. They had learnt to value her feelings over time.

After breakfast, Maa called her in. The cooking pot was already placed on the fire, and a container of rice lay on the floor beside it. Maya's hands were unsteady; she was still a kid. Some of the rice spilled beside the pot. Maya was scared stiff and dared not look at her mother directly. She was disappointed; every morsel of rice counted in their household. But Maa did not shout or scold.

Instead, she hurriedly pushed the fallen bits away with her foot because it could be dangerous if they fell into the fire. A gentle smile followed.

Then, who should appear at the kitchen door but Bhai! Why did he have to? Maya felt like lunging at him. In two minds, he added insult to injury by laughing raucously—the boisterous laughter he was famous for. Maa too joined in, their boisterous laughter echoing off the distant mountains. Maya felt relieved.

'You must be very careful in the kitchen, but more so when near the fire. The fire is our obedient servant; it makes life easier for us, but when it erupts in fury, it can wreak havoc. Now you realize why I do not allow you in? At your age, your hands are still unsteady. You'll need a few more years before you're ready to cook. But since you have started, you should finish it.'

'So, no lunch for us today,' was Bhai's two cents, delivered with a sparkle in his eyes. The rice Maya cooked was not just edible but also tasty. And surprisingly, Maa's mood also changed and she soon returned to her chirpy self.

Maa smiled as she looked at Akaash. She was confident that he loved his sister and would protect her from any ill fate that might befall her. Even though he was only a few years older than her, he was far more mature. He read between the lines and wasn't carried away by anyone's fake charm. He believed in simplicity, and his heart was pure.

A sumptuous meal and a family to love are all we need from life, for life is fleeting, and our needs should be few and far between. Akaash's simplicity was hard to match in today's materialistic world, an old soul with a heart of gold. Yet, the only dampener was that everyone but his father recognized the true value of his heart.

This was just one of the many cherished memories Maya held of their kitchen. Of course, there was another day she would never forget in her life—a dark memory.

★

Lazy Sunday afternoons called for lazier naps, and Maya was one gorgeous little lazy girl who loved her beauty sleep more than anything else. Weekends were meant for sleeping and eating, and some more sleeping and some more eating. She loved good food; it was one of her many weaknesses. Born into a disciplined family, she was the black sheep; she enjoyed disorder and entropy. For her, lack of order symbolized creativity. She would mess things up not out of laziness but because she hated things that were in order and symmetrical. Asymmetry was what she loved. It epitomized the inner soul, the urge to scale mountains. For Maya, those who loved order and balance were banal. She yearned for upheavals and was the only contrarian in their house. She sometimes wondered if she was her parents' genetic child, so different was she from them and Bhai. Yet the unconditional love shown by Maa and Bhai reinforced her faith that she belonged to the family.

The first incident to disturb her peace of mind occurred when she was just a child. Her Papa had perhaps restrained himself before. She later found it surprising because he was not made that way. Consideration for a child was somewhat alien to his nature, and it would not have crossed his mind to spare a child from trauma. He must have shouted and hit Maa before, which Maya had perhaps not realized as a child.

She had been just three or four years old at the time, neatly arranging twigs from the tiny bushes in a corner of the field next to their modest dwelling. Her neighbour had called her inside. The affectionate, childless lady was like an alternate mother to her. She offered Maya sweets, various types of novel foods, toys to play with and let her lie in her lap while she caressed her hair. Was her mother envious? There was no way to know now. It was highly unlikely because Maa was the unsuspecting type; even if a ruffian snatched away her purse on the road she would think the man was playing hide-and-seek.

Maya would never forget that day in her life. She had been

playing with a new toy Auntie had purchased from the market—a small helicopter that soared into the air when pulled by its strings. It made her wish to fly far above the ground at a height where birds flew, but she did not know how to acquire the skills.

And then, through the window, she spotted many kids rushing towards her house. Auntie told her to keep playing and ran outside. Maya also tried to go out to see what had happened, but the door had been locked from the outside. Auntie returned after a while and asked her to have lunch, but by then, Maya wanted to go to Maa. She was told that her mother would return only after an hour.

Maa had come later to pick her up, wrapped in bandages. Maya started weeping on seeing her state but Maa reassured her, 'Don't worry, Maya. A monkey entered our house. I went to the hospital, and the doctor said I can remove the bandages in three days.'

After many years, Bhai told her what had really happened that day.

But then things improved. She started loving her Papa also; he had become affectionate. They would all go out as a family to adjoining towns or to the meadows for picnics; he would play with them, listen to music together and even dine out at a *dhaba* close to their house. Papa would also take Maa to the movies or the market; they even held hands! Maya forgot about the incident after a few days.

But then it all started again within a few months! And when it happened, it would go on and on for days together.

It was another weekend when Bhai left to play cricket right after lunch; Papa had yelled at Maa and left home after his siesta.

Maya had thought hard; 'I think Papa hits Maa sometimes. She looks black and blue on those days.' Bhai always discouraged this conversation when Maya brought it up. But there was no proof; Maa was always upbeat and never complained. Maya was too young to ponder over the thoughts that criss-crossed her tender mind for long; she carried on with her life, forgetting what Maa must be going through.

It was a pity that the kind Auntie passed away when Maya was just seven years old. The death must have been sudden because she had met her just the day before. They managed to hide it from her, and she set off towards Auntie's house as usual when Maa came rushing to drag her away. Maya had violently protested, yelled, torn her hair and spat on her, but she had still been carried indoors.

The situation was explained after she cooled down. 'She has gone to the plains far away. She will return only after a few months.'

'But she did not tell me anything yesterday.'

'She had to go away suddenly. You were asleep. Don't worry; she will be back. And you will be starting school in a few days, so in any case, you will not miss her so much; you will be busy making new friends.'

★

The sun fell on her face whenever Maya slept in the afternoon, sharp at half past two. The window and curtains in her room were always open. The golden sun rays would make a desperate attempt to wake her up but she loved her naps and would roll over to the opposite side of the bed and continue sleeping. But that afternoon, she was not so lucky. The sun emerged victorious, managing to wake her up. Even though she was awake, the laziness didn't creep out of her body; she was like a cow that refused to move till someone shoved her away. So she lay in bed just like that.

From her bed, Maya could hear the jingling of bangles and anklets announcing the arrival of Maa's friends. They had come over for tea and khari biscuits—a traditional Indian snack that tasted like manna from heaven when paired with masala chai. The centre table in the sitting room was laden with samosas, kachoris, pakoras and other mouth-watering snacks, while aunties draped in vibrant saris sat around, chatting and laughing.

The exhaustion on their faces, from all the hard work at home, was unmistakable. They all looked forward to these afternoon gatherings—occasions to open up their minds and commiserate with each other. Their tired eyes, once full of youthful vigour, now carried deep sorrow behind dark kajal, reflecting sleepless nights and years of hardships. Their hands, rough and calloused from labour, showed the toll of menial tasks. Among them, Maa stood out, her back bruised from unseen struggles.

Despite their hardships, their smiles shone like stars, illuminating their weary faces, filling them with dreams and hope. In Ranikhet, their hopes remained bright, unaffected by the wealth around them. Even the riches of nearby Almora couldn't dim their spirit. They clung to intangible treasures—love, hope, faith, compassion and laughter—with only a small hint of sorrow, like the sugar Maa added to her tea. Their chatter provided an escape from the harsh world as they found solace in shared stories. Their children, their greatest joy, brought warmth to their lives. Their humble homes were symbols of pride and community, anchoring them in a sense of belonging.

Maya couldn't help but notice a common thread that connected the women seated on the chairs and sofas—they possessed an innate desire to give and share. Despite their own struggles, they found solace in extending a helping hand to those around them, finding strength in their interconnectedness. In their acts of generosity, they discovered a profound sense of purpose and fulfilment, their hearts overflowing with the joy that comes from uplifting others.

In these women, Maya found a living testament to the power of resilience, hope and the unwavering strength of the human spirit. Though their eyes betrayed the pain they carried, their smiles shone brightly, defying the burdens of their existence. They stood as beacons of inspiration, reminding Maya of the remarkable capacity for love and compassion that lies within each and every one of us.

Pinky Auntie was a sight to behold in her radiant red sari,

with a big round red bindi on her forehead and her trademark jhumkas tinkling with every movement. All the men in the town, young or old, could not walk past her without a second glance. She had an undeniable magnetic pull, exuding an aura of strength and allure that could both attract and intimidate. Yet beneath this fierce exterior she was one of the warmest persons Maya had ever met. She had a heart of gold, unlike some women in the room who fed on the gossip and miseries of others. But somehow, Pinky Auntie was always misunderstood as a rude, abrasive and egotistic woman. Maya secretly wished to be like her—the centre of attraction but with an attitude that sent a clear message to anyone trying to take advantage of her that they would be burnt at the stake.

Shakina Auntie was eternally joyful—she was always happy and cheerful, no matter what happened. She also had the innate ability of making others laugh, and everyone eagerly awaited her presence to kick off the fun; she was the life of every party. She would talk about her boys and dogs, sparing a few words for her husband in the middle of a conversation. She was hilarious and, at times, the only one speaking.

Shanti Auntie was the one who always found faults in the stars. A firm believer in astrology, she only stepped out after seeking the opinion of her brother, who dabbled in the mystical arts. People like her had little confidence in humankind. They always needed external advice for every small or large decision in life. They were, at the same time, carefree, according to Maya, as they rarely thought or analysed; they outsourced this to others. They were followers and needed gurus in life. Shanti Auntie, too, followed some of the malicious gurus who pepper the nooks and corners of this country. To Maya, a machine had mass-produced these *gyanis* with no *gyan* to share. She hated them with her heart and soul, but it was the only profession that seemed to be blossoming of late.

Even Maa had been a devotee of such a guru till a few years back—a bearded man in saffron robes who lived in an ashram.

Maa used to visit him every Monday morning, after Papa had left home for the day. Maya used to accompany Maa, who had sworn her to secrecy. Even a child as innocent as Maya was surprised when he asked Maa to arrange his belongings scattered across his room. The thought that bothered Maya was whether her mother was his maidservant. But Maa seemed elated at the opportunity to serve her guru. Maya would sit silently in one corner of the room, and was sometimes offered cheap chocolates that got stuck in her teeth.

One Monday, the guru asked Maya to clean his room, but Maa took over; Maya started hating the guru from that day, and even refused to accept the chocolates. The next week, when Maa told her that she would be going to the ashram alone, Maya pleaded once or twice but felt relieved in her heart of hearts. That man by then had become the embodiment of evil to her. Later that day, when Maa returned home, Maya noticed her sari was slightly torn and she looked dishevelled. Maa refused to explain what had happened.

The following Monday, when Maa did not go, the guru sent one of his disciples to their home. The man talked about the *atman*, the transient body, the Almighty and of the guru as His emissary—following his words would put one on the path leading to salvation. In a fit of rage, Maa suddenly picked up a flower pot and threatened to throw it at the man if he did not leave that very instant.

After many years, Maya was finally able to understand what had happened in the ashram that morning. She had never confided in Bhai about the incident because her mother had asked her not to. And Maa's word was always final for her. Maya had no soft corner for any of those godmen after the incident and would have loved to break their heads with flowerpots.

To return to that afternoon, Shanti Auntie was anything but *shant*. She was persistently depressed about something or the other, a neurotic. Nonetheless, her dry humour was entertaining, although direct and lacking in sarcasm. The women's topic that day was the bashing they received from their husbands and mothers-in-law, as if there was a competition to establish who was the most tortured. Maya wondered how women could be so docile and submissive, as if the Almighty had sent them to this world to suffer beatings by their husbands and in-laws. It seemed to her that they accepted it as a divine mandate, almost as if they believed enduring such pain was their ticket to heaven.

Her second source of wonder was how her mother could be so involved yet indifferent. It was a struggle to understand the other side of her personality. There was a bond that tied these women who would converge for the afternoon sessions, and that bond was being taken for granted. Women across continents feel exploited at various stages of life by their loved ones. To many, it might sound like a repressive attitude, but for most, it was the reality against which it was futile to fight. They failed to comprehend that the fault lay in their attitudes, not nature. Maya was exasperated at their submissive attitudes and their tragic stories. She would always scoff, 'These women and their lack of expectations from life!'

The lingering lethargy in her muscles prevented her from crawling out of bed; she continued to laze in the bed despite the harsh summer sun that flooded the room. But something bothered her—something was distinctly off that day. Pinky Auntie wasn't her usual self at the tea party. She was narrating an episode to the rest, who were all sombre and listening with concern. Maya got up from her bed and ambled towards the door. Hiding behind it, she pressed her ear against the door, trying her utmost to catch snippets of the conversation. She could hear the others gasping and then she finally heard Pinky Auntie.

'I entered his room the other night with his food *thali*. I was wearing a red sari because it was weekend—I thought to brighten up the dull house with some colour. The old man was half asleep in his wheelchair... He must have caught the scent of the jasmine flowers I'd worn, and woke up to stare at me lustily with his drowsy and bloodshot eyes. Even a child could have discerned what his motives were.

'I have always wondered how he managed to smell so well with that crooked nose of his. My mother-in-law once mentioned that his brother beat him black and blue when he was 10; since then, he has lived with a disfigured nose. I am told that noses can be operated upon at the hospital in Nainital these days…they call it plastic surgery…but he has never attempted it. He and his father were stuck in poverty until my husband started working. He has been a cursed man since his birth.' Auntie paused after uttering the sentence.

Everyone in the room, including Maa, seemed to know what was coming, yet they pretended to be oblivious and curious. This was another aspect of these women—polite to a fault. Auntie seemed reluctant to divulge more, but continued after a few moments of silence. Maya could make out that she was perspiring. She also understood that the matter was serious and that she should refrain from eavesdropping on such private conversations, but curiosity got the better of her. She sat down on the floor, next to the door, and stared blankly at the space inside the room. *Who could Auntie be talking about? Some guest in her house? Someone in her household?* Maya was exasperated yet massively curious.

Pinky Auntie continued. 'His room is so dingy and dull! His body odour is always a concern in the house… Just walking past his room at times makes me throw up. The old hag never bothers to take a bath. When I first got married and came to this house, I would dread entering his room. At that time, I only feared him. Now he disgusts and repels me.'

Maya by now understood that Auntie was referring to a family member. By the theory of deduction, she concluded that it was a man who was old and invalid. Realization dawned on Maya that Auntie was referring to her father-in-law. She had only faint memories of him, which was why she had not remembered him easily. Usually, her mother avoided taking Maya to her friends' houses, but on that particular occasion, Maya had been allowed to tag along. Maya had once ventured into his room but Pinky Auntie had dragged her out, warning her not to enter that room again. Later on, Maa had explained that he was a sick and immobile man and wasn't allowed to come out too much, nor could anyone enter his room. Family members also did not bother to wheel him out, not even his wife. They were sick and tired of seeing his sullen face the whole day.

'When I was about to leave the room, he called out to me—"Pinky"—a call loud enough to be heard from outside the house. I looked back at him in horror. I knew what was coming. It had been some years since he had done that to me, but this was it. His voice had given him away…the boundless lust resonating through it. I tried to ignore it and aimed to escape as soon as possible, but this time, he called out even louder, with aggressive male dominance. I was scared that someone might have heard him, because if they did, my punishment would be even more severe. Although they hated him, they would never tolerate petulant or insolent behaviour on my part. After all, I am the *bahu* of the house, subordinate to everyone, including the old man.'

At this point, Maya's mother let out an exasperated sigh. Maya peeked out from behind the door and noticed the expression on Maa's face—it seemed to Maya that she was in no mood to listen to Pinky Auntie's story any more; she was plain disgusted with not just the episode but also the manner of narration. More importantly, she didn't want to believe that her friend was constitutionally weak. Maa always liked strong women around her. Not that she was very successful with her husband, but she believed she had the power never to let him cross the limit; she would revolt at the right moment. She also believed that she was inherently rugged and robust.

The expression of disgust was consciously removed with some effort. What followed was a sympathetic look. Pinky Auntie continued after Maa's expression conveyed her sympathy, which was what the ladies of Ranikhet expected. They expected sympathy, not empathy, not on equal terms, but as a superior woman to a hapless inferior. They suffered from a peculiar form of masochism. However, Maya spotted her mother looking down again out of shame and disgust.

'I have told you earlier what transpired last Diwali. I might not be able to handle the same incident again. So I stood where I was and waited for his edict. He told me to turn back and stand in front of him. He then raised his voice and commanded me to look at him.' At this point, Maya thought she should stop eavesdropping. It was getting murkier by the minute. She pressed her fingers to her ears, but again, she could not restrain herself. The words rang in her ears.

'He smirked at the terror in my eyes. "*Nikalo*", he said. My hands trembled, but before he could raise his stick, I thought it was better to obey him and let the nightmare pass. I started removing my sari and he shrugged in disgust. He told me that my body had sagged and wasn't "juicy". I felt relieved at the "compliment" but after that, he asked me to remove his pants and go down on him...'

And then she sobbed. Her cries echoed throughout the entire house. It was not just the ladies. It seemed even the walls had heard her and started weeping, shedding tears that were not only painful but also filled the room with a deep, throbbing sorrow.

It was a feeling that Maya had never experienced before. The room had gone silent for what seemed like an eternity. All the women wore downcast expressions. When they glanced at the weeping woman, their looks were not of pity, but they all seemed to be pondering on something. Maybe it was a regular thing for the others too, or they faced similar situations, although not identical. They did not bother to question her, they did not accuse her of being too submissive and docile, nor did they try to console her. And from the look on their faces, they were not even shocked!

On the other hand, Maya felt a swirl of shock, disgust and nausea. She was rattled and perplexed, her heart racing with palpitations that made it difficult to swallow. The sickness clawed at her throat, and the urge to vomit loomed closer with each passing moment. She needed to cough or stick her fingers down her throat; she had to get to the bathroom. There was no alternative.

She walked to her study table like a lifeless automaton. Maa noticed her and hastily came to her room to shut the doors. She wasn't aware that Maya had already heard whatever had to be heard.

That day Maya could not eat. She had nightmares for the entire week. Wherever she went, she could hear the echoes of Pinky Auntie's insult at the hands of her father-in-law. She saw flashes of Auntie's smiling face in her dreams, but as she looked closer, she realized that she was not smiling but weeping inconsolably. Each night brought a new dream and further misery. She wanted to speak to someone about it, to reduce the intensity of the pain inside her, but that would amount to disgracing Pinky Auntie and her family. No, it was not the family, only Pinky Auntie! And it wasn't, after all, Maya's story to share; the story had not even been shared with her. She had just overheard.

One thing was sure—the next time she met any male member of other families, she would feel disgusted towards them. Irrespective of their deeds, she would look at them as if they were culprits. If one apple was rotten, the entire bag was sure to have turned so. Had she started to despise the male gender? In her heart of hearts, she did understand, however, that it was just not fair to generalize.

Yet there was one person she would always view in a different light. It was Shiv—the one she had been warned to stay away from by her protective brother. And Bhai spoke as if Shiv was his worst enemy.

2

The people of Ranikhet led a slow and laid-back life. They would pause to talk on the roads and spend hours chatting at teatime. There was no hurry; no one was going anywhere. Sometimes, not being ambitious could also be a boon—it saves you the heartbreak and the stress of constant performance. The charm of small towns is always something to be cherished.

Ranikhet was a town of festivals. Holi was celebrated by everyone, and that year was no exception. The *Holika* bonfire on the night before Holi illuminated the mountains with its vibrant flames, fuelled by wood gathered from the jungle. Minstrels danced around the fire, their incessant chants of 'Holi Hai!' signifying the onset of spring. While the weather didn't change as rapidly as it did in the plains, there was a definite recession of extreme winter conditions. The heat from the fire was sufficient to warm the souls.

As Maya looked at the speckles of wood dancing out of the flames, she wondered whether it was an escape or a natural progression to another form of life. She sat by the fire with her friends, dressed in red, oblivious to everyone around. The colour of the fire had mesmerized her, and its warmth kept her trapped in a state of hypnosis. She felt a strange unity with the Creator, the bright stars above, the full moon casting its glow on the night sky and the entire cosmos. She also felt one with the fire, which seemed to cleanse her of any negativity or wrath or other feelings, leaving only love and positive vibes. The festival was a celebration of the triumph of good over evil.

The sprinkling of colours was anathema to Maya. The bright shades of *gulaal* and the dissolved pigments refused to go away. The boys used this once-a-year opportunity to get as close to the girls as possible, smearing them with colours. The *thandai* sent all of them cruising into a parallel universe, lasting at times till early evening. The sweets were of varied tastes, and gifts were exchanged.

The mild scent of hibiscus hung in the air, the flowers blooming like little red light bulbs across the town. Maya and her friends, dressed in colourful clothes—imbibing the festival's spirit—wandered through the small lanes on Holi, trying to escape the excesses of this festival of colours.

As they stood at the crossroads, in her bright clothes and with a sparkling smile that outshone her clothes, Maya spotted him.

He had a captivating presence—his striking features combined with an innate charm made him a sight to behold. With an air of confidence surrounding him, he exuded a magnetic energy that made heads turn and drew attention wherever he went.

He briefly vanished from sight, but just as quickly as he disappeared, he reappeared. Walking along the road, he held a few books in his hands, lost in his own world. Seemingly unaware of his surroundings, he didn't notice the observer, or perhaps he did, but it was the observer who couldn't tear her eyes away from him.

There was something about Shiv that captivated Maya, something beyond his physical allure. She continued to gaze at him, her eyes fixed upon his every movement. She felt an inexplicable karmic connection; it was as if their paths were meant to intersect, and the universe was conspiring to bring them together.

No one had ever stirred her emotions quite like Shiv did. Though he was a stranger, he held an inexplicable power over her. In that moment, he was not just a singular person but a representation of everyone who had ever held sway over her heart. As he continued on his way, unaware of the effect he had had on her, she couldn't help but wonder if their paths would ever cross, if their lives would entwine in a tale that transcended mere chance encounters.

Tamara had diagnosed it as a case of infatuation. Although Maya was too young to appreciate the difference between infatuation and love, she understood the attraction she felt for Shiv. It was also true that instead of a sweet feeling, her heart ached whenever she spotted him, sinking to unfathomable depths. To her, it felt as if she had been deeply in love with him even before she had seen him for the first time—perhaps from some previous birth. It might just be an attraction, but a fatal one. Maybe she felt so because she had been instructed by her brother to stay away from Shiv or, for that matter, any other boy. Bhai was aware of how boys spoke about girls and what they discussed among themselves; he hated his sister being the topic of discussion among lusty boys sipping tea in the marketplace or perched on the railings of the mall. But, still, Maya couldn't stop being blinded by Shiv's presence.

'Shiv!' Her heart sighed.

But Shiv had never seemed to notice her before; he wouldn't even spare a passing glance. Yet, that day was different. His gaze lingered, capturing her in a moment that seemed to stretch on endlessly. Maya's pulse quickened, her heart thundering with a fervour that echoed in her ears, each beat pulling her deeper into the thrill of it all. But despite the warmth in her eyes, his gaze held only a quiet curiosity—a look that fell just short of mirroring the intensity in her own.

Maya's eyes brimmed with an unmistakable and indomitable love. She was willing to defy the world for him. There was just one small problem—she had never been able to express her emotions to him, for they had never exchanged a single word. Still, deep within her heart, she knew he held the power to either make her blissfully happy or crush her utterly. She felt that their connection surpassed anything she had ever experienced. He was the knight in shining armour who would rescue her while vanquishing her greatest enemy. What she felt for him was no ordinary infatuation or mere affection; it went far beyond that. It was an intense longing to be his, to belong to him, no matter the cost. She kept this burning desire locked away, hidden from everyone, aware that it was a profound sentiment beyond the comprehension of the outside world. How could others possibly understand! How could she feel such intense emotions for someone she had never spoken to or met? The answer eluded her. All she knew was that it wasn't a fleeting crush or a commonplace, mundane love; it felt as if he possessed her and she, in turn, possessed him.

Bhai had noticed, not once but many times, and always tried to suppress it, perhaps sensing in his heart that Shiv would cause her much misery and sorrow—a premonition Maya also harboured. But who knew the future. In that moment she felt that he was the only reason for her existence, and nobody, not even Bhai, could stand in her way. All she yearned for was to be fully present wherever he may be. Anywhere—in any corner of the world, the solar system, or even the universe. They were meant to be together, embarking on life's journey hand in hand.

Maya gazed at the deep blue sky devoid of clouds. Rain on Holi was a rarity and that day was no exception. The sky appeared flawless, like a masterpiece; it seemed motionless, as if time itself had come to a halt. She wished for the world to freeze when she locked eyes with Shiv; let everything else fade away, perish and evaporate. They would gaze at each other for eternity, encapsulated in that instant and suspended in time. He would beckon her into his sturdy embrace and she would dash towards him—just like the scenes from the movies she had watched or the fairy tales her mother had narrated during Maya's childhood. She also knew one undeniable truth—the only person she could ever truly be with was him and him alone.

Maya was about to sprint towards Shiv, ready to surrender herself in his arms, when she heard a loud commotion and blaring car horns, snapping her out of her daydreams. As she surveyed her surroundings, she realized she had caused a traffic jam—numerous vehicles were stuck behind her. Her friends were calling out to her, attempting to pull her away from the middle of the road, while onlookers stared at her with a mix of astonishment and resentment.

All eyes were on her when she stole a glance at Shiv. There he stood, a vision of perfection, his gaze piercing through her very soul. A smile adorned his face, a smile that spoke volumes, revealing a glimpse of the enchantment she held over him. In that moment, it felt as though time had frozen, the world around them ceasing to exist.

Their eyes locked in a dance of emotions, an unspoken connection that transcended words. She couldn't help but feel a surge of nervousness coursing through her veins, causing her to avert her gaze momentarily. When her eyes found him again, a profound transformation had taken place. No longer was he merely smiling; his countenance was now painted with an expression of profound love.

Locked in the silent exchange, Shiv yearned to convey his thoughts and emotions, but the words remained trapped within him. Still he persisted, his gaze unwavering, as if etching his love into her very being.

Try as she might, Maya struggled to maintain her composure. Unable to hold his gaze any longer, she cast her eyes downwards, a blush adorning her cheeks like the rosy hue of a bride meeting her groom for the first time. Yet, it was a moment worth cherishing, an ephemeral dream that felt more real than reality itself.

Maya's friends tugged at her arm, pulling her away, and the world around her resumed movement while her heart refused to comply, soaring towards Shiv even as her physical form was led away. The lingering sensation of his unwavering gaze sent shivers down her spine—a deliciously haunting reminder of the profound effect he had on her.

Her hands turned cold, her mouth parched and goosebumps rose on her skin—every pore alive and tingling with anticipation.

Shiv smiled—an enigmatic smile that could be interpreted as amusement or perhaps an acknowledgement of her audaciousness.

She couldn't tear her eyes away from him, for in those deep, enchanting hazel eyes lay her sanctuary, her refuge from the chaos of the world—a place where her love resided, unyielding and eternal. Nothing and no one could ever snatch that away from her. It was her and him, nobody else. The gravity of his gaze was a magnetic force, drawing her in, compelling her to reside in his gaze forever. It was a glimpse into a realm where emotions reigned supreme, where their connection defied logic and reason. In that moment, she did not care for the perils that surrounded her; the probability of being run over by a passing car seemed insignificant compared to the depth of her connection with Shiv.

This was a moment where the illusory world transcended reality, a parallel universe where the mundane and the banal were left behind. Maya was a fervent believer in the power of love at first sight. From the moment she first laid eyes on him, at just 11 years old, an inexplicable intensity surged through her veins. Her youthful innocence couldn't grasp the enormity of this emotion, yet it consumed her entirely. At first, she dismissed it as a fleeting notion, but it resurfaced with an unrelenting force, refusing to be ignored.

Maya was willing to sacrifice everything to catch a glimpse of him each day. Her heart fluttered every morning as she left for school, deliberately taking the route that would go past the store where he worked. Though Shiv's family owned the shop, he worked as a humble assistant in their modest establishment, weighing goods, handling cash, packaging items and serving customers.

Over time, Maya became convinced that Shiv waited to see her each day, yearning for the moment she would pass by. Even on days when school was not in session, she contrived reasons to go down that path, to steal glimpses and peer into the depths of his eyes. Her mother never questioned her intentions, but her brother often intervened. Maya persisted, finding opportunities whenever Bhai was distracted or engrossed in work. Sometimes alone, sometimes accompanied by her loyal companions, she would stealthily make her way to Shiv. The days when she was not able to see him were unbearable trials. Her heart sank and her thoughts wandered aimlessly, lost in the absence of his presence.

While every boy in school had his eyes set on Maya, her heart raced only for Shiv. Perhaps it was all preordained; perhaps it was not. Maybe he knew, and maybe he did not. How did it matter? That was not in her hands; what was in her hands was to love him, and she did just that. Whoever said that love had to be two-sided? Whoever said that love had to be mutual?

It was a peculiar kind of love, all weird. Maya never wanted to communicate with Shiv, never felt the need to express her feelings directly. She was merely happy to look at him from a distance and steal a few glances. And she continued the same, day after day, never feeling the compulsion to break new ground. Never. She was in a one-sided relationship and content. Perhaps the complications of mutual love were too much to bear. If another person was involved, pain and suffering were bound to erupt; on the contrary, if there was only her, her love for him would not be painful.

Maya was young but precocious. Though she could not articulate it properly, she understood why she believed in this one-sided love. Her analytical mind that could conceptualize the future fooled her into believing there was no need to act on her feelings. However, as time passed, her love for Shiv was no longer willing to remain confined to the boundaries of a karmic love, and she needed his presence. Being a spectator of Maya's pining, Bhai tried to keep her away from Shiv as much as he could. But no one can keep a person away from a disaster waiting to happen; no one can alter destiny when you are your own biggest enemy.

She looked across the road, and he didn't take his eyes off her this time. While he would usually shy away whenever she looked at him with longing, that day he looked back at her with the same intensity. He looked at her as if there was no one around, as if there was no world, no sky, no sun, no passers-by, no cars, no honking, no trees and no snow-clad peaks watching over them. Maya felt struck by Cupid's arrow when their eyes locked. Standing in the middle of traffic, being tugged back by her friends, the only thought that crossed her mind was to run to him and melt into his arms like someone who belonged to him, just like in the movies.

'What happened to you there? Do you know that a car could have run you over?' one of her friends exclaimed. Maya turned a deaf ear to her; in that moment, she was above death, above mortality. She just wanted to feel his presence.

As she continued walking down the street, Maya came across a mosaic artwork that spoke about love. Was this a sign? Was a superior power trying to convey a message or was her mind playing games with her? The artwork was beautiful and mesmerizing—an image of a mother in black and white, watching her children play hopscotch, painted in glorious colours. The painting had faded over time but still shone. Further ahead, the same mother was depicted in colour, now old and haggard, while the same children, now grown up, were rendered in black and white. They had swapped places. Maya didn't understand why the artist chose to depict the role of the provider in black and white while the recipient's role was in colour. What was he trying to signify?

And then she read the inscription: 'Happiness is black and white. It might look faint to others, but it is the universal colour of life.'

It was now crystal clear; happiness lay in giving.

Did she start believing in this maxim from the day she first saw Shiv in that shop?

Shiv's gaze pierced through the distance, fixated on her with unwavering intensity. Across the street, on the sidewalk, he remained rooted, his longing to catch even a fleeting glimpse of her burning like an inferno within him.

Against all expectations, Shiv drew nearer. Was he approaching her to speak, to bridge the chasm that separated them? Or was it a mischievous act of teasing, a tantalizing game meant to stoke the flames of desire? The air crackled with anticipation as he closed the distance, leaving Maya's heart suspended in a precarious dance between hope and uncertainty. Maybe he was coming to kiss her. She didn't know. All she could see was a smirk on his face. Her brain screamed for her to move away, yet her body refused to budge an inch. Her heart yearned to feel him closer to her.

Inch by inch, he moved towards her. The mosaic work on the wall was hinting to her to look at Shiv through the colours. He then faded away and his image became black and white. She thought that maybe her mind was playing games with her until she heard her friend whisper, 'He is coming here'. It was more of a gasp of horror, but to Maya it was an affirmation that it wasn't her imagination and wishful thinking; he was really approaching.

Maybe he was heading towards the other side of the road; maybe he needed to go somewhere right past me to some store behind—she was now rationalizing with her analytical brain—*maybe he is going home. This isn't a dead end after all; many others are walking past me. It isn't only him.*

Shiv's arms swayed as he crossed the street. His face was a shining bronze beneath his stubble-covered cheeks and chin, highlighted by the white *Pathani* clothes he wore. His hazel eyes with long eyelashes were innocent but held deep-seated pain. He was coming right towards her.

'He is coming here, Maya. Let's go!' her friends cried out again.

But their voices were lost on her. Her heartbeat was so loud that she couldn't hear anyone; it drowned out their voices. She was sure that Shiv could hear her heart beating from the distance. He was a few feet away, his eyes glued to hers. He kept walking, until he was right in front of her. Closer than ever before, he looked a lot like the man she saw in her dreams. Of course, now her mind was hallucinating and making up things.

He bent down to retrieve something from the ground. It was her dupatta that had fallen; he picked it up and draped it around her neck. He immediately turned and started walking back but not before smiling at her with his soft, loving eyes. As her kohl-lined eyes locked with his hazel ones, it felt like the whole street was looking at their first-ever union, at two souls merging into one.

If a day you expect to be disappointing turns out to be the best day of your life, well, even once in a lifetime, it is a day to remember. That is what happened to Maya on the day of Holi. Her encounter with Shiv in the morning had left her stumped; she could still smell his scent. She didn't want to remove any garment from her body as it made her feel his presence but had to since they were wet and stained with colours. She didn't put her clothes in for washing; she tightly hugged them and buried her face into the dupatta.

That afternoon, as Maya slept, she only dreamt of being in Shiv's arms. But in every dream, she caught a glimpse of Bhai's angry face whenever she was with Shiv. She was terrified of what Bhai would say when he found out about what had happened that day. Ranikhet was a tiny hill town and there were too many folks on the road today. It was tough to keep secrets here; gossip spread like wildfire.

When Maya woke up, still pondering about her dreams, all she could do was manage a faint smile. Waking up in love was one of the best feelings.

She heard loud chatter and laughter outside. Maya wanted to close her door and continue sleeping, but she also knew that Shiv would be out there anxiously waiting for her. On Holi, everyone met on the main street in the early evening and played again with colours and water. She got dressed in a white salwar kameez and pink dupatta, lining her eyes with kohl that Maa made each morning.

She could now hear her friends looking for her inside the house. 'Maya, Maya!'

Before she could go out, they came barging into her room. She was already blushing and they did not spare her.

'Look at you! Are you ready for some dupatta-pulling again?' one of them said while the others giggled.

'I can't believe he came so close to you. What if you had pushed him away?'

Not everyone knew how crazy she was about him. She had dreamt of that moment even before she knew what love was. Something had always drawn her towards him. She wasn't someone to ask for anything, content to love him from a distance. She didn't care whether it was reciprocated. All she knew was that she couldn't stop loving him. It didn't even occur to her that she needed him to love her back as she had concluded that her love wasn't selfish, or so she thought. Another perspective was that she loved her idea of love and being in love with him. She had never thought further and now that it was moving to the next step, she felt shaky for the first time. It was as if she was being pushed into the deep waters where the end was unfathomable, beyond her comprehension.

She took a deep breath and decided to let time play its cards; she would surrender herself to fate.

3

'Shiv,' Maya called out as he headed towards her with a fistful of gulaal. Maya didn't know where to go; her heart was racing. She was closer to him than she had ever hoped or expected.

She wanted time to pause and let the moment stand still; seeing his mischievous smile that could break a million hearts was going to break her. Thoughts swirled through her mind as he approached. *Yes, I'm sure we will break each other's hearts. There is no chance this will work but I can't stop myself. I can't stop this disaster, for it's the sweetest fruit I've ever tasted. I am even willing to drink poison from his hands—if I die, it will be a life well lived.*

It's rare when the journey itself proves more pleasurable than the destination. Arriving at the destination is a brief affair, a sliver of frozen time, a final denouement—perhaps a signifier of the union of souls. Yet, after a while, it becomes lost on the traveller, who then yearns for those days, months, or years spent undertaking the arduous journey—memories resurfacing as reminders of that sweet destination, cherished moments etched in the heart.

Did she not hear stories of many united through love marriages recounting the days of courtship with nostalgia? The days they meandered hand in hand through the valleys and mountains, beneath the trees, half-buried in the snow?

Focusing only on the destination can lead to a craving for instant gratification, which often results in stress—whether during an intense courtship or preparing for examinations. Focusing on the journey—those moments of bliss, the subjects one is studying, and the gifts of nature on a stressful trek, on the other hand—brings joy and happiness.

Her mother also quoted from scriptures like the Gita to emphasize this lesson throughout her childhood.

As Shiv came closer to her, Maya felt his breath falling in rhythm with hers. He approached her and smeared her with gulaal. It was the first time he had touched her. He was mindful of the moment; his expression conveyed it. Maya could visualize her mind ascending gently into the starry night, soaring into a parallel universe. Was this the moment she had been waiting for, despite her earlier protestations about one-sided love?

It felt as though he had touched every part of her body, even though he had rubbed gulaal only on her forehead and cheeks. Oh! That touch! Electric signals flashed through her like lightning tearing through the darkness on a stormy night; he had penetrated her heart and soul. He gingerly caressed her face, using his finger to trace the pink gulaal across her cheek, over her forehead, to the other cheek and finally down to her chin, before returning to where he had started. He repeated this three or four times and the pathway remained the same for each. His hands did not falter once; they were as steady as the boatmen's rowing up the lake in Ranikhet. He then touched her hair, a mischievous and charming smile playing on his lips. The strands falling on her face and obstructing her eyes were gently stroked away so that he could look her straight in the eyes like he had done earlier in the day.

In her mind, Maya imagined herself standing there, eyes brimming with longing, yet in reality, she remained frozen like a statue. But she didn't care—she craved the experience, and more than that, she wanted him to feel the same way. The entire street now focused on her. In a small town like theirs, where everyone knew each other, there was no room for privacy or secrecy. Yet she was unconcerned. This wasn't the moment to worry about what others thought or gossip spreading through the town, or how her brother might hear of it, or what whispers might eventually reach her mother. This was her moment, a precious sliver of time she wanted to treasure for the rest of her life.

The man she had wished to love from a distance till a few days back had now stepped into her life; she now wanted to not only love him but also be loved by him. Shiv had kindled in her a kind of desire she had never experienced before. He was holding her, touching her, rubbing gulaal on her face, playing with her, smiling at her—the only comparison that came to her mind was the amorous game of Holi played by Lord Krishna with none other than Radha. In that moment, she could feel what love was with all her senses. The love that emanated from him was so deep and pure that no mortal being could touch, see, feel or even smell it. It lay buried deep within her, and she wondered if he, too, felt this intensity in his heart and soul.

This was the way she loved him in that instant, and she knew she would continue to love him for eternity. It was a kind of love that poets, novelists, short story writers and lyricists had failed to define for so many years—not that she was able to either.

She didn't blink and kept looking at him; Shiv also couldn't keep his eyes off her. It dawned on her that he too felt for her; she saw it in his eyes, in the manner he stared at her, in the softness of his touch as he smeared gulaal across her face. He wished to move closer; he was desperate to express his feelings more intimately. His lips quivered but he perhaps felt that the moment was too sublime for mundane words. Words were always banal, be it from the pens of bards or the teenage lover next door. Even gestures could be misconstrued. But the stream of messages that flowed straight from one heart to another through two pairs of eyes would always be clear.

His warm palm on her cold cheeks felt like the first breeze of spring that rustled the leaves of trees. 'Shiv,' she almost moaned when he touched her. She wasn't sure if he heard her, but his heart seemed to have picked up the signals. The love from him that flowed in torrents was a lifetime of desires being fulfilled for her. The more he played with her, the more her love for him multiplied. She could happily live her life without ever wanting to be with anyone else. She would live for these few moments. Just these few magical minutes! Those fleeting seconds were a lifetime of happiness for her, the flame of which would burn forever. She still didn't know whether such a denouement was ever attainable, but she could feel it as she lived the moment of sublime love.

She felt him sliding closer after she had inaudibly uttered his name. They were wrapped in each other's arms, held tight not by physical strength, though his body was muscular and hands strong; instead, it was a magnetic force that emanated from deep within them, from some indefinable and unreachable point of their intangible anatomy.

For Shiv, it was different. He had never felt anything for Maya before. She was just another girl in town for him—a girl he had occasionally noticed walking past his shop on her way to school, and Akaash's sister. But now, she had transformed into Maya. It was undoubtedly a two-way love for Shiv, who would have walked past her if he had not sensed her feelings for him. She spoke through her eyes, communicating in a language only he could understand.

Shiv's fingers brushed gently across her cheeks, her shoulders, her neck and finally, down to her arms and wrists. He was finding it difficult to exercise self-control, to keep his hands off her soft and supple skin. He couldn't help himself; her beauty had left him mesmerized and spellbound.

How can anyone be so beautiful? he wondered. And why had he not realized it earlier?

In the golden rays of the setting sun, Maya seemed to glow, her face radiating with love. She was nubile and sensuous. Shiv stared at Maya as if she was an angel or *apsara*, a celestial being from heaven, who needed to be protected from the devils on earth. He wanted to shield her from the adversities and protect her by wrapping his arms around her, covering her completely and carrying her away from the wicked world straight into his world, where only love existed, where it was just the two of them. He would stand by her during times of need, when she would be overwhelmed and on the verge of succumbing to misfortunes that had come her way. At that moment, he was willing to offer himself as the person who would guide her through life, through the rugged hills and valleys to the safer sanctuary of the plains. That was his mission in life—germinated at that very moment but sure to persist throughout life. At that moment, Shiv vowed to destroy any demon that would ever dare trouble Maya. It wasn't easy to fathom the depths of these feelings he was experiencing because he had never felt them before. However, one thing that he was sure about was that the intensity of his feelings could never be replicated in his life.

One's first love is always unique; it stands out forever in one's life and an individual rarely lets it slip out of their mind. This one was just as unique in character. He knew it was not like any other love; its intensity was rare and unmatched.

It was a strange and alien feeling. He was known to be heartless among his few friends—a boy bereft of normal emotions and incapable of experiencing love because he was not made that way, as if he was missing some amorous gene. Unlike other boys of his age, he never teased girls while walking past them and never even thought about any girl. He did not speak much to anyone other than his close friends and family members; the only girl he had ever spoken to was his younger sister.

He respected women, but along with that respect was interwoven a reluctance to get close to any girl's heart. Perhaps it was insecurity, or perhaps he was just shy! Deep down, he often wondered what it would feel like to be with a girl. But he only thought about the ordinary, approachable ones, not someone like Maya. She had appeared distant on the few occasions he had spied on her, and he felt she was too beautiful for a regular person like him to even dream of being with. Forget loving her, the thought of even approaching her was far-fetched. He never indulged in fantasies because, in his opinion, that was disrespectful to the girl. It was like pulling her into the depths of the subconscious where desire and lust reigned supreme.

The occasional dreams that crept upon him invariably led to panic attacks and a splitting headache. He was a strange boy, somewhat out of place in the 21st century. But then that was Shiv—the same Shiv who now gazed at Maya as if she was a long-lost lover who had suddenly appeared from obscurity. He was living a fantasy he never thought he would even have the gumption to dream; the idea of experiencing it through his five senses in real life belonged to the realm of make-believe.

Shiv wanted to grab her by the arm and take her to some isolated spot—there was no dearth of such spots in the desolate town of Ranikhet and its environs. She sensed it in his eyes and wanted him to voice his desires, but she also knew he was too noble. He was Shiva, the protector of the weak and downtrodden.

Maya's mind took a surreal turn and she saw Shiv as Shiva in her stupor:

> *In the cosmic expanse where creation meets destruction,*
> *Emerges the mesmerizing spectacle of Shiva's dance.*
> *With flames engulfing his divine form, a celestial inferno,*
> *He dances with primal fury, a symphony of cosmic rhythm.*
>
> *His matted locks whirl in wild abandon,*
> *As the universe trembles beneath his thunderous steps.*
> *Each movement, a stroke of destruction and renewal,*
> *Unleashing the forces that shape existence's eternal tapestry.*
>
> *With each beat, the ground quakes, mountains crumble,*
> *As Shiva's dance ravages the limits of mortal comprehension.*

The symphony of creation and annihilation resounds,
Echoing across the boundless realms of the cosmos.

His third eye blazes with an all-knowing fire,
Piercing through illusions, revealing truth untamed.
In the vortex of his dance, galaxies are born and perish,
Life's transience celebrated amidst the eternal dance of time.

In this cosmic dance, Shiva moves with divine purpose,
A cosmic choreographer, the embodiment of cosmic balance.
His dance, fierce and unyielding, bestows liberation,
A transcendence of mortal limitations, a union with the infinite.

Witness the awe-inspiring majesty of Shiva's dance,
And be consumed by the intensity of its divine embrace.
For within it lies the essence of existence,
A perpetual cycle of birth, death and ultimate liberation.

Shiv would not want people around to defame her and show disrespect through shadowy gossip that pervaded the nooks and crannies of the small town. And, of course, he would prefer to keep this news from reaching Bhai's or Maa's ears. Ultimately, he left after picking up her dupatta that had once again fallen on the ground. It seemed to Maya that the dupatta, too, was disappointed. It exhibited a look that conveyed frustration at not being able to witness something it wanted desperately to happen.

Later that evening, Maya played Holi with her friends while Shiv did the same with his; since they were playing in close proximity, their eyes remained fixed on each other. Not once did he take his gaze off her and she also tried her best to keep up with him. She blushed, feeling embarrassed, unable to look directly at him because she knew others would be watching—discreetly, if not brazenly. It seemed like he was making sure no boy got close to her—as if he would kill anyone who dared to do so with just his stare.

She hadn't been able to wash off the colours from the morning, but the only colour that mattered to her was the one Shiv had applied. She had not washed as vigorously as she usually did because she feared his colours would wash off. She wished to preserve them for a few days; they symbolized the colours of rebirth to her. A colour smeared on a momentous day of her life, a day that would never be repeated. It was also a reminder of the tender touch that had sent shivers down her spine.

As soon as she reached home, she took off her clothes. Standing in front of the mirror, she gazed at the colours Shiv had smeared on her—colours that would remain hers forever.

A knock on the door broke her stupor; it was Bhai. 'Come, Maya! It is time for dinner!'

At the dinner table, Maya was oblivious to what was being discussed. Still, she somehow managed to sport a stupid grin to hide her lack of concentration. Bhai suddenly threw a napkin over her. 'Where are you?' he asked, his eyes smiling.

He had sensed her lack of focus. So typical of Bhai! But Bhai and Maa didn't press the issue. Maya just smiled and continued eating, wondering where Bhai had been at the time of Holi. She was glad he hadn't been there; this had been her first Holi without Bhai and the first with Shiv. What a coincidence! It had played out exactly how she would have liked it to.

Her friend Rani called to tell her that Shiv and Maya were now the talk of the town. It was only a matter of time before Bhai would come to hear of it and Maya hoped that he would forgive her, and respect the feelings emanating from her heart. After all, he always had her well-being in mind.

Maya could not sleep that night and was sure Shiv couldn't either. Her thoughts were consumed by him, the few moments of their communion revolving a million times in her head as she relived it again and again. She tossed and turned in her bed; at one point it seemed to her that it would be a sleepless night, which was fine to her. It was not like any other night after all. The memory of Shiv, his touch, smell and soft touch pervaded her existence. To sleep now would amount to disrespecting a day that would forever remain holy to her. It seemed he was right beside her, tucked under her blanket, keeping her warm with his body heat and looking fondly at her. The bed was not very large but it did not matter.

Shiv, too, thought deeply of her. He wondered about the mysterious girl who had suddenly taken over his thoughts, flooding him with feelings he had not experienced earlier. He had seen her around—it was a small town—but had yet to enquire about her.

He stared at the stars above him and wondered if this was what love felt like—he had never experienced it before. Although he had witnessed some of his friends in love, his connection with Maya seemed more profound, far deeper than what others had experienced. He could also sense that this was the beginning of something bigger, which, perhaps, hadn't fully begun yet, but it would, sooner rather than later. He could brook no delay. He was desperate to meet her again, if possible, under the dark cover of night.

Shiv was perceptive and knew this was not a passing infatuation. This wasn't a fleeting crush but a love unlike any other; it wouldn't fade. He had been lonely for so many years, a naysayer, but today, something within him had transformed. It was as if Maya had brought light into his life. He had never longed for love because he had never experienced it. But then the dormant pessimist within him awoke to proclaim that everything that had a beginning would have an end. He was sceptical and apprehensive about diving into an ocean where both the depths and shores were unfathomable. It was like chasing a shoal of fish, his feelings drawing him deeper and deeper into the abyss. Maya had enchanted him—much like the ocean that entices one to immerse their soul in it. Her beauty hypnotized him—the clear dusky skin, the rosy cheeks, the lips that could convey a thousand words without moving an inch. Her eyes conveyed a distinct innocence and were capable of wounding a million hearts and launching a thousand ships.

Shiv remembered the first time he saw Maya. She had passed by his shop while he was busy with customers. He had noticed her deep blue eyes, but that was all. Then he had forgotten about her. Another day, he had noticed her in the doorway of a restaurant where he had gone for tea. It was unusual for girls to dine alone, but she had sat at a table near his. As he had been ill that day and was not feeling well, he had ignored her.

A torrent of memories kept flashing that night—memories that were once considered insignificant, trivial, forgettable. Another day, Maya had stormed inside a restaurant, this time with a friend. He had looked up from his tea and samosas, but decided to ignore the coincidence. There was nothing unusual about it since the restaurant was famed for its samosas and many gathered there.

He had wondered whether she had recognized him—a thought persisting just for a few seconds. Was she deeply embedded inside his subconscious? Did he dream of her face, flailing arms, soft eyes and long, curly hair tied in plaits? He had removed her from his conscious memory immediately after leaving the restaurant.

Then there was the Holi from last year. He had gone to buy colours, and he had seen her again in the market. Her hair was lighter, her eyes sadder than before. He was once again curious whether she had recognized him, though her expression conveyed not a glimmer of familiarity. He was not even sure whether she had noticed him in the crowd. *Why should she recognize me?* he had thought to himself. He was aware of his ordinariness, his plebeian roots and his social status.

After purchasing the colours, he had left almost instantly. There was no one to help him at his shop, and he had to rush. Hobnobbing with young girls was a luxury he could ill afford. There was also the lurking fear that if he peered into her eyes, it would open a path leading into uncharted territory where he would get lost, unable to find a way out.

Time seemed to have come to a standstill as the memories surfaced one after the other with a vengeance. Today, he could hear his heart pounding loudly like a staccato of bullets, and feel his mind racing down the hills—he wondered whether it would stop at the valley below or reach the plains near Kathgodam.

4

Maya's driving force in her life was her brother, Akaash, and she was apprehensive about him finding out about her encounter with Shiv. She believed in Bhai's intentions; he did not have any ulterior motive. It was not as if he wanted to dominate her to fulfil some sadist urge. It was just his deep affection for her; he always had her best interest in mind. At times he could be overbearing but Maya did not resent it. Yet, after her encounter with Shiv, she felt it would be nice if he could leave her alone sometimes! How would he ever realize the depth of her feelings for Shiv!

Very few in Ranikhet liked Shiv. He appeared grumpy to the majority who failed to see through his tough exterior, whose understanding was skin-deep. Most of the time, he kept to himself, giving the impression that he was arrogant and scornful of others. It was farthest from the truth. He could also be rude at times, which was why he was disliked. Maya was the only one who was able to see through him.

Shiv had never been able to taste the sweetness of a carefree childhood. He had been forced to take up responsibilities and start working very early in his life as his mother was drunk most of the time and his father had abandoned their family long back. He had a younger sister whom he loved and adored, and he lived for her. Maya had heard stories about him and his family from a friend who lived near him.

His sister studied in the same school as Maya, and it was there that she spotted him the second time. It was just days after she had first seen him inside his shop. She noticed the gentle care and affection that radiated from his eyes when he handed the school bag to his sister and stood there, transfixed, till she disappeared inside the building. That minor detail would have escaped most, but Maya had picked it. Shiv's sister hadn't looked back or said goodbye; instead, she had playfully run towards her classmates upon spotting them. Maya had noticed tears gently streaming down Shiv's cheeks.

Initially, she thought it was an illusion, a product of her imagination, but she realized he was genuinely sad. The sadness that he carried in his eyes was often misconstrued as anger but Maya recognized it as the tragedy in his life. She had woven a narrative around those tears. Perhaps they came at the thought that he had lost his sister, or maybe because she had not bothered to look back at him, bid him goodbye or display a modicum of gratitude for dropping her off at school despite being deprived of the opportunity to study himself. What would happen when she grew up? The thought of separation after she got married or went off to the plains to study or work had perhaps played on his mind.

Of course, Maya couldn't be certain of any of this. His tears might have been caused by an irritation in his eyes; he could have contracted an infection. Or maybe he was reminded of his family's tragic past. It was just conjecture.

The workings of Shiv's mind were difficult to decipher. A person's mind is one of the greatest enigmas; Maya had never understood hers, let alone others'.

★

Shiv had not even noticed Maya that day. After all, she was just one of the many schoolgirls who loitered in the school's playgrounds. He suspected that they looked down on him and scorned him for being a poor kid and not attending school. Who would bother to know more about his predicament? Who was interested?

Maya was different. She was the one who had gauged the

depths of his mind, who had heard his heartbeats like drops of water falling on a drum, who had communicated with his soul without bothering for a reply. It was an intangible love extending beneath layers of their conscious existences.

She often saw him with books in his hands. What surprised her was when she spotted him with a book of poems by famous poets sticking out of his cloth bag. She wondered why he was carrying them.

Sometimes, she was tempted to ask him but refrained. It was taboo for girls to talk to strangers; besides, she was aware that she would not be able to utter even a few coherent sentences. The moment she spotted him, she would feel her knees weakening and tongue getting tied. She would blush like a rose at the very sight of him, even if from a distance. No other boy could elicit such reactions from her. Speaking to him was out of the question, and she had yet to muster the courage.

Sometimes Maya would arrive at the school when he was expected—about 15 minutes before she would normally have, as he had to open his shop—so that she could study him from close quarters. However, those would be the days he invariably did not show up; instead his mother dropped off his sister. At times, she wondered if there was some supernatural force warning her that their paths were not destined to converge.

One day he came to school with a book of Kabir's poems. She, too, had been reading Kabir at the time. The joy of seeing him with the same book was boundless. She initially attributed this to their karmic connection but soon dismissed it as a coincidence. Back then, she had not realized that she had fallen in love with him. After all, she had no clue of how Cupid played games with human beings. What was love? How did one define it? Was it different from Bhai's affection towards her? Maya just had a faint longing to catch a glimpse of Shiv—at his shop or the school when he dropped his sister off.

★

For Maya, school was like heaven. In the morning, she got to see Shiv, and then she learnt things that she always felt blessed to know. To her, school was a place to expand her imagination, make friends, gain new perspectives, and, of course, knowledge.

She travelled to far-off places around the world during her geography lessons. During literature, she entered into different realms inhabited by strange people, getting transported to distant England or India during the times of Kalidasa and Mirza Ghalib. Sometimes, Maya imagined herself standing alongside Bhagat Singh in the freedom struggle, waiting to be hanged. At other times, she imagined competing against P.T. Usha in the Olympics. She also honed her skills in various extra-curricular activities. For Maya, the purpose of education was not just to score marks to land a good job and earn pots of money. She lived her education, unlike others who just studied for their exams. The ritual of going to school every morning was not a burden to her; it was an experience she cherished. The thought of vacations made her feel dejected.

She was known among her classmates as a nerd, but a gorgeous one. She was an all-rounder, taking part in drama, sports, rock climbing, dancing, quiz and story-writing competitions. She was famed for her sprints, and sometimes ran half-marathons, barefoot and uphill.

Maya's passion for running had originated one fine afternoon when she had run away from home for a short period. Upset over an argument with Bhai and after shedding buckets of tears, she stormed out of her house and soon found herself running at top speed. She had been only six years old then but ran as fast as she could along the lake where tourists often gathered. It was off-season and the area was desolate. She soon forgot her sorrows and wished to run faster than a stream flowing down a mountain. The very act of running fast was intoxicating for her, and the argument with Bhai slipped her mind. She was captivated by the sound of the rushing water, feeling an urge to merge with the lake's gentle flow. She forgot she was running along its edge, yearning to leap from rock to rock with the grace of a deer. The lake held a mysterious allure, as though it might lead her to a world of fairies and angels. Even at such a young age, it had brought a rare calm to her mind—a profound realization for a six-year-old. She felt joy in running alongside the lake.

Bhai had set out to locate her but had been unable to find her. He had returned home, wondering whether the police should be informed. In their small town, it would have instantaneously made news, which he was keen to avoid. Little did he imagine that Maya would be running along the lake. He had wept copious tears as it suddenly occurred to him that he had lost the most precious person in his life. He swore to never quarrel with her or hurt her again. If he ever fought with her, he would stick to limits. As an older brother, his duty was to take her failings and eccentricities in his stride. Those long hours of agonizing suspense and tension were unbearable for Bhai.

Fortunately, Maa had not been at home and only heard about the incident later that evening. Just as Bhai had finally decided to reach out to his mother, Maya appeared in front of him. That was the day he realized how much he loved her, and she realized how much she loved him.

Maya chuckled when she saw her brother standing in front of their house, about to depart for the police station. He wept bitterly and hugged her tight, muttering through gritted teeth, 'I will never let you go again.' He had held her so fiercely that it had hurt her, the pain lasting till the next day. Not that she minded it. It was the first time she had witnessed her brother weeping; Bhai was known for his fortitude and ability to stand like a rock during storms and tempests. She had also wept loudly, nestling in his embrace.

But Maya was not the type to linger in sentimentalities. Without wasting time, she caught her puzzled brother's hand and ran. Akaash was not in the mood to run but had played along, so overjoyed was he to see his sister again. He noticed that she was wearing chappals, which had given way. Eventually, he managed to stop her and bent down to fix the chappals she wore on her tiny blister-peppered feet. They continued again, and she stopped when they reached the lake. She wished to share the sublime experience with him. They both started running along it, briefly stopping to listen to the sound of the swirling waters, the chirping of the birds and the myriad musical notes. Like a well-rehearsed orchestra, the music synchronized and the setting sun created its magical aura. She pointed to the floating clouds, imagining them as their protectors from the vagaries of nature.

He held Maya's hand as they rested by the lake and remarked, 'Don't you ever run away again, okay?' Maya smiled and promised not to repeat the act ever again. She had been too young to be able to gauge the depth of his anxiety.

As the years passed, Bhai grew more and more possessive about her. While she was mostly fine with it, she sometimes felt it was an obsession. Not that she was trained in psychology, but there were times she felt it was a strange kind of possessiveness and love, and once in a while, she even resented it. She could also feel it getting more and more intense with the passing days. Was he trying to step into their father's shoes, who had neglected them? Or was it because he had never tried to cultivate relationships with other girls, despite most of them swooning over him? Was it the manifestation of an unmet emotional need?

★

Maa had once decided to take them to visit an astrologer—the one everyone in Ranikhet visited at least once in their lifetime. The astrologer lived far away, inside a cave high up in the hills; it was quite an adventure getting there. Maa rented a blue-coloured diesel hatchback car with an engine that purred softly. They had left home at dawn, when it was still dark and freezing outside. The surroundings were desolate; not a soul stirred. A faint orange hue was visible on the eastern horizon; the sun was yet to rise fully in its resplendent glory. The occasional bird chirped.

A solitary goat wandered near their car. Its eyes seemed sleepless and bloody to Maya. It appeared like a carnivorous animal, reminiscent of the tiger they had once spotted on a visit to Corbett—one of the few occasions her father had taken them on an excursion. The goat looked homicidal, bloodthirsty, as if it was about to pounce on them. She knew it was all in her imagination, possibly emanating from her sleepless night. Nonetheless, the uncanny feeling persisted during their journey.

Maya believed in premonitions. The day had not started on the right note; the goat's red eyes had felt ominous. She also believed that a day that did not start well would not go well or end well. She had a hunch that this trip would either make or break her. She was a kid, being dragged outside the limits of her haven. She wished to return to the comfort of her bed. The lake she had seen flowing with water a few days back was now frozen, covered with ice. Not a soul moved on the surface; the fishes were all below, invisible. The thought that they were imprisoned under the ice made her feel claustrophobic and suffocated.

The sun did not rise that day; the clouds obscured it, as if confining it behind their dark cover. This time the feeling was different, and Maya did not feel claustrophobic. Her mind spun vivid fantasies, imagining the sun had voluntarily surrendered to the clouds, perhaps in response to a long-held plea. The sun was enjoying the confinement.

It had been a bleak day for Maya. The cold wind seeped through the car windows, chilling her to the bone. Her skin was pale, her nails brittle, and her face felt drained of life. They travelled in silence, captivated by the desolate landscape, without a single vehicle passing by. Maya, who normally dismissed ghost stories with a laugh, felt a strange energy in the air that day—a fear of the unknown, which was both unsettling and vivid.

They finally reached Dunagiri after a tiresome journey, and stopped at the foot of a hill covered in Amrutha, the climbers pulsating with life even in peak winter. From there, they had to trek for 10 km to reach the astrologer's cave. The trek felt much longer—almost 50 km—to Maya. It's not that she was averse to walking—she could walk much more effortlessly—but that morning was different; it was filled with apprehensions, deep forebodings and a thousand thoughts crowding her young mind.

They spoke very little as they made their way to the cave. Bhai did most of the talking, warning her and Maa to watch their steps as the path grew rocky and uneven. They walked together, supporting each other and keeping an eye out for potential dangers. When they finally reached the cave, they had to bend and crawl through the narrow entrance before being able to walk upright. Fortunately, all of them were rather short in height, making it easier to navigate.

The temperature inside the cave was −10°C. Despite being at a higher altitude than Ranikhet, it felt cosy and welcoming, which helped ease their fear of heights. Maa squeezed Maya's hand, offering reassurance and a sense of familiarity. The cave was unlike anything Maya had ever seen, with stalactites and stalagmites rising and hanging like natural sculptures. Many devotees often likened their shapes to deities, and Maya thought one resembled Lord Shiva.

The impeccable flowers and dainty-looking fruits jutting out from the walls contrasted with the starkness of the surroundings. Maya was at a loss for words to describe the beauty within the cave when they, all of a sudden, stumbled upon a waterfall cascading down one of the walls. The source of the waterfall was nowhere in sight; it just threw pearl-like droplets on Maya's face, as if to welcome her. Maya was overwhelmed with gratitude for nature.

It was a novelty for Maa as well, despite having visited

the place before. She had previously come with a companion to know what the future held for them. Some predictions had come to fruition, while some had not. Now that she had brought her daughter along to this palace of wisdom, it was a different experience for her.

They walked through the cave for half an hour deep into the mountains. Not a soul was in sight; it was futile to expect other visitors in this extreme weather. Maya removed her jacket and tied it around her waist. The blood coursing through her veins pulsed with life again, echoing the rhythm of the waterfall. Her face was damp with sweat droplets and her heartbeat settled back into its regular pattern; she had sprung back to life.

Maya had followed Maa like a little duckling trailing its mother until, at a distance, they finally spotted a sadhu sitting erect, unbothered by the freezing temperature, draped only in a saffron cloth around his legs. Maya was unable to comprehend how the man could withstand such cold; it momentarily reinforced her faith in a divine power that often felt fickle and prone to disillusionment. She had seen many holy men in her town, but most failed to command respect. She was reminded of her mother's bitter experience, but this one seemed different. He radiated luminescence; he didn't just reflect the surrounding light; it seemed as though he *was* the source of it. The entire environment around him glowed with an unearthly brightness, as if animated by the fire within him. It was surreal.

The sadhu's eyes fell on Maya as they approached, and his face melted into a faint smile that conveyed a profound insight. Pointing at Maya, he said, 'So this is the one; she, right there, is *Jeevan*.'

Maya felt as though she was in a trance. Was it a dream or a manifestation of her fecund imagination? Would it turn into a nightmare? She had yet to figure it out. She sat down next to him on the floor, which was damp and cold. She was wearing a salwar kameez and could feel the wetness of the floor seep through the material and on to her skin.

Water droplets continued to fall on Maa and Bhai, like a divine petal shower, much like people showering flowers at candidates during election campaigns. Yet the drops touched neither Maya nor the Sadhu.

The sadhu spoke in a soft voice, which Maya found to be incongruous with his personality. She had expected it to be gruff or deep, but it was comforting, as if to reassure them of the future. At times, it sounded like a lullaby. He repeated, 'You are Jeevan.'

Maya needed clarification; had he mistaken her for someone else? He gazed intently at her, his eyes piercing through her being and touching her soul. The smile on his lips grew more enigmatic, which stirred a sense of foreboding within her.

'When I say "Jeevan", I mean life. You will experience life in all its extreme forms—from the darkest depths to the highest joys. You were born to live fully, to embrace both the glories and the agonies of existence. But to attain this ultimate bliss, you will have to traverse the seas, experience volcanic eruptions, and endure tempests and rough earthquakes. You were not born to live an ordinary life; angst will be a constant companion in your journey. You will have to follow your heart, take risks in life and suffer pain. Once you start following your heart, there is no looking back.'

Maya had glanced at Maa and noticed sweat trickling down her forehead despite the freezing cold. Her face had lost colour. She appeared terrified—as if she had spotted a ghost—and she seemed to regret bringing them on this excursion. Her expression conveyed that she had reached a point of no return, of imminent disaster. Such is the nature of tragedy: if we don't expect it, we don't know about it, but if we know it, we expect it till our last breath. There is no scope to rest or relax; it does not allow you to live or die. That is what life is all about.

Bhai, on the other hand, was unruffled. He had not lost his composure and sat there with a slightly amused expression, at peace with himself. Such was his nature; he was not prone to getting carried away easily. He was unbothered by this sadhu, whose age and antecedents were undefined, sitting on a pedestal—a cut above mortal beings, aloof from the ordinary vicissitudes of life. Suddenly, the sadhu seemed insignificant to Maya; his utterances were to be taken with a pinch of salt. However, as she stole another sidelong glance at her mother, he regained significance. There were two parallel sources of energy at that moment and she was right at the centre of that whirlpool, spinning round and round, unsure of where to settle down. Maya felt torn between two conflicting energies—one source emanated from Bhai and the other one from the sadhu. Ultimately, she closed her eyes, seeking clarity, and chose Bhai. The sadhu smiled, which she construed as a reprimand.

It had started snowing on their way back, as expected given the time of the year. Only a few lights were visible in the distance, piercing through the darkness and the thick clouds. They had reached home around midnight, had a quiet dinner and never spoken of the encounter again. Maya had absorbed whatever she wished to, and it was an encounter Maa was only too willing to brush off or perhaps bury deep inside the crevices of her mind. Bhai had displayed incredulity and disbelief; it was a non-event for him.

The future lay in the hands of the divine power that Maya vaguely believed in.

5

'Maya! Maya!'

Someone seemed to be calling her name, but there wasn't anyone in sight. Her deep blue eyes scanned the surroundings, darting left and right, but she was unable to spot anybody. Was she hallucinating or was it a ghost? Her mind often dragged her into the realm of phantasmagoria. Eerie as these moments were, she enjoyed them.

After a while, she realized that there was nobody around.

Maya had an extraordinary mind—one half was a volcano spouting lava, with the tectonic plates of her brain brushing against one another, while the other half was reserved for peaceful meditation, at one with the cosmic universe, but somehow they balanced each other out. She was a bundle of contradictions, a confluence of extremes.

'Maya!' her best friend, Tamara, called out once again. This time, Maya felt assured that it must have been Tamara calling before and not something she had imagined.

Then she remembered that an examination was coming up and they were studying by the lake. Maya blinked twice and replied, 'Yes, Tamara!'

Tamara, smirking mischievously, suddenly touched Maya's face and ran. Tamara was known as *toofan*—she could run faster than the wind and soar like an eagle—a toofan that one could not catch, that had no independent existence but manifested itself through the sheer velocity of the moving air. She was Maya's confidante, someone she could trust with her exclusive secrets and darkest thoughts, someone she knew would remain faithful to her—like her Bhai. Tamara was, in many ways, Maya's soulmate.

Tamara was the one person Maya wanted to be around all the time. They were in synergy and could sense each other's energies; Tamara triggered the power within Maya and vice versa. They made each other stronger to overcome the trials and tribulations of life.

Maya suddenly remembered a particular summer evening. It had been unusually hot in Ranikhet, and 10 of them had gathered by the lake. They had waded into the shallow end, letting their feet sink into the brittle rocks beneath the cool surface, the water tickling their skin. They pranced around as the sun went down, then lay down on the grassy bed, singing and watching the birds return to their nests. As dusk set in and the shadows grew longer, the sky became dark and serene. The banks felt like their private domain, even though many tourists and locals often strolled past, unaware of this particular spot. It remained largely secluded—not out of fear, but because few found it enticing enough to pause and linger.

Maya could not understand why the memories of that evening suddenly popped up because her mind immediately digressed to another incident. A few days after Holi, which would remain a milestone in her life, they had gathered by the lake. They had been lying on the bed like any other day, singing songs in tune with the chirping birds, when Maya heard a faint sound—as if someone was crying for help.

She sat up with a jolt and looked around but could not detect anything out of the ordinary. After a brief reconnaissance, she lay back when she did not hear the sound again. Just as she was convinced it was all in her head, she heard the sound a second time and realized it was coming from the lake. What initially seemed like a branch in the water turned out to be a girl. Tamara had also heard it, and before Maya could react, she had dived in to help.

The current was particularly rough that evening; the branches, leaves and flowers swirling violently did not make for a pleasant sight. After some time, Maya noticed that the girl and Tamara were also being swept away. Tamara, an expert swimmer, was helpless against the strong current. Maya screamed for help; she could not bear the sight of her soulmate being carried away. She wanted to jump in and save them but she had never learnt to swim. Bhai had tried to teach her many times, but she had never been interested as she found it boring. She was also a tad terrified of water, having heard ghastly stories of folks drowned by the undercurrents.

While others stood there, flummoxed and unsure of what to do, Maya sprinted off in the direction she was confident help would be readily available. She desperately needed an expert swimmer willing to help and ran as fast as her legs could take her.

She located Shiv loitering by the side of a fig tree at some distance from the lake. She cried at the top of her voice, 'Shiv! Help! Tamara is drowning.'

Shiv had been concerned when he saw Maya running towards him barefoot but could not initially hear what she said. He did, however, realize that something was drastically wrong.

'Shiv, two girls are drowning there. Do you know how to swim?'

Others would have responded with 'Who are the girls?' 'Why did they jump into the water?' 'Did they fall?' But not Shiv! It was not in his nature.

Maya saw Shiv as a saviour—a person who was constantly at the service of humanity. But what was this now? It was not the image of Shiv she held in her mind. He kept staring at her. Had he not heard her? Or was he so carried away by her sight that nothing else could penetrate his mind? Her heart skipped a beat but she realized it was not the time for romantic sentiments. She grabbed his hands and pulled him towards the lake.

Neither of the girls was in sight. The others had given up hope but pointed in the direction the current was flowing. Maya and Shiv sprinted along the banks; Shiv was, of course, way ahead and running at a speed faster than light. As he plunged into the swirling waters, Maya chanted a short prayer. Her mind was also in a dilemma. Was this the right thing to do? Was it right to expose Shiv to a life-threatening risk?

Of course, Tamara was her dearest friend, but Shiv was special. Then, as if by some divine intervention, she had spotted them—three heads bobbing up and down in the turbulent waters—but they disappeared again. Maya's heart pounded wildly, a deafening *Dhak! Dhak! Dhak!* She couldn't bear to look back at the water. For a moment, she was certain this was the end. There seemed to be no hope, as five agonizing minutes had passed—minutes that felt like an eternity.

But then, Maya noticed movement in the distance and could make out a few figures. As they drew closer, she identified one as Tamara and the other as Shiv, supporting another figure, their outlines becoming clearer with each passing minute. They were safe and sound! Shiv had achieved the seemingly impossible. The stress was slowly dissipating, but the aftermath of the tension lingered. Maya felt faint.

The others rushed towards them, cheering and hugging Tamara and the little girl whom Tamara had dived after to save from drowning.

Shiv had managed to save them. This wasn't to take credit away from Tamara—after all, who would have dared to impulsively jump into the lake to save someone? But, of course, Shiv was, for Maya, the incarnation of Lord Shiva.

She spotted Shiv at a distance, watching the celebrations as if he had played no part, as if he was just a bystander.

Maya had run to Tamara and hugged her tightly, whispering, 'I was so scared, Tamara. Please do not ever do that again.'

'What are you saying, Maya? The girl would have drowned, and her parents would have been devastated.'

Tamara's reply made Maya regret the thoughtless statement she had made. As she closed her eyes, the image of Tamara jumping into the lake, followed by Shiv, appeared like a bad dream; she wanted to erase it from her memory. It later dawned on her that she had hugged Shiv much tighter than she had held Tamara. He, in turn, had raised his eyebrows and stared at her in a way no one else ever had. Pure passion had oozed from his eyes. Yet, he had been hesitant to hold her tighter and shower her with kisses from head to toe. He would perhaps have done it if others had not been around.

It had been impulsive; Maya would have hugged even if it had been someone else. After all, he had saved two lives, one of whom happened to be her best friend. Yet the intensity, perhaps, would not have been the same, it would not have lingered. Perhaps hugging any other boy would have caused her skin to erupt in goosebumps, her mind would have floated in the sky for a few minutes and she would have also been aroused—but not to this extent. Shiv was special. He was unique.

They had interrogated the little girl. She was five years old and a resident of Nainital. She had come to Ranikhet to visit her maternal uncle, who was very strict. The girl had managed to sneak out while he was sleeping, and she beseeched the group not to disclose the incident to him. They refused; it was their duty. And how would she explain her drenched clothes? Did she not deserve a thorough spanking?

After dropping the girl off, Shiv left as he had to get back to his shop. The rest of the group discussed it for a while and decided to keep the incident to themselves because their parents would surely stop them from visiting the lake if the story got out.

Maya's mind had been preoccupied with only one thought—had the other girls sensed lust in the way she had hugged Shiv, holding on for a few minutes? Or had they construed it as mere gratitude for saving two lives? Lust was not the word—she was passionate. Passion and lust are two distinct characteristics of the human mind but are often used interchangeably. One keeps you preoccupied with the physical aspects, concerned only with the fulfilment of hidden sexual desires. Sometimes, it is a desire to dominate the other person, to display one's strength, to be aroused, to shower kisses on the other and indulge in various other acts of playfulness.

She had witnessed the act long back with sleepy eyes. She had almost screeched in fear and had felt unsettled for a while. She had wanted to call out for Bhai—Maa had to be rescued—but her instincts had advised against it. She had been relieved to see Maa hale and hearty the following day. The incident was never mentioned.

But passion originates in the mind—it is a desire to integrate with the other person, to become one and share each other's lives. It is about feeling the gentle touch of the other. Just being in each other's presence lifts you to the seventh heaven of delight. Only the couple truly understands the nature of the attraction; others can only speculate and gossip endlessly.

Maya could feel Shiv in her bones, through the blood coursing through her veins, in her neurons, in the beating of two hearts, in the unity of a pair of minds. She realized again that day that there was magic in his presence—in the mere sight of him, his smell, his touch, the sound of his voice. She was mesmerized by his aura, his being. These feelings can't be described; they have to be felt. The depth of these emotions can't be fully expressed through prose and poetry, no matter how talented the writer is. Maya strongly believed that, at best, one could attempt to articulate the maelstrom of thoughts and feelings inside one's own mind, but no one could fully convey someone else's feelings—no matter how much they tried. It was for the individuals to feel.

In that moment by the lake, Maya had felt as if she and Shiv had slipped into a world of their own, where only they existed—two bodies and two hearts, with everyone else fading into insignificance. Did anyone else even exist there? It was not a tangible place, but a metaphorical one, where others were mere specks on the horizon.

She wondered why the little girl had been by the lake that day, and why the currents had been unusually strong. The lake was typically calm, and the weather had also been clear. What had drawn Shiv to the fig tree near the lake? Maya and her friends often visited the area but had never seen him before. Were these odd occurrences mere quirks of the universe or was something larger at play? Though Maya leaned towards scepticism, moments like this made her question her agnostic stance. She had always believed that every phenomenon had a rational explanation, a cause that could be understood if examined closely. But this? How could she explain the strangeness of it all? For the first time, Maya felt her belief in a higher power deepen.

Maya was usually focused on her studies, aspiring to become a doctor, but her recent emotions had disrupted her concentration. Sensing her turmoil, Tamara advised her to shape her destiny through hard work and determination, dismissing the idea of fate. Yet, she also suggested that Maya's feelings for Shiv were significant and should not be ignored, leaving Maya deeply conflicted.

No matter how hard Maya tried to focus on her exams, her thoughts kept drifting back to that fateful day at the lake, to her connection with Shiv and to Tamara's words. Troubled by the events that had unfolded at the lake, Maya resolved to overcome her fear and learn to swim. She briefly considered asking Tamara or Bhai for help, but dismissed the idea; this was something she wanted to do on her own, something she needed to accomplish for herself. Every morning, she walked down to the lake, determined to teach herself. There weren't many swimmers around, so she tried to learn from the fish. She watched them glide gracefully and studied their tranquil movements and postures. The way they took to water as men took to earth fascinated her. It seemed that they were one with the water, the corals and other creatures in the water—a harmony pervaded their universe. Human beings are far more complicated. They are not so harmonious; they bicker and quarrel and lack cohesion. They are crooked at times. Yet they are supposed to be the most intelligent species on this planet. The ways of nature are truly inscrutable!

There was another motivation behind learning to swim; she wished to surprise Bhai one day by jumping into the lake, sparking panic in him and forcing him to dive in and rescue her. Yet, the thought of even a split second of panic affecting Bhai's health worried her. Bhai could handle anything that happened to him, but when it came to Maya, he was vulnerable. Yet, the thought of pranking him kept her amused and entertained.

Maya strongly believed in the importance of family ties. She felt that families should support each other through both good times and bad, remaining devoted to one another. Friends might come and go, relationships could falter, but families are bound together through an invisible force—blood ties were unbreakable. No one runs away from their blood; even if forsaken for a while, families come back together as soon as the wounds heal. Her father, of course, had been an exception. He had a history of broken promises and pretences.

Eventually, Maya decided to execute her plan on Tamara and Bhai. She called them over to the lake one evening. The sky radiated a beautiful orange streak with shades of red visible at the far end, the drifting clouds adding a touch of mystery. The lake reflected the shifting colours, creating an ethereal atmosphere, one Tamara usually loved to gaze at.

'Why have you called me here today?' Bhai was upset whenever he had to be around Maya's friends; he did not get along with them. Maya thought it was because of his tendency to be overprotective of her or his difficulty in connecting with people, especially women.

Tamara was the only person who found Bhai rather endearing. The perpetual smile plastered on her face made Bhai even more annoyed. He thought she was mocking him, but Tamara remained unfazed.

Maya told him she wanted to show him something, and the three of them began walking along the lake as the water shimmered. Although a little nervous, Maya was resolute about carrying out her plan. She felt reassured knowing that there were two skilled swimmers with her in case anything went wrong. They eventually stopped and lay down on the grass, taking in the beautiful sunset.

All of a sudden, before they knew what was happening, Maya jumped into the lake. Bhai and Tamara sprang from the bed of grass they were relaxing on and rushed towards her. What Maya hadn't anticipated was the force of the current that evening. It was stronger than when she had practised, and she soon found it tough to push back and fight against the current.

She struggled to stay afloat and had almost given up when she felt a manly hand on her waist, pulling her towards him—from the touch, she knew this wasn't Bhai. His hands curled around her belly as if it was where they belonged forever. The familiarity of his grasp was incredible; it created a different sensation even in the swirling waters.

But how did she realize it was Shiv? She had not seen him. How did her body whirl towards him at his one touch? How did she surrender herself to him as if she had been his for ages? What magnetic force had pulled her towards him? What was this force that was trying to unite them? How did he manage to reach her whenever she needed him?

Her mind reverberated with these thoughts as water gushed into her system and she found it tough to breathe. The world around her dimmed until she could only hear muffled voices, distant and fading.

'Maya… Maya!' The voices came and went.

'I see her eyes opening,' she heard Bhai say. The dread of facing Bhai made her want to return to her unconscious state. As she opened her eyes and slowly gained consciousness, she saw Tamara, Bhai and, towering above them, Shiv! The bulging vein on his forehead spoke of his concern for her. She wished to stand up and hug him, but the sight of Bhai was a dampener.

Once fully conscious, she looked at Bhai and offered her lame explanation. 'I just wanted to show you that I can swim now. I had been practising all week. I didn't mean to scare you. I had not realized that the currents were so strong.'

Bhai stood up and said, 'You have shown me enough for the day, possibly my entire life.' With that, he turned and left. He did not speak to her that night, and Maa was not told about the incident. In any case, suffering from her periodic bouts of depression.

6

Maya could not sleep that night. The mystery of Shiv appearing from obscurity and jumping straight into the lake to save her from certain death was not something that offered a ready explanation. His appearance the other day could be rationalized—perhaps he had decided to take a walk to relax or shake off fatigue. Just because he was not seen in the vicinity on other days did not necessarily point to clairvoyance, and it could have been sheer coincidence.

But Shiv's appearance that day had several thoughts criss-crossing Maya's mind. Was he so mesmerized by her that he had been secretly following her? Was he looking out for her? Did he wish to convey some message to her? Did some supernatural force pull him towards the lake, warning him of an imminent disaster? Or had he simply been strolling around and just happened to be there?

Or was he planning to murder her? Perhaps he had noticed her practising swimming every day and had secretly planned to drown her in the lake. But with Bhai and Tamara present, maybe he had failed to execute his plan. Perhaps rescuing her was a cover; nobody would ever suspect him if he did something to her later. There would be no plausible reason to suspect him of murdering her unless he was caught red-handed in the act.

But if he wanted her to die, why not just let her drown when she was already struggling in the water? He would not have been blamed; it would have just been a natural death. Bhai or Tamara would have jumped in to save her anyway.

But why would he even consider killing her? What could she

possibly have done to him? The only reason she could imagine was that he wanted to erase his feelings for her, knowing these would be impossible to overcome as long as they were both in the same town. The disparity in their social statuses made it clear that they could never be together. Perhaps the thought of loving someone he could never be with was unbearable for him. And in his despair, he felt the only solution was to eliminate her—out of sight, out of mind.

The more Maya considered this, the more sickened she felt. Her throat tightened as she fought back the urge to vomit, feeling a surge of acid reflux from her churning stomach. But then, as quickly as these dark thoughts had surfaced, they began to recede. She was ashamed that such thoughts could even come to her mind and brushed them away. In her heart of hearts, she knew that these had no basis whatsoever.

Maya's thoughts shifted to more comforting possibilities. Perhaps Shiv had followed her to the lake, unaware that Bhai and Tamara would also be present. Maybe he had wanted to talk to her about something important—perhaps to clear the air between them, to share his feelings, or even, to propose?

Now, she was sure. She believed that he wanted to tell her something important. Love could make even a sane person behave foolishly, and men are known to jump the gun. They are, by nature, impulsive and impatient, anxious to upgrade initial fondness to the state of a relationship to consummate their desires. Maya had seen many boys behave similarly. Was that not the case with Ashok, Tamara's admirer? When Tamara rejected him, he was devastated. The entire town knew about it. It had taken him almost a year to get over it. Maya had also felt these strong urges about Shiv, but being a girl, she would wait for the relationship to develop, to flower naturally. Possibly Shiv, as a man, could not.

She slept fitfully for the next few days, in a state of unrest, reliving the moment when Shiv had touched her waist. She would wake up in the middle of the night, feeling his touch on her skin. She wondered how, struggling between life and death—almost sure that her last moments were nearing—she had felt the touch and recognized it as Shiv's and not Bhai's. It was, after all, just the third time in her life that they had touched each other. The first time had been when he had smeared gulaal on her during Holi; the second time had been when she had pulled him towards the lake to save Tamara and the girl, but she had been too tense that day to feel anything.

Maya's body still carried the memory of Shiv's touch that had drawn her towards him and right into his arms. He had pulled her close as if he had done so many times before, by the meadows or at a secluded place up in the mountains. Shiv must have jerked her towards himself using all his strength—there was no scope for gentleness amidst the swirling currents of the lake—but to her, the memories were of a soft and tender pull, almost like how a lotus is plucked out of water.

She also wondered why Bhai had not jumped in to save her. Had he been scared? Or had it just been the primordial urge for self-preservation? Did he feel that losing both of them would have devastated Maa? Was a man capable of thinking logically at such a crucial moment?

Maya remembered a story her teacher had once shared. A man and his wife were both drowning in the sea, the wife holding on to her husband tightly. The husband realized he couldn't reach the shores with her tugging him, so he had just shrugged her off and made it to land all by himself. Ultimately, most human beings are selfish and self-centred. They love themselves the most. The romance found in novels and poems from time immemorial remains confined to the pages of the books. A whole lot of balderdash!

She consoled herself with the thought that Shiv just happened to be swifter. Before Bhai could jump into the lake, he had seen Shiv diving in and felt there was no point in both of them jumping in to save her. That explanation was more plausible. She decided to remove other thoughts from her mind, to think positively. Negativity ultimately harms the individual and disturbs the peace of mind.

Maya then thought of Bhai's reaction after the incident. He had barely spoken to her since, and hadn't even mentioned the incident. How much did he know? Had he attributed Shiv's heroic act to a deliberate and pre-planned drama to convert Bhai and make him more malleable and accepting towards Shiv? The thought of Shiv appearing at the right moment must have crossed his mind. After all, Maya's own mind had entertained fleeting doubts about the timing of Shiv's rescue, and Bhai could not be blamed for harbouring such thoughts.

Maya was a dreamer and believed in magic. When unable to comprehend or explain events, she sought mystical validations. This fact was unknown to most, even Bhai and Maa; only Tamara knew it. She believed in angels, in clairvoyance, and in events that had no rational explanation. Not that she necessarily believed in the supernatural; she was, at heart, an agnostic; she loved her science classes but just believed that certain events were beyond rational explanations and logical reasoning.

Memories surged unexpectedly as she sat motionless on the intricately carved wooden chair by the beautifully crafted console. These pieces of furniture had been passed down for three generations on Maa's side and showcased exquisite craftsmanship. The chair itself was adorned with carvings of lotuses, some in bloom, others closed, each petal etched with painstaking precision. The table, matching in its beauty, featured Brahma Kamals, carved so realistically they seemed almost alive, as though freshly plucked from a garden. The rare, fragrant wood, faintly scented of flowers, added to the illusion of being surrounded by nature.

Maa had once explained that special paints and rare woods had been used to craft the furniture, believing they would promote sound mental health for the girl of the house. Maya often wondered whether the belief would hold true for her. The scepticism had only magnified after her unsettling encounter with the astrologer and her recent encounters with Shiv.

Maya hated the table and the chair, but for practical reasons. If she accidentally brushed against it, her feet would bruise from the carved edges, the pain lasting for several hours. They would sometimes bleed, and she would have to keep them bandaged for several days. The number of such bruises had increased recently because she had become more absent-minded. Were the chair and the table intentionally punishing her for a perceived misdemeanour, or was it the outcome of crimes committed by her ancestors, picking her simply because their blood flowed in her arteries?

Bhai had also, many times, voiced his reservations about the furniture, but never in front of Maa. He hated to hurt her, aware as he was of her sentimental attachment to it. Only recently he had joked that the 'hard' chair hurt his buttocks, but she had laughed it off.

★

It had been a scorching Sunday afternoon, just a few days after they had visited the sadhu. Although Maya initially felt a sense of relief after hearing the soothsayer's prediction about her future, fear still gripped her from time to time. She was only nine years old, and the weight of those words had left her anxious and unsettled. Bhai, noticing the turmoil in her mind, had been furious with Maa for exposing such a young child to the unsettling words of an insensitive astrologer.

Bhai had passed a remark that ignited a spark within her. 'Remember, you are the author of your destiny. Nobody else can guide you on this; you can either make it or break it. You are to blame if experiences are traumatic, and you will get the credit if they turn out pleasant.'

He made a pithy comment—'You make your magic!'—and gently smiled before walking out of the room. Bhai's smiles were always mysterious but also serene, reminding one of the Buddha. His words were even more inscrutable. Maya felt that the comment was likely meant to alleviate her apprehensions arising from the astrologer's predictions and not to allow them to bother her. They had sparked another thought within her—even if fate played games with her, it was she who would be blamed.

Bhai's comments had triggered the arrival of a soulmate in the form of an angel. The dawn had been cloudy, with the sun struggling to make its presence felt through the clouds, when Saria made her appearance. The angel was a solace on the days when Maya felt depressed, bringing tranquillity when her mind swirled with the tumultuous waves of uncertainty and indecision.

Maya was fond of entering a state of suspended disbelief whenever fears overcame her, in a deliberate attempt to wash away her apprehensions. Saria had floated in through the window, wearing a shimmering white dress, followed by a trail of clouds. While it was common for clouds to enter houses in Ranikhet, these were different. They illuminated the room with flashes of incessant blue and red lightning, like fireworks on a Diwali evening.

At first, Maya had dismissed Saria as a dream or an illusion, but her figure soon turned clearer. Saria claimed she had existed for the last 500 years. They engaged in a conversation, discussing life in general. Saria had asked about Maya's feelings, having known what the astrologer had predicted. She had asked Maya not to worry, assuring her that she would ultimately emerge victorious. They had spoken until the clouds cleared and sunlight streamed in through the drapes. Since that day, Saria continued to visit Maya—not every night but quite often, especially when Maya felt overly depressed.

Maya had never told anyone about Saria, not even her mother, and she knew Bhai would have laughed it off. She also was apprehensive that if she mentioned Saria to anyone, she would never reappear as Maya had sworn to an oath of secrecy.

Saria seemed to grow with time, keeping pace with Maya. They were of identical height, size and shape. If Maya gained weight, Saria would also! She was Maya's alter ego!

★

As Maya lay in bed, relentless gusts of wind tore through the air, unleashing a tempestuous symphony of nature's fury. A tantalizing coolness infiltrated the room, along with the intoxicating scent of *raat ki rani* flowers filling the air with their hypnotic perfume. In the midst of this sensory assault, Maya found herself utterly powerless, her heart heavy with a sense of impending doom.

Like a blossoming flower, the love that had once held promise and hope now seemed to be withering before her eyes, condemned to a tragic demise. This fleeting thought filled Maya with fear, as she worried that what once brought her joy might now only lead to heartbreak.

Maya often found herself longing for the simpler days when her love for Shiv had been one-sided. There had been a certain comfort in the unrequited nature of that love. She had believed that remaining in that state would safeguard her delicate heart. Yet, fate—unmoved by her hopes and dreams—had intervened with an unforgiving hand that fateful Holi morning, irrevocably changing the trajectory of their lives.

Now, standing at the precipice of no return, she found herself teetering on the edge of despair. The scent of him lingered in the air, an intoxicating blend of desire and anguish that relentlessly taunted her senses. A firm grip on her waist—a physical reminder of their entwined destinies—tugged at her, echoing the irrepressible pull she felt towards him.

A gentle breeze, carrying the warmth of his breath, caressed her cheeks, igniting a fire within her that threatened to consume everything she held dear. In the recesses of her mind, his image loomed ominously, accompanied by the haunting presence of Bhai and Tamara, their terrified eyes etching themselves into her very being.

In this harrowing tableau, she stood alone, a solitary figure trapped in a labyrinth of emotions, grappling with the agonizing consequences of her choices. The weight of her decisions, the fragility of their love, and the ever-present spectre of those petrified eyes merged into a cacophony of torment that threatened to engulf her entirely.

The white lace curtains with floral accents swayed in the breeze, while the rustle of the trees outside created a soft backdrop for her thoughts. A sweet melody filled her ears, resonating with each heartbeat, but it was not just her own heart that thumped—it felt as if two hearts were intertwined, alternating between slow, steady beats and a faster, romantic rhythm. She sensed that this rhythm was not solely her own; it seemed to come from an external source, perhaps the Almighty, in whom her faith was growing stronger with each passing day. She believed that only He could guide them through the uncertainties of the future.

Theirs was a silent love story, not meant to be broadcasted to the world, nor captured in the pages of romantic novels, nor imprisoned within the soft strains of a Bollywood song. They had both listened to their hearts and spoken to each other with their eyes. It dawned on her that they had not exchanged a word till now. She had called him by name only on the evening she had implored him to save Tamara's life. She had not even heard his voice. But did they need to speak? Was not love expressed on a deeper level? Did it not manifest through expressions, the gentle movement of eyebrows, the flutter of eyelashes, and the intensity of a gaze? She had no clue; perhaps theirs was unique. All relationships could not follow a set template; if one attempted to, it would explode into a thousand fragments. There was no need for grand declarations like 'I can die for you' or 'I love you from the core of my being'. Words sounded too banal, mundane and commonplace. She could feel him in his gentle footsteps, the fragrance of his body, and in the aura that preceded him.

Maya felt she was going insane. She had heard that love could drive people to madness, and now she was experiencing it firsthand. Sleep had deserted her, but she felt perfectly comfortable staying awake through the night. Did Shiv feel the same way? Every conscious thought seemed unreal to her; the only reality was Shiv. His thoughts elevated her to heights of desire, igniting a longing for his physical presence, but it was entrapped under a blanket of foreboding.

She had pinned all her hopes on him, but what if he did not feel the same? What if he wanted to escape from this unreal world? What if this entire episode turned out to be a waste of time, an exercise in frivolity and childishness? Her situation had changed; she now needed his validation at every stage. Until a few days ago, she had been content with her one-sided love, placing him on a pedestal to be worshipped and adored from a distance. Now, she had become greedy; she wanted them to possess each other. There was no desire for material wealth, no longing for a luxurious life. He could continue the way he was, helping out in the shop. Maya imagined Shiv hiring an extra hand to help; he could then go home in the afternoons to relax, sleep, walk by the lake, trek up the mountains or read his favourite Kabir poems. She would drop by on her way back from school. The evenings were meant for them, savouring each other's presence. She found herself looking forward to that life. Marriage seemed immaterial; it was just an institution, a certificate from society. In that moment, she did not care about the surroundings, about Ranikhet's gossipy residents, or even Maa and Bhai. They were free to accept or reject them; she did not seem to care.

It was just him, standing in front of her, in flesh and blood, walking in the house, sitting at the table for breakfast, lunch and dinner. A smile plastered on his face, his long fingers picking up the covers of the bowls containing rice, lentil or chapattis. She needed him close to her, caressing her, sharing sweet thoughts, reciting Kabir, cooking vegetables or the occasional sweet dish and laughing heartily at an odd joke. Did he know that she pined for him, yearned for his golden touch to apply soothing balm on her cuts and bruises, to sing lullabies till she fell asleep?

Maya rubbed her eyes.

Shiv stood there, smiling and oblivious to her disbelief, inching closer from the kitschy cactus table they had bought at a fair.

'Is this you?' she whispered. *Is this the real Shiv?*

He smirked and edged even closer. She could hear his deep breath and heartbeat as she stood near the wall, her intense gaze studying him. Now so close, she could almost touch him. His hand brushed against hers, sending a tingling sensation through her body. Blood rushed to her head, causing mild vertigo, as if she were on a roller coaster. Her stomach tightened at his touch as he gently rubbed his thumb along her palm, their fingers intertwining naturally. Goosebumps rippled from her toes to the top of her head, making her hair stand on end.

Shiv didn't stop; his movements seemed endless. His fingers traced her shoulders and other parts of her body, igniting a lingering heat that refused to fade even after he withdrew. Uncertainty flickered across his face as he contemplated his next move. Maya understood his feelings without words; he wanted to hold her tightly, and she wouldn't mind dying in his embrace.

As passion overtook her, thoughts of life and death faded. All she desired was to become one with him, to be as close as possible. She longed for him to kiss every inch of her body and soul. She craved ecstasy, the ultimate joy, feeling as if she had yearned for it her entire life.

Maya wanted this moment to last forever. She craved him, needed him. Yet, all he had done was hold her hand, caressing it gently and gripping it tightly, without daring to venture further. Time seemed to freeze; they had lost track of the earth's rotation, oblivious to the arrival of the moon and stars on the horizon.

For Shiv, Maya was willing to sacrifice everything—Ranikhet, Maa, even Bhai—if they opposed their relationship. Their bond had been forged not through physical contact but through the deep connection in their eyes—the instant she had looked into his and seen the love and care radiating from him. On that fateful Holi, he had vowed never to abandon her, promising to care for her for all eternity.

That was their pivotal moment, marking the point of no return. It was a realization that their love could either plunge them into despair or lift them into a blissful existence free from the daily struggles for food, shelter and clothing. In that world, they would stroll hand in hand, expressing their feelings through silent glances or pursuing shared dreams—a perfect love story yet to be written in this world.

'You are a goddess,' Shiv whispered into her ear.

Suddenly, there was a knock on the door. Maya heard Bhai calling her from the other side, breaking the enchantment of the moment.

Shiv appeared unruffled, not a crease of concern on his rugged face.

Maya urged him to leave, but he refused. 'I have not come here to leave.'

Maya could hardly believe her ears.

Bhai continued to knock, wondering if Maya was all right. She enjoyed her afternoon sleep but usually woke up after a few knocks.

'Bhai, I'm changing; give me a few minutes,' she called out.

She then turned to Shiv and said, 'You have to leave, Shiv. Bhai will not like it.'

Shiv replied without a trace of fear in his voice, 'Now that we are together, no one can stand between us. I will never be unfaithful to you. But I can't hide my love for you, not from anyone. I love you, Maya.' He said it with such ease; his thoughts were uncomplicated, transparent and in tune with his personality.

'I'm not scared to express my love for you, Maya. You were a maya for me till the evening I jumped into the lake after you, until I held you in my arms and pulled you to safety. Now you are both maya and reality.'

Maya pushed him out of her house through the window.

She quickly opened the door for Bhai, but he had left.

Her heart raced; she felt numb with joy but also wary of how this episode would play out. When Bhai got to know about it, would he approve? What about Maa? Would they be able to see through Shiv's exterior and witness the loving soul beneath? Or would they still consider him an uneducated vendor, a boy who had never attended school, who belonged to a low-income family whose father had forsaken them early in life and whose mother survived on liquor?

The future was uncertain. She took it as a challenge, aware that the war consisted of innumerable battles—bloody, fierce and prolonged.

Suddenly her phone rang, and Shiv's name flashed on the screen. Her Shiv was calling. She peered at the phone, checking it from various angles to ascertain whether she was reading it correctly. Seeing his name flashing in her mind made her heart pound, and it skipped a few beats. She was so carried away that she forgot to accept the call. After many attempts, a message appeared. She pinched herself, wondering if this was merely a dream.

Suddenly, a figure emerged from the depths of her subconscious—a vision she had longed for. It was Saria. Maya held a steadfast belief that Saria would grace her with her presence, especially during moments of profound joy or inconsolable sorrow.

Saria, a constant pillar of support, possessed a unique bond with Maya that surpassed even the latter's friendship with Tamara. Saria had an extraordinary quality—an absence of judgement. No matter the circumstances, she would extend her hand, ever ready to aid Maya on her path. The mere thought of Saria's arrival filled Maya's heart with euphoria; it had been years since they last met, and now, like Maya, Saria had matured and blossomed. They stood shoulder to shoulder, their physical attributes mirroring one another's with uncanny precision—a striking resemblance that bound them together.

Maya, always curious, often found herself pondering the mystery of Saria. While some might dismiss her as a mere figment of the imagination, Maya knew otherwise. Saria was a tangible presence, a living embodiment of angelic grace. Today, she wore a stunning pink dress that seemed to elevate her beyond the earthly realm. The delicate lace flowed and twirled, capturing the ripples of existence as it pointed towards the radiant moon above. It was as if the fabric had been summoned to dance among the celestial bodies, guided by the soft glow of the moonlight, enchanting distant galaxies with this extraordinary spectacle.

'So, Shiv,' Saria's voice echoed from the walls. She smiled at Maya, her expression imbued with a magic and charisma that was unmatched by any human being.

Maya blushed at his name. 'Yes. Do you like him?'

It was important for Maya to gain approval from Saria, as she was her only hope. Saria did not belong to this materialistic, unromantic world; she came from the realm of love and abundance. She had scaled mountains, was lighter than the clouds, her eyes twinkling like stars, and her expression conveying magnanimity.

Pride had no place in her world.

'He belongs to our world. Unfortunately, he landed on earth and isn't valued here. I have come to warn you; if you take this path, disaster awaits you both. He will not be accepted because he is a non-conformist and unconventional; he will never bow down to traditional norms. You should also know that he won't wait to be accepted over time because he is impatient and uncompromising.'

Maya fought back. 'What you do not comprehend is that he will do anything for me; I see it in his eyes. I need someone like him.'

Saria retorted, 'If he were conventional, then you wouldn't love him. He may bow down to your love but will you love him then?'

Maya didn't want to hear the truth. 'Yes,' she said abrasively. 'Saria, whenever I have seen him, I have noticed an indomitable power within him. It is unnatural and overpowering. Our love is not to last one lifetime; it is eternal and transcendental. Perhaps its origin lies in our previous births. Some mysterious energy pulls us towards one another. We are meant for each other.'

Tears rolled down her eyes but Maya did not even realize it. 'It's cast in stone. I've never felt like this about anyone; I have not heard such intense emotional sentiments expressed before, neither read them nor seen them in deeply passionate love stories. My body has no control over my actions, and my soul and heart override my mind.'

She was almost wailing now. 'We don't crave each other's bodies; we pine for an ultimate and everlasting union. We have already experienced each other in our lives, and this is just a logical continuation of our past union.'

Saria sat upon the ancient chair that had been in Maya's family for three generations, its jagged edges casting eerie shadows that seemed to pierce Maya's very soul. The intensity in Saria's eyes was overwhelming, as if she held secrets too profound for mortal comprehension. Though Maya sensed the weight of Saria's words, their gravity threatening to consume her, still her heart found itself ensnared in a tempestuous dance of longing and passion.

Her desire for a love transcendental and other-worldly burned within her, igniting an insatiable craving for a connection both sublime and divine. With every fibre of her being, she yearned to immerse herself in an ethereal realm of love that surpassed all earthly bounds. Nothing could restrain her now; no force in existence could halt her pursuit.

Saria vanished into the impenetrable embrace of the night, leaving Maya alone in the dimly lit room. But this solitude did not weigh upon Maya; the presence of Shiv, her steadfast companion, offered solace and a temporary respite from the relentless passage of time. Maya fervently wished for the night to stretch eternally, unwilling to face the impending dawn that would mercilessly thrust her back into the clutches of reality—the reality she dreaded, for it was unyielding and cruel.

7

When the first rays of sunlight grace our faces after a harsh winter, our skin seems to glow, embracing the arrival of spring. The trees shake off the snow with pride, singing a melody that alternates between the dew and the leaves. The amalgamation of the disparate notes sounds like a natural union, creating a seamless harmony.

Maya went to the lake, as always, one evening with Tamara and their friends. Tamara wasn't herself; she initially refused to swim in the lake, which was a strong indicator. She relented after Maya urged her. Maybe it was due to the pressure of studies, or maybe she was feeling down for no apparent reason, but there was something in the air; Maya's instincts were rarely wrong on these matters—she never missed a beat with Tamara. Maya looked at Tamara with deep concern. This was unprecedented. Maya also knew asking Tamara directly would do no good; Tamara hated to burden others with her feelings.

Usually the group's unofficial coach, Tamara did not scold anyone for their mistakes that evening. Instead, she swam alone, as if the others did not exist. Yet, she was always alert, ready to help anyone in trouble or in danger of drowning. This tension was a result of the previous incident, and Tamara always tried her best to prevent any recurrence, keeping a watchful eye on everyone.

But beyond her physical alertness, she seemed otherwise unconcerned. She didn't attempt to correct anyone's posture, style or swimming technique. Nor did she retort or counter anyone. Her wet hair, covered with bubbles, formed delicate crystalline patterns that she untangled with her dainty pink fingers. Her skin, shimmering in the reflection of the lake, gave her an illuminated, pearl-like glow. Tamara's radiance was famous in Ranikhet—even Bhai, who rarely noticed girls, had once commented on it.

A heavy sigh escaped Tamara, a sound that reverberated within the confines of her own being. It was a sigh drowned out by the clamour of everyday life, concealed from the world around her. To the casual observer, her melancholia might have appeared as a fleeting phase of the human psyche, easily dismissed and forgotten. But for Maya, it was an entirely different story. Only she recognized the unprecedented nature of Tamara's despondency—a departure from her typically eccentric mood swings.

Although Tamara was good at masking her inner turmoil from prying eyes, Maya could see through the façade. Her heart ached to approach her friend, to envelop her in a tight embrace, to shower her face with tender kisses. Maya longed to reassure Tamara that she was never alone, that as long as she stood by her side, no harm could befall her on this vast earth. The love that Maya felt for Tamara was profound and boundless.

At times, Maya pondered the distinction between her feelings for Tamara and her affection for Shiv. She had realized that what she felt for Tamara was, in fact, love—a profound connection that surpassed ordinary bonds. What it lacked was passion—unexplainable energy that one could sense but never quite articulate.

Maya, at last, found the opportune moment when the others had dispersed, leaving just her and Tamara. 'Okay, now tell me!' Maya demanded.

Tamara looked at Maya incredulously. 'Tell you what?'

Maya then witnessed something she had never seen before—the tough Tamara had tears in her eyes. Tamara tried her best to fight them, to hold them back, wiping them away with the back of her hand. It was a rare vulnerable moment, and though the roads were empty, they were not devoid of the occasional passer-by. She did not wish to expose her weakness to the world. But she knew she needed Maya.

Maya gently took Tamara by her shoulders, guiding her towards a huge banyan tree by the side of the lake. She glanced around to ensure there was no one watching them. The spot felt abandoned, a place where even the wind seemed hesitant to tread. Maya absent-mindedly kicked at the dry leaves scattered around her, an instinctive act devoid of intent. Deep within her, a quiet urge thrummed—a desperate attempt to end the suffocating silence. A foreboding sense crept into her heart, whispering of an impending storm, much like the unpredictable tempests that sometimes swept through Ranikhet. Until the moment of impact, all appeared deceptively normal, the forecasts merely idle chatter and dismissed as nonsense. But when the storm broke, it unleashed chaos, sweeping through like a harbinger of destruction, leaving only debris in its wake. The horizon had darkened, yet most remained oblivious, unaware that a reckoning was at hand.

Tamara sat at the base of the tree, knees drawn to her chest—a pose she had mastered during her yoga sessions—as if her legs were guarding her heart. She fiddled with the dry, withered leaves on the ground, tearing them one by one—a clear sign of nervousness. She traced shapes in the damp mud, her gaze downcast as the sun prepared to retire for the day.

'Do you know we are a lot like plants?' Maya asked Tamara, peering into the distance.

The philosophical question soared above Tamara's head. Tamara kept looking at the ground, hiding her tears as if afraid they might cause Maya pain. Or maybe she wished to keep up the appearance—after all, she was known in town as a tough girl. She had stood unbroken when her relationship with Ashok crumbled. Ashok had cried, but not her.

Maya sat still, trying to maintain her composure. She knew that in that moment, she was perhaps Tamara's only source of support.

She breathed quietly, so as not to distract her friend. What was needed now was absolute tranquillity.

'How is it so?' Tamara queried. The question had been rhetorical, and Tamara was aware of it. She was in no mood to discuss the similarities between plants and humans. During such moments, no one wanted answers to questions; they just wanted to be heard. Maya did not bother to respond; she wanted to be an avid listener.

Tamara tilted her head and took a close look at the roots as though she were an expert botanist trying to identify its species. Her strange behaviour was beginning to unsettle Maya. She knew Tamara was in trouble and needed empathy, but Maya was not in the mood to entertain it beyond a point. She was there to listen and offer solutions, but Tamara had to open up too.

As Tamara kept silent, Maya decided to reply. 'Well, we both have roots,' she said, glancing at the gnarled roots of the banyan tree that seemed to spring from the earth and seep into it, depending on how one looked at it.

Tamara remained silent, so Maya continued. 'We cannot change our roots so long as we are alive. The leaves might fall and the bark may peel away, like the cells in our skins, but the roots remain as they are. We are born with them, and we shall die with them. It is not something we choose, yet it remains with us until we the end.'

Maya was surprised at her own eloquence. She wasn't typically one to delve into philosophical musings, but today, she seemed to be in a mood to go on and on. She felt that perhaps the time to detach herself from her own roots had come. Why, though, this sudden revelation? Why did she feel that her roots could cause immense sorrow and pain?

However, this was not the time for random thoughts; they were there for a definite purpose. After careful contemplation, Maya said, 'Roots can't be changed, but they can be interconnected. Trees are known to connect beneath the surface, sharing strength.'

Tamara scoffed at her. Maya's optimism wasn't something she was in the mood to entertain.

Maya stayed quiet after that because she sensed Tamara was ready to reveal her secret.

'I'm getting married.'

A deafening silence hung in the air, suffocating Maya's desperate mind. The wind stopped rustling through the leaves, the lake turned still, and even the distant sounds of life faded into nothingness. Maya felt the roots beneath her shift, as if they were wrapping themselves around her, eager to offer consolation. The very earth trembled beneath her, as if sympathizing with her anguish, while the stars and half-moon wept in solidarity. Even the moon, veiled by ominous clouds, seemed to hide its light, mourning alongside her. The atmosphere itself exuded a sinister and foreboding aura.

Maya's gaze remained unwavering, filled with a mixture of determination and desperation. She gritted her teeth, clenching her fists so tightly that her palms bore the marks of her nails digging into her flesh. With each scrunch and uprooted blade of grass, her fury intensified. She seethed with anger, feeling a surge of indignation, restlessness, disturbance and profound shakiness. She felt as if she had failed in her duty to protect Tamara, as if she was unworthy of her role as a close friend.

Words eluded Maya, slipping through her grasp like sand as she desperately searched for the right ones. In certain moments, words prove inadequate, unfit to be uttered, for they hold no solace for those who have suffered. In such situations, the options are starkly limited—either a deafening silence or a gentle, comforting touch. Or perhaps an eruption of frenzied turmoil, a tempest unleashed upon the world.

When she could, at last, find a word, it turned out to be interrogative, framed in a simple question. 'When?'

'As if it matters.'

Maya raised her eyebrows at Tamara's blatant acceptance.

She knew Tamara had no choice—no girl had. They were all like puppets—in the hands of their parents, their husbands, and even their sons. Did a sage not say that long ago?

A pair of bright golden eyes glowed in the dark, possibly an owl. It had overheard the conversation and wished to offer its sincere condolences. Every creature on earth seemed to pity girls. The wildflowers had also dropped into a deep sleep, their petals closed as if in mourning. The world itself seemed to have come to a standstill upon hearing Tamara's news.

The question that Maya asked next was a dreaded one. But it had to be asked—it was tied to Tamara's future, and she was a loyal friend. There was no escape. She pondered whether it was appropriate. Would it be better not to? After all, it would only add to Tamara's sorrows and Maya hated to be the cause of it. But what would be the right time to ask? Maya ultimately decided to shoot the question in the hope that it might unburden Tamara.

She did a quick countdown. How much should she count till? 20? 50? 100? The silence and the suspense were both unbearable. And then she abruptly blurted out, 'Who is the lucky guy?'

Maya found herself hoping, desperately, that Tamara's groom was, at the very least, someone young, handsome and from a good family. She had seen too many of their friends being married off to older men, many of whom had been married multiple times before. These men had either lost their wives to illness, had wives who had committed suicide, or who ran away. And yet, they remarried. Maya sincerely hoped Tamara's fate was not similar. The idea of an older man marrying Tamara was not just inconceivable, it was preposterous. An accomplished girl like Tamara married off to an old hag!

She chanted a prayer in her mind. 'I pray to you, God, please let it not be an old man. Please give her the best man in town! She deserves the best. Please protect her from misery. She does not deserve it. If you are still adamant, transfer her fate to me.'

She squeezed her eyes shut like a small child praying for good results, as if she was asking for herself and not for a friend. She kept praying relentlessly as tears rolled down her cheeks. Tamara sat beside her silently. Could she hear Maya's prayers?

The look in Tamara's eyes suggested that something ominous was about to be disclosed. It was not solely about getting married at the young age of 14. There was much more to it. Even in the darkness, it was so obvious. The focus was now shifting. Tamara was concerned about something. Could it be connected to Maya? Why was she hesitating? What was stopping her from disclosing a few details about the boy? That was all she had asked of her.

And then, Tamara stated something that would change Maya's life forever. Words that were unutterable and sinister.

'It's Shiv,' she said softly.

Maya moved closer, straining to hear the faint mumble, needing to be sure of what she thought she had heard. After all, she was just human, prone to mistakes; she could have misheard.

Tamara spoke louder this time, looking straight at Maya and fighting off tears from her once intrepid, vibrant eyes. 'It's Shiv I'm marrying.'

Did Maya's prayer come true? It would be the only time she was heard. She had prayed for someone nice, someone whose parents were lovely, someone young. Folks said that Shiv's mother was nice and sweet, despite her propensity for drinking. His father had deserted them long ago. And Shiv was young, handsome—a gem of a boy. She could now breathe freely. Tamara, her friend, had got the best.

But did he love Tamara with the same passion he had for her? Doubts started creeping into Maya's mind. Tamara was not to blame. But would Shiv stand by Maya? Would he refuse to marry Tamara? Was he even aware of this arrangement? Her head spun at the thought of seeing Tamara and Shiv getting married at the *mandap* and mocking her. She imagined Tamara smiling as Shiv held her, the seven rounds around fire, the incessant cheers from the guests, the witty comments, the guffaws.

Maya's vision blurred and a searing ache pulsed through her temples. As the world around her darkened, she felt herself slip, lose consciousness. When she finally opened her eyes, she caught sight of Tamara curled into a foetal position, weeping softly, striving to remain unheard. Yet, her gut-wrenching sobs conveyed an inconsolable melancholy, echoing a deep tragedy. The lake, serene and silvered under the waning light, suddenly stirred to life. Water churned, breaking into chaotic ripples that filled the air with a deafening, discordant roar. Amid this sudden upheaval, the world seemed muted to Tamara. The only sound she perceived was the raw, wrenching sobs deep in her chest—silent, yet betrayed by the shudders coursing through her body in rhythmic spasms.

Maya's surroundings became a disorienting spectacle where nothing seemed anchored in place. She had momentarily forgotten that they were beneath the sheltering embrace of an ancient banyan tree, seeking solace in its protective shade. Tamara, her loyal companion, was also there. She had even forgotten that Tamara was the true victim and not she. The pledge she had made to support her friend had evaporated from her mind, overshadowed by the stark reality that her own life was irreversibly slipping out of her grasp.

Tears filled her eyes, blurring her vision with a veil of grief, mirroring the torrents of emotions surging within. Sobs wracked her body, each convulsion shaking her with a profound sense of fear. The memory of that fateful Holi celebration replayed in her mind, a forewarning she had failed to heed. With her worst fears now realized, her emotions shifted; fear alone no longer gripped her—it was replaced by an urgent, desperate need to act, to break free from the tightening snare around her.

Maya yearned to seek refuge in Shiv's comforting embrace, to release her anguish upon his sturdy shoulders. Simultaneously, she craved the solace of Tamara's presence. Neither Maya nor Tamara knew the full weight of Maya's feelings for Shiv, or were aware of Shiv's reciprocated affection for Maya.

With her legs still trembling from the shock, Maya stood up and walked towards Tamara, who also rose to meet her. They hugged each other, weeping and mourning together. The unforgiving reality of life had struck them for the first time, shattering their once carefree existence. They were only 14—the age to swing wildly on the branches of trees, swim in the lakes, play games, play *antakshari*, go for picnics and enjoy life. But it was a cruel world that they were now facing. The oft-repeated words they had heard from adults—that life was hard—now took on a weight they could feel in their hearts and souls.

The two teenage girls had no clue what lay ahead, nor what steps to take. And as they wept, the entire world seemed to mourn with them—the clouds, the moon, the trees and the wildflowers. A lone goat ambling by paused for a while, as if to commiserate.

8

The evening unfolded like a sombre painting of two souls bound by their shared pain and empathy. Despite their long-standing friendship, Maya and Tamara were overwhelmed by emotions, unable to think clearly about their future. They realized that they faced a challenging situation, and their fate was intertwined. They could either support each other and overcome the obstacles together, or succumb to the pressures and hardships they would face.

For these two helpless girls, individual resistance would be futile. They could only register their protest, but they knew that society, including their own families and the people of Ranikhet, would stand united against them. The weight of social honour and prestige took precedence over their personal feelings and desires. This raised questions about the balance between individual freedom and the constraints imposed by societal structures. By standing together and supporting one another, they could create a ripple effect that might eventually lead to a broader shift in perspectives and attitudes.

Ultimately, true fulfilment and happiness lie not solely in material advancement or outshining others, but in the journey of self-discovery, personal growth and meaningful connections with fellow human beings. It is a complex and multifaceted endeavour, but by cultivating empathy, cooperation and a genuine desire for self-improvement, one can strive to be a better version of themselves and contribute to a more harmonious and compassionate world.

Maya's thoughts turned to Shiv. What stand would he take? Doubt gnawed at her. To what extent would he risk his neck and stand by the girl he loved? Did he love her at all? Was it a misjudgement on her part? Had she misconstrued his feelings? He had applied gulaal on her face with a soft, tender touch. He had stared at her intently with what she thought were loving, tender eyes. Had she misunderstood the message she thought he sought to convey through his eyes? Maybe it was lust that she had mistaken as passion. He had saved her that day from drowning, but perhaps he would have done it even if it had been someone else. Had he not saved Tamara's and that little girl's lives just a few days before?

Tamara was due to marry Shiv. The match was fixed; a done deal. People rarely backed out of commitments in Ranikhet, and the party who did would be severely reprimanded and even ostracized. Here, an engagement was equivalent to a marriage. There were certain norms in the social fabric that everyone was expected to adhere to.

If it were any other girl, Maya, in a fit of rage, might have slit her throat. She was capable of that. She was known for her aggression, and during those few moments of anger, she lost sight of context and possible ramifications. Both Bhai and Maa had warned her several times—it was widely acknowledged that she could go to any length when furious.

But she knew she could not do the same to Tamara. Tamara was a helpless prisoner of a hypocritical and insensitive society. She needed Maya now more than ever.

★

Maya reached home quite late. Fortunately, Maa and Bhai were not there; she remembered that Bhai was supposed to escort Maa to a *kirtan*. She quickly scribbled a note saying she had eaten at Tamara's house and was feeling slightly under the weather, so she was going to bed.

As dawn broke, the simple act of leaving her bed proved to be an arduous challenge for Maya. She delved deep within herself, exploring the uncharted corners of her heart that she hadn't known existed. It was a place consumed by sorrow so profound that it weighed heavily upon her soul.

Maya's night had been restless. She had dreamt of a terrifying descent from a majestic mountaintop, spiralling down into a desolate valley. The fall was not swift but agonizingly prolonged. It felt like an eternity, as she descended further and further into a perilous abyss, with no glimmer of hope or rescue in sight, utterly helpless. No Bhai, no Shiv—no one was there to offer solace or extend a helping hand.

Shiv had always been her lifeline, her anchor in times of turmoil. In the past, Maya had embraced her unrequited love for him, finding contentment in loving him from a distance. She had never expected anything in return, cherishing the mere sight of him, even if it was a fleeting glance during her daily journey to school. It wouldn't have mattered if he had chosen to marry Tamara or anyone else, as long as she could continue to catch a glimpse of him and ensure his well-being. But the events on Holi had changed everything. It was no longer a one-sided affection; it had evolved into true love that was reciprocated. Love, in its purest form, is all-consuming and unwavering, setting its own rules that cannot be bent or tailored for convenience. True love demands possession of one another.

With a sudden burst of resolve, Maya forced herself out of bed, determined to shake off the thoughts clouding her mind. She knew she had to be with Tamara in this time of distress. However, an invisible force seemed to tug her back towards the comforting embrace of her bed sheets. She was drained of energy and motivation, hanging on by a frayed thread—one snap and she feared it would all give way. Fortunately, no one witnessed her weakened state. Her family had already departed for their own errands, their whereabouts unknown and unimportant to her in that moment. She was utterly alone.

But their return was imminent and Maya dreaded their arrival, for Maa and Bhai would surely discern that something was amiss. Their perceptive eyes would unleash a torrent of questions she couldn't possibly answer. How could she explain the storm that had broken within her at this delicate juncture? The weight of her unspoken truth seemed insurmountable, crushing her spirit beneath its unyielding burden.

As she walked past the worn wooden console, she felt a sharp sting—the familiar sensation of the rough edges scraping her skin. She winced, noting how frequently these small injuries had been happening lately. She couldn't help but wonder if it was her growing absent-mindedness or maybe her skin had become more delicate, susceptible to the slightest touch.

Regardless of the cause, the physical pain in her leg paled in comparison to the anguish that gripped her heart, a searing ache that seemed to permeate every fibre of her being. The intensity of her emotional pain was overwhelming, an unrelenting torment that consumed her soul. Each step she took, each breath she drew, was accompanied by a heaviness that seemed impossible to shake off. It felt as if a cruel force was mercilessly tugging at her core with a pair of sharp clippers. The throbbing ache in her abdomen mirrored the one in her heart, amplifying the agony she felt with every passing moment.

The pain of separating from Shiv was unbearable. The longing for his presence gnawed at her relentlessly. It was as if a vital part of her had been torn away, leaving a void that no amount of time or distance could fill.

She saw him—Shiv was there, climbing through the same golden window as the other day. But he was in rags! His clothes, though never spectacular, were now torn and soiled like those of hard-working labourers. His hair was unkempt and eyes bloodshot, with his body covered with cuts and scratches, blood oozing from multiple wounds. Blood had stained his shirt. He kept looking over his shoulder and then staring blankly ahead.

Suddenly, his expression turned calm—a look of contentment appeared on his face as he spotted her. For a moment, Maya thought that goons had accosted him on the road and beat him black and blue for daring to refuse to marry Tamara. She tried to run towards him because she felt he needed her at this hour. She had to stand by him. He was, after all, hers. But her injured leg refused to move, and her pain surged. She kept chanting his name like the Gayatri Mantra, but he didn't respond; he just kept smiling at her.

As Maya struggled with the searing pain in her leg, she wondered why he was not rushing to her, lifting her off the ground and taking her to lie on the bed. There was no risk to his life now; he only had to inch forward, take a couple of steps. She then noticed a detached look in his eyes. It was not the same Shiv who had saved her from drowning just a few days back. Why was he staring at her with helpless eyes? Had something changed? Had the two souls drifted apart? Was that what he was trying to convey?

And then, he was gone—vanished into thin air. She remembered overhearing his neighbour once say he was known for his quiet, enigmatic presence—a boy who rarely revealed his thoughts or intentions. For a fleeting moment, she wondered if he was hiding nearby, silently watching, testing her patience. She searched around—under the bed, behind the console, beneath the chairs. He had disappeared.

Maya's unconscious body hit the floor with a heavy thud. She hit her head and blood started trickling down in gentle streams. When she regained consciousness, she could see the bloodstains and even spotted a bit of vomit on the floor.

She realized she must have vomited and then passed out for a few moments out of sheer exhaustion. She was in a worse state than she had initially anticipated. She was now hallucinating and vomiting. Her physical fitness was declining alongside her mental sanity; they were, after all, twins. It was a different experience, unprecedented for Maya. The cut on her head was not deep, but she kept lying on the floor. She needed sympathy, people to fuss over her.

Fleeting in and out of consciousness, she woke up every few minutes and whispered Shiv's name, sometimes even screaming it out. The intensity of the pain and agony in her heart was unrelenting. She found herself trapped in a world where time stood motionless, and every tick of the clock belonged to a reality she had transcended. Her existence had become a never-ending cycle of being stuck in limbo.

Realization hit her with a force—she needed to seize control of herself. She needed to be the Maya who had been fierce, defiant and resilient. She could no longer afford to languish in this paralysing state.

In one abrupt movement, she broke free from the inertia that had engulfed her mind and body, and stood up, walking purposefully towards the bathroom, her each step brisk and resolute. The yellow-stained tiles on the floor and the white-and-pink-lily-painted tiles on the wall appeared bleak. Loneliness and desolation seeped into her being.

A few flies hovered above the sink, darting around the faint traces of vomit, avoiding them as if repulsed. It was no delight for them either. Perched upon the toilet seat, Maya noticed bloodstains on the floor—dried droplets that had fallen long ago, yet they now filled her with an inexplicable terror. Panic gripped her as she frantically searched for scars on her face and body.

Maya possessed a penchant for discerning marks on her body. These could manifest as scars that required time to heal, birthmarks, skin growths, allergic rashes or black spots. To her, these marks symbolized a lack of cleanliness and her unwavering goal was to maintain immaculate purity. This fixation was almost bordering on obsession. In addition, she had a tendency to unconsciously inflict harm upon herself, resulting in scars. Bhai and Maa would mock her for this behaviour, labelling her as a reincarnation of the Devil or calling her a 'walking time bomb'. Though they would jest at her expense when such incidents occurred frequently, their demeanour suggested a certain degree of concern, albeit not excessively displayed.

Standing unclothed in front of the mirror, Maya scrutinized herself. The internal unrest she felt was even more pronounced now. Dark patches under her eyes and a fresh black spot on her cheek became apparent. Turning around, she strained her neck to inspect her back. As her fingers glided down, she suddenly discovered it. There it was, situated precisely at the bottom of her neck. To examine it more closely, she pulled out another mirror. An injury mark was discernible—an ominous dark blemish. She possessed no recollection of when this injury had occurred—perhaps during a swimming session or the evening Shiv had heroically rescued her from drowning.

Maya wanted to believe it was an injury mark from months ago, or even years. The pain had subsided, yet the mark persisted. Logically, this should not perturb her; with time, it would heal naturally. Alternatively, she could seek her mother's assistance in visiting a doctor; applying a few healing balms would likely alleviate the issue. However, she found herself overcome with emotions and broke into a sob as she continued staring at the mark.

And then it struck her like a bolt of lightning—Tamara, she concluded, relied on her far more than she depended on Tamara. In that moment of clarity, Maya recognized the urgency of Tamara's predicament, which compelled her to get up and confront the challenges that lay before her. She decided to finish her bath.

As the water cascaded over her body, a searing sensation engulfed her, reminding her of the pain she carried within. The crimson hues of the water—her own blood—trickled down her body, flowing past her thighs, legs, feet and even the very floor beneath her. The hot water became her refuge, soothing not only her body but also her mind. Memories of her mother's counsel resurfaced; she recalled how Maa had always advised her to take a bath or engage in physical exertion whenever anger consumed her. Both water and sweat had the remarkable ability to quiet the storm raging within her. Maya faithfully followed her mother's wisdom as it had never failed her.

As she stepped out, a salwar kameez, the one she had worn on Holi, beckoned to her. It bore the indelible mark of Shiv, carrying the scent of his masculine essence and encapsulating his very being. The vibrant stains of colour served as a testament to their connection, forever imprinted upon her garment.

Casting a fleeting glance at the mirror, she carefully applied the black kajal that Maa had lovingly prepared in the morning. Its dark pigmentation would add depth to her eyes and cheeks, effectively concealing the traces of her injuries. This was the version she had chosen for herself, aiming to embody a heavenly presence. After all, beauty lay in the eyes of the beholder and her longing was for that one person who would appreciate her allure and validate her self-assessment. Alas, that person now belonged to another.

Maya chose to forgo the application of a rose blush as she firmly believed that her skin possessed a natural radiance surpassing that of any cosmetic. Her complexion bore the imprints of mountain girls, a testament to their resilience in the face of harsh weather. The glow that emanated from her skin outshone that of her friends', even Tamara's, blossoming like vibrant flowers eagerly welcoming the advent of spring and summer.

But beneath this curated façade of her appearance, her eyes betrayed the existence of deep-rooted pain. With just one look,

Bhai would be able to discern the depth of her anguish. But for now, Maya brushed aside these contemplations, choosing to wage her battles one at a time, relying solely on her own fortitude. No external assistance was needed; nothing could alter the unwavering expression etched upon her face.

For the first time since the shock of last evening, she attempted to make more sense of Tamara's news, to ask the right questions. Thoughts crowded her mind. *How did this match come about? Who could have thought of Shiv for Tamara? Wasn't he somewhat uneducated for her? Did Shiv know? Would he approve of this union? He must have agreed; otherwise, how would Tamara categorically tell her she was marrying him? Even Tamara must have agreed, albeit reluctantly. Not that her acquiescence mattered, but still…she must have agreed.*

In her heart of hearts, Maya knew that the bride's and groom's views hardly mattered in their society—this was not Mumbai or Delhi.

What happens next?

This question drove her out of her wits. Tears once again flowed in gentle streams before becoming torrents. She could feel the persistent lump in her throat, a constant reminder of the heartache since last evening.

She tried to imagine the wedding night. Tamara dressed in red bridal finery would look like a princess straight out of a storybook. She would smile cheerily on her way to the mandap. Only Maya's life had been wrenched cruelly and heartlessly out of her body, leaving her to gaze listlessly at the cloudless sky.

★

Tamara's house was ancient. Her family was not too well off, and her father had somehow cobbled together a new building over the remains of a past structure—the relics and ruins of the previous construction still partially discernible. Nobody knew for sure the exact year when the original had been constructed and when Tamara's ancestors moved into the village. They had come in long before many others, but the family tree remained a mystery.

Maya walked into their open-air veranda and it was as plain-looking as on any other day. Her mind shifted to the wedding evening, as if the ceremony was happening before her eyes.

The fairy lights shimmered and twinkled, casting vibrant hues of blue, green and red that danced against the evening sky. Maya, the epitome of grace and beauty, stepped on to the open-air veranda, her bridal finery flowing around her like silk in the evening breeze. With every step, she exuded a sense of tranquillity, her calm smile radiating warmth and contentment.

The veranda was filled with Maya's loved ones gathered from far and wide, their presence a reflection of the significance of that day. Her parents beamed with pride as they stood beside her, their eyes filled with a mixture of joy and nostalgia. Maya's grandmother, adorned in traditional attire, offered a silent prayer for her granddaughter's happiness. Countless other relatives from Uttarakhand, their faces a mosaic of love and anticipation, surrounded Maya, their collective energy infusing the atmosphere with a sense of celebration.

Carefree children darted around like shooting stars, their laughter and excited shouts filling the air. Their playful innocence starkly contrasted with the imperfections marring the otherwise enchanting setting. Loose wires snaked their way across the veranda, their unsightly presence a blemish against the backdrop of meticulously arranged flowers and the warm embrace of the setting sun's rays. Their ugliness was overlooked in the jubilant chaos, eclipsed by the radiant love that filled the hearts of those in attendance.

Nearby, vast bamboo scaffolding stood tall, its sturdy structure supporting a thick, billowing cloth to form a makeshift enclosure to accommodate guests and serve dinner. The fabric appeared weathered and worn, hinting at the temporary nature of the arrangement. It symbolized the transience of the moment, a reminder that life's grandest celebrations are fleeting and ephemeral.

Glass bulbs adorning the scaffolding, once pristine and sparkling, now bore the marks of time and neglect. Dust and grime clung to their surface, obscuring their clarity and causing their light to diffuse unevenly. The air's moisture added to their murkiness, as if mirroring the hazy nature of the marriage itself. The symbolism was not lost on Maya; her heart weighed heavy with the realization that the union she was about to enter was far from perfect, marred by circumstances beyond her control.

Amidst this vibrant tapestry of emotions and conflicting realities, a young boy stood out, his presence a poignant reminder of the complexities of love. He belonged to someone else, yet fate had chosen to intervene, tearing him away from his rightful place. The clashing forces of desire and duty played out before Maya's eyes, her heart torn between the longing for her own happiness and the understanding of the pain she was inadvertently causing. It was a bittersweet reminder that sometimes, even amidst joyous celebrations, sacrifices must be made.

As Maya embarked on this new chapter of her life, she couldn't help but feel the weight of these juxtapositions. The flickering fairy lights, the imperfect surroundings and the boy being snatched away all symbolized that life's most intense and meaningful moments often arose from the interplay of light and darkness, joy and sorrow. It was in these complexities that Maya found the strength to move forward, to embrace the uncertainty of her path and to strive for a love that would transcend the murky glass bulbs and the hazy uncertainties of her marriage.

Maya's world suddenly shattered, as if an unseen hand had struck her countenance with brutal force. The impact plunged her into a temporary abyss of unconsciousness. As she slowly regained her bearings, a relentless vertigo seized her senses, leaving her teetering on the precipice of sanity. It was a disconcerting awakening to the harrowing presence of depression that had stealthily infiltrated her very being.

With a grim realization, Maya acknowledged the gnawing emptiness that had taken residence within her. The pangs of hunger had not been quelled since the previous evening, casting a shadow of doubt upon her fragile mental state. The deprivation, it seemed, had contributed to this unsettling encounter with her inner demons.

Her gaze fixated on Tamara, her companion in this sombre tableau. Tamara's face bore a similar burden of anguish and inconsolable sorrow. As they stood side by side, an unspoken connection tethered them in their shared desolation. Maya's eyes remained unblinking, the weight of her melancholy etched upon her lips in a wry, joyless smile. Through her silent understanding, she discerned Tamara's façade of pretence, a mask that failed to deceive her. Their bond was as untainted as the delicate petals of wildflowers, an unbreakable connection woven with threads of honesty.

And then, as if the universe conspired to unveil a cruel tapestry of despair, Maya's gaze fell upon Tamara's mother, whose once vibrant eyes were now clouded with the same profound sorrow. In that moment, Maya knew there was no turning back. The decision had been irrevocably etched in the annals of fate—a wedding cast in unyielding stone.

With a sigh, Maya retreated into the sanctuary of her imagination.

She clutched Tamara's shoulder, trying to break her stupor and wake her to reality, but she remained unresponsive. The smile on her red lips failed to reach her eyes. Tamara's beauty was unblemished yet indefinable. It flowed seamlessly, like a river descending from its source. She was alluring, but her charisma had died over the last few days; she was like a doll on display on the wedding night that people would look at, appreciate and gently walk away from.

Maya felt revolted and asked Tamara's mother, 'Why is she sitting there like a doll? Why is the groom not sitting next to her? Why is she not moving around?'

Tamara's mother was not to blame. She was a docile lady without much say in family matters, compliant and compelled to follow the diktats of their family. She was stuck between the chaotic wedding arrangements and her daughter's refusal to display any signs of happiness. To outsiders, Tamara was smiling, but only her mother and Maya were aware of the sorrow that lurked under the surface.

'I don't know, beta,' she replied submissively.

'Auntie, why didn't you say anything?' Maya questioned her. She, like Maa, hated submissive women. Why did Tamara have to be married off so early? Was she a burden on the family? Why this drastic step?

Maya did not wish to rankle Auntie any more. She knew that given a choice, Auntie would not have allowed this to happen; she was just another puppet in the household. The orders came from her husband and father-in-law. Instead of chastising Tamara's mother, Maya enveloped her in a hug.

That day, Maya chose to sit beside Tamara and hold her hand, sometimes squeezing it in a gesture of reassurance and support. It was the day they reached adulthood—adulthood that did not evolve as a natural course but had been thrust upon them.

As they sat together, Maya noticed a tinge of despair in Tamara's eyes, but it passed like a flash and a cold, bright smile replaced it.

Maya was surprised at Tamara's acting skills—she was known to be a good actor but the skills displayed on her wedding day were unparalleled. She opened her mouth if someone offered her a sweet, but the stony expression soon reappeared. Maya sincerely hoped and prayed for a happy life for her friend, who was marrying the only man Maya would ever love.

On one side of the veranda, an older woman sat with a sari seller who displayed a vibrant array of embroidered fabrics while flashing his red, tobacco-stained teeth, while on the other side, a sweet vendor haggled with Tamara's grandfather. Younger married women went around with tea and snacks for the hungry men from the groom's side who demanded to be served promptly. Some of them had been in school with Tamara and Maya until they were married off. They had forgotten their studies and how to play, their routine now consisted of lighting ovens, fanning them if powered by coal or biogas, cooking dal, vegetables, rice, the occasional fish or egg curries, mending clothes, sometimes cleaning the floors, making beds, massaging the tired feet of in-laws and rushing to the market to buy the necessities. Today, their responsibilities expanded to include catering to the whims of the groom's family and the demands of the bride's side.

Maya did not know what to say but tried to placate Tamara. 'Shiv will be a different husband; he will take care of you.' Upon hearing this, Tamara burst into hysterical tears, and soon Maya joined her. As Tamara hurriedly wiped her tears and resurrected her smile, a few kids gathered there, as if to comfort them. They had heard that brides typically cried on the day after the wedding, just before they left their parents' abode—the home that had nurtured them and seen them grow up.

Not one adult came to console Tamara, not even her mother. We think parents love their children, and we are right, but they fail to stand up for them when it is most needed—an opportunistic kind of love. They fool themselves into thinking that whatever is happening is for their daughter's good; they refuse to understand what is going through her mind or ask her what storms she is weathering.

Maya and Tamara retreated into the latter's room, away from the festive drummer and the wedding songs, the noisy runny-nosed kids and the sight of fake happiness. Tamara sat motionless, her eyes glazed as if she were drugged. Perhaps that is what they had done to her.

'Tamara, tell them that you have dreams; you want to be a swimmer, not just a wife. Tell them. You want to study, not just be a wife. Tell them. You want to work in an organization and earn independently, not just be a wife. Tell them. You want to explore adulthood, not just be a wife. Tell them. You want to achieve something in life, not just be a wife. Tell them. You wish to fulfil your dreams, not just be a wife. Tell them. You want to be anything but a wife. Tell them that!' Maya urged her friend.

Tamara remained frozen as Maya voiced her feelings. 'Just tell them, Tamara. Why aren't you telling them?' Exasperated, Maya punched the wall.

'Because no one cares,' Tamara finally said and then hugged Maya tightly. They cried holding each other, unaware of how long they clung to one another. The pain was incomprehensible; they died inside a million times at that moment. Maya decided to stay with Tamara and not let her out of her sight. She held her like an older sister, mother, father and brother—the family that had deserted her at the time she had needed them to understand her. Maya was ready to endure the ordeal with Tamara till she was handed over to her husband.

'I am very sorry, Maya,' Tamara said sullenly, tossing the duvet across the bed.

9

The sky was infested with thick, dark clouds as Maya made her way towards the forest. The leaves of the dense trees had gained a pale greenish hue.

If only the lake had been still that day, she would not have faced this situation. She could have remained passionately in love with Shiv, but not to the point of no return. It would have stayed a one-sided love, where she would have been the giver but not the receiver.

Maya kept walking towards the dense forest, lost in a haze. Her legs moved like an automaton or one of those wind-up dolls that keep jumping until they run out of wind. As her eyes fell on her bare legs, she realized they were remnants of what they once were—unshaven and neglected. Her mother had also not pestered her, which she found surprising.

A baffled Maya raised her hands to touch her face; her jawbone was shattered, her ears partly scuffed and her cranium seemed fragmented.

It struck her that perhaps an animal had attacked her, its hunger satiated for the time being, but it would come back later, only to realize that a mutilated Maya had fled! As she ran—breathless, wheezing, huffing, puffing—she was dumbfounded about how she was still alive. How had her body retained life? How had she not lost the stamina to run? She touched her chest to check whether she was breathing at all. Unconvinced, she took her skeletal fingers to her nose. Yes, she was breathing! Amazement washed over her at her own courage.

Far away, she spotted a sliver of light consisting of a singular ray. It was the lake from where Shiv had rescued her just a few days back. She quickened her pace. Maya had made her mark as an athlete and was determined to sprint the remaining distance with all the stamina a half-eaten body could muster. Her discoloured legs ached; her heels looked scrawny—this was the first time she had laid her eyes on them. Pain throbbed through her limbs; in all probability, the wild beast had broken her bones, but that would not deter her—she had to reach the lake. The lake was sacred to her.

When she arrived at the brightly lit banks, not a soul was in sight. She remembered that the lakeside had been illuminated a few months ago to attract tourists.

At that point, she realized that she was no longer the Maya everybody was familiar with—this was a different Maya, one who had transcended life on the planet and attained an ethereal existence. The paths to return to her familiar world were irrevocably blocked like mountain roads after landslides stranding passengers on their way. She did not care whether life persisted after death; all that mattered now was that she would never again return to her Bhai, Maa, Tamara, or…Shiv.

She scratched at her body but could not feel her familiar exterior—her nose, ears, hands, knees, soft skin—but she felt something burning. Her organs seemed to evaporate into the atmosphere, expelled in constant streams from her body, the ash dispersed in the gentle breeze. She felt agile; the clumsiness had disappeared.

The crescent moon peeked through the clouds. Maya peered into the lake, but there was no reflection of her to be found. The reflection of the trees was visible; she could even make out the gentle swaying of the branches, but her outline was not to be seen. The vacuous surroundings stared nastily at her. In that moment, panic gripped her as it again dawned on her that Maya no longer existed.

She tried to hold her body, but it was now an empty vacuum. Eeriness engulfed her. She wanted to vomit but found herself unable to. The non-existence of Maya the human and the existence of Maya the spirit—the very transcendence her teachers had so often explained with spiritual fervour—swirled in her mind.

A body floating in the still water drew her attention. Despite her disembodied state, she could sense that it was a person, a living human being. On closer perusal, she recognized it to be Shiv. Shiv, the person she loved; Shiv, the person she had placed on a pedestal; Shiv, her version of Shiva—the Shiva to whom she was willing to dedicate her life. She noticed that his body lay still in the water, failing to create even the faintest ripple; he appeared to be in deep sleep, his breathing heavy—but why were there no ripples? How could he float without disturbing the water? A body displaces water, and the displaced water buoys up the body. Archimedes' principle, which they had been taught only recently, stated so. The incongruity startled her. Yet, even in this surreal state, she felt a flicker of pride that she could recall a bit of physics. But, Shiv, at that moment, was the focus of her attention.

She thought she had spotted him smiling, but uncertainty gnawed at her. She kept staring till she was sanguine that he was, indeed, smiling—that gentle smile of his, the smile that had swept her off her feet on Holi, the faint smile she had witnessed as he was lifting her from the water, the smile that was her companion in her dreams, in states of introspection, procrastination and hallucination. Yes, it was the same smile.

She wanted to utter his name softly, but could not quite articulate it. She tried again, louder, and when that too fell flat, she decided to scream it out loud. 'Shiv!'

The mountains echoed her cries, but Shiv did not respond. The gentle smile felt like a sweet dream, but the silence was deafening.

Determined, she tried once more, her voice reaching a desperate pitch. 'Shiv!' 'Shiv!' It was now a loud yelp, sufficient to stir the lake's waters, but Shiv remained unresponsive. He kept smiling—it seemed he was mocking her. How could he? Could someone who loved her as much as Shiv did ever mock her? There was no trace of love, no hint of feeling or empathy in the cold smile.

She could not take it any more; she now wanted to strike him. In that moment, for her, he was a traitor—a wicked individual who had betrayed and manipulated her love. He had played with her emotions. He was a sadist, a monster. In intense desperation, she jumped into the lake's still waters and tried to reach him, to smack his face, pull out his teeth and gouge his eyes.

And then it was a repeat of that day. Although the waters were still and she had learnt a bit of swimming over the past few days, this time it was not the currents that pulled her under, but the thick weeds below that ensnared her legs. She desperately tried to extricate herself, screaming and yelling Shiv's name. Not once, not twice, but three times...five times...seven times...countless times.

She struggled to keep herself afloat, forgetting for a few moments that she had already passed away and was just a spirit. A dead person could not drown. Yet, such is the human urge to live—to cling to this world, experience a full life and continue to exist for tens and hundreds of years. In a flash, she realized that life, indeed, was beautiful. Its sublimity lay far above the cosmic permanence that priests and philosophers often debated. She wished to live here on this planet, in this country, in Ranikhet—with Maa, Bhai, Tamara, her friends and her aunties.

As these thoughts crossed her mind, she spotted Shiv slowly swimming towards her. He was not very far, yet his movements seemed infinitesimally slow. Despite his almost imperceptible progress, she was happy because he was inching towards her. The smile on his face had become more prominent, and now, it no longer seemed to mock her.

Shiv was coming to her rescue, a replay of the past; the same cycle kept repeating itself. The endless cycle of life—birth, death, resurrection—the eternal journey of the human soul.

She questioned herself—was it possible to turn back the clock? To revert to childhood? To start life all over again? To the day she first spotted Shiv at his shop, packing a customer's groceries, accepting the payment? Or the first day she had seen him dropping his sister off at school? Yes, it was possible. She would repeat her life, learn from the mistakes she had committed and live life to the brim once again. She would be gutsier and proclaim to the world that she loved Shiv and that he loved her. He had indicated this in no uncertain terms. There are ways of conveying other than just words. The person who is addressed understands them.

He had almost reached her, his hands stretched towards her; she could feel his touch on her waist—the firm grip. Let him pull her out first, and then she would tell him. She would confess her love for him in words, sweet words, just three English words she often heard in those movies on cable television. She would immediately force him to go with her to Tamara's parents and tell them to call off the marriage. She would tell him that he had to tell Tamara and her family the whole truth and nothing but the truth.

But just then, it struck her that the feeling was all in her mind—a phantom sensation. She had no body, no skin, and the touch she felt was not his or that of any human being. It was a gigantic hallucination. She was unconscious. Her body was like a massive stone, an inanimate object with a mass, but devoid of nerves, neurons or a brain. The thought that he might not be able to rescue her this time terrified her.

Yet, he managed to pull her out of the water, removing those weeds one by one and placing her on his firm, broad back. She was soaking as he laid her on the limp grass by the lakeside, beneath a powerful lamp, and began to resuscitate her. As she slowly regained consciousness, he seemed to produce a towel from nowhere and began drying her.

But why was he screaming her name? Why was he crying for

help? She was right before him. Only the hooting of owls and the barking of stray dogs greeted him, angry at being woken up from deep slumber. Not a soul responded. Maya could have sprung back to life but was not in the mood. She preferred the state of sublime unconsciousness. She could hear his loud wails, his shrill screams, but alas, there was no one to help!

It had been a long day.

Maya looked around and noticed the tall trees and the brightly coloured flowers staring pleasantly at her, letting off their afternoon fragrance. She was in Tamara's garden. She looked down at her hands and body. What had seemed disfigured, non-existent just moments ago now appeared whole and intact. She was breathing. She wasn't drowning in the lake, struggling to breathe, waiting to be rescued by Shiv, but alive and kicking. It was Tamara's wedding, and the entire family and guests awaited the bride's arrival.

The chattering of the guests, the clatter of utensils being moved to the small shamiana-covered enclosure in the corner of the garden reserved for cooking, the kids in their playful mood, shaking off the vestiges of the afternoon nap they were forced to take by their parents, the majestic chair where the groom would rest before proceeding with the religious rituals—everything seemed to be in place.

She would have enjoyed the day—the day her best friend was getting married. A day to celebrate because she was to begin a new chapter in her life, but was not moving to a different town; they would continue to meet, swim and play as regularly as before. Yet it was a horrific day, a nightmarish day for her, a day that would remain a black spot for the rest of her life, a day that would be cast in stone. All because the groom was none other than Shiv. She turned back to her dreams once again.

Maya was attending Tamara's wedding; that meant Shiv had managed to rescue her, bring her back to life like the eternal creator Shiva. She wanted to tell the whole world, but who would listen! Her friends were scared to laugh in her presence, and she knew they hated her for her domineering nature; they would likely have a hearty laugh later. It was not the right time to tell Tamara, and Bhai would scold her for daydreaming. Maa still did not know about the turmoil in her mind, or perhaps she preferred to ignore it. To whom could she disclose her secret?

Then it struck her—Saria, whom she had not met for some time. She usually made it a point to turn up during moments of crises, and tonight, Maya felt sure that she would.

In the garden, the men tied two ends of a rope to two burly gentlemen, setting the stage for the tug-of-war. This was a game invariably played on the evening of the wedding, and was a vital component of weddings in Ranikhet. It would soon be played out between the bride's and the groom's families, accompanied by loud cheers, merriment and witty comments. The game always reminded Maya of Darwin's theory—survival of the fittest—the weak slowly faded away while the strong survived.

Maya and Tamara had always participated in the game, revelling in the merriment. But that day was different—a dark day in Maya's life. She spotted Tamara, who was moving with sluggish determination, still dressed like the schoolgirl she was. Maya reached out, pulling Tamara into the room designated for dressing the bride. She locked the door behind them and fixed Tamara with an intense gaze—eyes filled with an unsettling, almost threatening steadiness.

'What is wrong with you?' Maya fumed.

There was a sudden change in her mood—like clouds clearing to reveal the bright rays of the sun. Tamara was giggling like a child. Who could say, looking at her, that she was to get married in a couple of hours?

'*Kya hua?* (What has happened?)' Maya asked again.

Noticing a glass of milky liquid on the dressing table, Maya assumed it was lassi. 'Why don't you drink it up? You need it for strength; it's going to be a long night ahead.'

Tamara's giggles were now overwhelming. She was beside herself, but somehow managed to utter the words, 'Silly, it's not lassi; it is bhang.'

Maya remembered the last few years, the days they had sneaked bhang leaves or liquid during Holi, the intoxicant making them giggle and laugh uncontrollably.

'You disappeared for two hours. You left me, so I found this—a leftover stash from Holi,' Tamara snapped at Maya, before laughing again.

Maya felt an urgent need to reclaim her ground, to cling to sanity. The whole situation felt hopeless. She had only decided to attend the wedding to support Tamara, though she sometimes wondered whether Tamara even needed her. If God were an accountant, keeping track of the debits and credits of every individual, neither Tamara nor Maya would be handed what they did not deserve. But the Lord was whimsical and his ways whimsical.

'Where's mine?' Maya demanded.

'Didn't you say you wanted to go for a swim when you walked out of the veranda, leaving me alone? I could not figure out where you disappeared, Maya. I searched and searched, but could not locate you. How would I know that you were sleeping off somewhere in the garden?' Tamara replied, her voice tinged with concern.

Maya's dream twisted between clarity and confusion, a realm where emotions became tangible and voices from reality mingled with imagined echoes. She felt the weight of Tamara's gaze, an awareness that pierced through the haze. The town's whispers seemed louder here—knowing smirks and hushed tones dissected her pain, the gossip relentless and sharp. The spectre of Shiv and

Tamara's wedding loomed large, suffocating Maya even in this imagined world.

Tamara appeared in fragments, her concern palpable, yet in this dream it lacked depth and coherence. Maya's mind replayed the small, telling details she had noticed in real life: Tamara's eyes shadowed with worry, her hesitant steps, the subtle way she bit her lip as if holding back words. The cuts on Maya's own arms, which Tamara had seen but never mentioned aloud, felt both real and distant here, part of the turmoil that her dream-self struggled to escape.

Even in this dream state, Maya knew that Tamara wished to reach her, to comfort her without forcing a confrontation that could splinter their fragile world. The fear in Tamara's expression spoke volumes—a silent plea to keep Maya grounded. But the distance between them felt insurmountable. The dream shifted, as dreams do, blending moments of shared childhood laughter with the harsh silence that followed when Maya would slip into her coping state— eyes unseeing, heart detached.

If Tamara's voice existed at all here, it was a faint whisper beneath everything—a hope that Maya would return to her, that the dream would shatter before reality claimed something irreplaceable. And beneath it all, a persistent feeling haunted Maya: Tamara's silent wish to switch places, a wish that would never reach her ears but was understood in the unspoken language of sisters bound by a shared history.

It was evening, and the sun was setting on the western horizon.

The wedding bells would soon ring, sealing the fate of three individuals. The moon peeked out from the sky, intermittently covered and exposed by the clouds, as if desperate to witness the evening's events. It appeared heartless that night.

Tamara's face had turned ashen, as if mourning the loss of a near and dear one. She was angry at her family but then rationalized that they couldn't have known the depth of feelings Maya had for Shiv. Only Maya and Tamara knew, and Tamara lacked the courage to stand up and make her voice heard. It was easy to say it would have been fruitless, but she could have at least tried. Now, she was sick of herself, feeling a deep self-loathing and the urge to pull her hair out. For the first time, she feared what the future held for Maya. God only knew what she would have to endure.

Maya sat beside Tamara, her eyes sunken and shadowed. She appeared tired, despair-ridden and at the end of her tether. Then she noticed the shadow of a young boy, all set to celebrate the most auspicious day of his life, fall upon her. The boy dared to look straight into Tamara's eyes, as if nothing had happened, not bothering to look in any other direction. Silence blanketed Maya as she felt a wound deep inside her heart, cleaving it in two.

As she glanced at his shadow, she forgot to breathe. She needed to remember where she was and why she had come—to support her friend. She also needed support, but urged herself to stay strong for Tamara.

Tears rolled down her cheeks as she transcended into an imaginary world, a parallel universe where only she and Shiv existed. She wanted to live with his shadow for a moment. She closed her eyes, and screamed inwardly, 'Shiv! Shiv!' Her cries, though silent, echoed within. Realization dawned that she needed to take charge and overcome the alternating feelings of wrath, dismay, consternation, repulsion, vulnerability and hopelessness.

Then there he was, in the flesh, wearing a red kurta, his well-built arms bulging slightly at the sleeves. He had worn a half-sleeved kurta, which was a tad unusual. It seemed his eyes were searching for Maya. No, it was not her imagination; she was sure of it. Unlike what she had visualized earlier, he was not looking straight at Tamara. His eyes were roving, searching, probing. The intensity of his gaze made it clear. It was the same pair of eyes that she had spotted on Holi, at the lake the day he had saved Tamara and on the day he had saved her.

Maya was now sure he was looking for her.

She slipped out quietly to hide behind the lime tree at the farthest corner of the garden, a place where she was sure nobody would be able to locate her. It was dark and riddled with mosquitoes and insects that could be dangerous, but Maya was not bothered. She had selected her secluded spot; no one on earth could move her from there. Let him continue searching for her; she would remain invisible for the night. Let the message reach him. Let him also feel what she felt. Let this be a night of tears for him, not of joy and mirth. He was the cause of her pain; he was heartless and ruthless, without a trace of sympathy for her or her dire predicament.

Her soul was distressed, gripped by a deep and unrelenting agony. She had come to the end of her life, a life that had seemed pregnant with possibilities till a few days back. But now, she didn't know which direction life would take her, and she did not wish him to know his either. They had to float in the same boat, a boat that would only tussle in storm waters, run adrift and topple from time to time.

The suffering should be equally borne by them. The pain should be shared. They were both victims, not she alone. This was not an ordinary heartbreak. It was like a tectonic shift, a massive earthquake that had split the plates within her in two. Their teacher had once told them that the Himalayas had sprung from under the sea many million years ago. This was something similar. This was capable of destroying her. Tamara was her soulmate, but in this case, she could support her because she was also the cause of her pain. She had refused to stand up. She had only pretended to empathize with her. Sometimes, Maya felt Tamara's sobs to be false, her tears artificial. Tamara was a good actress. She had always stolen the show in their school dramas.

Bhai was the happiest person today because he had never liked Shiv and considered him to be an uneducated jackass. He would never have approved of Maya and Shiv's union if it had ever been proposed; Tamara had saved him the agony.

After a while, Maya perched herself in the centre of the veranda. The lime tree had served as a cover to hide her melancholy from the world, but she now felt the hide-and-seek business was for those who had committed wrongs. Her only culpable crime was to have loved someone.

At a distance, she caught sight of Shiv, accompanied by his mother and sister. As was the standard practice, Tamara's father escorted him, a broad grin stretched on his face. Maya walked stealthily towards Tamara, having spotted her expressionless, pale face. After Shiv's arrival, Tamara's misery had multiplied, yet she refused to shed a single tear. That would undoubtedly have shed some load off her, but she would not allow herself to be carried away or be overwhelmed.

Life could be hard at times, and this was one of those moments. Miserable for Maya, Shiv and Tamara. But was she imagining their misery? Was Tamara play-acting? As far as Shiv was concerned, there was no discernible trace of misery on his face. But Maya imagined otherwise; she liked to portray all three of them as victims of the social system they belonged to.

Tamara walked in, a *ghoonghat* covering her face, serving sweets to the guests as per custom. Shiv didn't even raise his eyes to look at her, as if he wished to avoid the unpleasant act.

Questions surged in Maya's mind:

Did he say anything?
Does he truly wish for this marriage to happen?
How could he give up on me so easily?
Can he not stand up for his own wishes?
Would he have spoken to his mother, tried to dissuade her?
Why did he agree to this? Does he lack a mind of his own?
As a man, could he not have protested?

Was he ever asked for an opinion? And even if asked, did they accord due importance to it?
Tamara is a great girl, much more talented and qualified than him. Did he feel it was a godsend?
Did he ever truly understand how I felt about him? Was the love I thought I saw in his eyes nothing more than an illusion? Did I fail to convey my own feelings?
When did he come to know about this arrangement?
Was he just a manipulator who loved to play with a hapless girl's feelings?

Though she expected no answers, each question deepened her sorrow, and her heart felt irreparably broken.

'So, Shiv beta, what do you do?' asked Tamara's father, trying to lead him into a conversation as if he was unaware of what his son-in-law did. He was never famed as a conversationalist and his attempt at breaking the silence was awkward at best. Maya wondered what motivated an individual to marry off his daughter to someone he hadn't ever spoken to and had very little knowledge of. For whom, the very act of marriage was to get rid of a daughter who would otherwise remain a burden on the family.

Soon, Tamara reappeared, dressed in a sari, which hung on her frail body, the blouse fitting tightly and the contours of her breasts visible. The sari possibly belonged to her mother. Maya was reminded of their childhood, when she and Tamara played 'house-house'; Tamara enjoyed playing the role of a mother, a dupatta tied like a sari around her waist.

The makeshift sari had looked excellent on her then, but today, when she was wearing a far more elegant and genuine sari, the effect was marred. Her grim, unwell expression stood in stark contrast to the beauty of the attire, rendering the ensemble incomplete. Her soul was not happy tonight, her appearance only betraying her inner feelings. She marched like an unwilling sentry walking towards the battlefield. She came and stood right next to Maya.

For the first time, Shiv raised his eyes. He was looking at Maya, and Tamara knew what he was thinking. Maya suddenly concluded that she had misunderstood him—he had not been looking happy and cheerful; it was a mistake she had committed. He appeared paler than Tamara. The one look gave Maya all the answers she had needed. She knew this situation could not be ignored—she had to intervene for the sake of her friend. She was now absolutely certain that Shiv also loved her, all previous doubts dissipating. His look had given him away. He had tried to penetrate her soul. His deep eyes had conveyed the message.

An epiphany struck Maya—he only wished to convey his apologies for not standing up for them, and that he genuinely wanted to be with her. This union was only for the sake of his sister. The alliance would provide his family with the stature they aspired for and would enable his sister to obtain a decent match. He had done it for his family.

As he silently begged Maya for her forgiveness and sought permission to marry her best friend, she accepted his apology and granted him permission for the marriage!

10

The red ghagra choli—her one and only, the colour of sunshine and hope—was Maya's favourite for celebratory occasions. She thought she looked great in it, and others seemed to agree. Her crystal earrings dangled and tapped gently against her bare shoulders every time she moved, tilted her head or spoke, while her skin shone in the golden sunlight.

Dressed in red, Maya felt like a bride for a few minutes. Her dream of being Shiv's bride would remain a dream, but she did not seem to care about that—she was surprised by her own indifference! Love was tender, sublime and surreal at her age, pregnant with possibilities.

Despite the momentary stoicism, she was worried and scared that the dormant volcano within her might erupt, spilling lava everywhere. She was surprised at her equanimity but realized it was a temporary phenomenon and the angst would reappear shortly. It was a façade meant for Tamara, but her friend was not a fool and would see right through it. She was petrified that an outburst could lead to immense difficulties for them both.

The once-spirited Tamara had become a docile little girl, moulded by her parents' wishes. She was not only unable to rebel but also unwilling to try. The swimming champion, who was the icon of her school even among teachers and the principal, would, in a few days, be making round chapattis for her husband, her best friend's lover.

To Maya, it felt as if Tamara had gotten the wrong end of the stick, not her. After all, she could still escape to a city and build a life for herself as soon as she overcame the trauma. Tamara, however, would be bound to Ranikhet, its traditions and the weight of a marriage that couldn't be so easily shrugged off in a place where conventional values reigned supreme. Maya could still go to college, make a career for herself and let time heal her heartbreak, while Tamara would remain in Ranikhet, confined by its stifling expectations.

Tamara had once confided to Maya that Shiv's mother struggled with alcoholism—a fact widely known among the townspeople, despite her attempts to keep it hidden. Maya had quipped to Tamara, 'If nothing, you will always have access to alcohol to drown your sorrows!' She regretted the joke later, knowing it had been harsh, though at that moment, they had both laughed heartily till their jaws ached.

Shiv's mother had promised Tamara she could continue her studies and maintain her friendships after marriage. Maya felt she had no reason to avoid Tamara; in her heart of hearts, she had accepted that Tamara was not responsible for her predicament. They would still meet in school like before, play games, study together and share notes. But how long would they be able to? It was a question that haunted them both. Maya promised herself that she would not spare any effort to forget Shiv, though she knew it was easier said than done.

Maya and Tamara knew, now more than ever, that they needed each other.

★

The wedding was to take place by the lake, where most town events usually took place—the same lake that held special significance for Maya. Around the lake, trees were draped with coloured bulbs and twinkling lights, while marigold garlands stretched from branch to branch, creating a festive, golden pathway. Relatives bustled about, adjusting the bamboo structure that would serve as the mandap, while caterers set up food stalls, preparing for the wedding feast. Peeled potatoes, freshly chopped green vegetables, vast bowls of dal makhani, a tandoor for the rotis and huge frying pans for the jalebis created a delightful sight when Maya visited the banks a few hours before the event was set to begin.

Almost all of Ranikhet was invited, and Maya wondered how Shiv's family had mustered the resources for the wedding reception; like many others, she had assumed they were poor. For the children of Ranikhet, the wedding season was a time of boundless joy and excitement. The air buzzed with the lively sounds of musicians, blending traditional Uttarakhandi folk songs with the latest Bollywood hits, breathing life into the otherwise sleepy and laid-back town.

Maya had been with Tamara since morning, helping her get ready. Naturally radiant, her soft skin gave her a natural glow, while her sharp features added to her stunning looks. Yet, that day, Tamara seemed far from her usual loquacious self. She barely spoke, cracked jokes or showed any emotion. It reminded Maya of a duck that had forgotten how to quack. Maya could feel the depressive atmosphere in the room; one look at Tamara was sufficient. Did her parents notice her state? Maya refused to believe that Tamara's mother hadn't noticed; she was sensitive enough, even if her father lacked the insight.

'I know what you are thinking, Maya,' Tamara said, while peering out of the window, not daring to look directly at Maya. She reminded Maya of a prisoner, gazing at the vast world outside her prison cell, dying to escape captivity.

'Maybe you do, Tamara, because I am transparent. But I have no clue what you're feeling. You are an opaque person.' The words came out harsher than Maya intended, and she regretted them at once.

She continued, hoping to make amends for her earlier comment but unwilling to let the topic go. 'You barely speak these days, and hardly express yourself. You have become this mute puppet. This is not the Tamara I knew. Where is your fighting spirit? And why do you not confront your parents? If not them, at least speak to me. Let your emotions out, Tamara.'

'I disagree with you. Talking can worsen things, especially when you know that words cannot change the situation. I would have expressed myself wholeheartedly if it meant I could change my fate. But for that, you cannot rely solely on your own strength—you need the backing of society. We'd have no support, Maya. Not one person in this would stand by us. Soon enough, I'll be Shiv's wife, bound to his house—a glorified maidservant to him and his mother. I will have to drop out of school; college would remain a distant dream. My only choice is to carve out my own small space. I'll play the devoted wife in front for everyone, but behind closed doors, in my room, I'll do as I wish. A novel form of protest.'

Though Maya understood what Tamara was trying to say, she, nevertheless, decided to protest. 'As much as I would have wished your plan to fructify for my sake, Tamara, I am not selfish. Since you have decided to marry, you should enjoy your conjugal life to the fullest. I want you to do that, and my best wishes are with you and Shiv.'

She paused, gazing intently at Tamara to gauge her expression, before continuing. 'Shiv is a nice boy, even though he has been through a lot in life. He could not afford to pursue his education. For what it's worth, I believe he is, by nature, benevolent, kind and affectionate. He can be the wind beneath your wings and provide you with support. He will understand your emotions and satisfy your needs. He is a thorough gentleman, and will be your friend and stand by you. He will support you during your weak moments and pull you up when you need it.

'I have seen him drop his sister off at school. I am not sure whether you have noticed the affectionate look he has when she disappears inside the building, the sad expression in his eyes when his sister does not bid him goodbye. I noticed these things, perhaps, because I had a crush on him.

'He is a partner who will remain steadfast in his duties and loyalty towards you. I am sure he agreed to this marriage solely out of responsibility for his sister. Please try to understand him, now that your lives are bound to each other's. He may sometimes appear callous, even rude, but try to look beyond and appreciate the real Shiv. His only problem is that he struggles to express himself because he's had little opportunity to learn how to.'

Maya paused, noticing Tamara's lips quiver slightly, as if she might respond, but instead, the latter turned back to the window. What followed was a long and heavy sigh. Maya was surprised at herself. From how she had been eulogizing Shiv, it was as though Shiv were a noble stranger rather than the man she deeply loved and believed to be hers. An onlooker wouldn't have seen the jilted lover beneath her words—a lover betrayed, yet one who still clung to the feeling that Shiv was somehow hers.

Maya continued, almost as if speaking to herself. 'He cares, mentors, teases, caresses, embraces and provides space to his lover. He is deeply possessive but would not hesitate to grant full freedom to his partner—he is a liberal at heart. He is protective, and will take you in his arms, nurture your desires and talents, and guide and support you to the hilt. He is someone whose presence will invigorate you. He is not someone who will easily let you go, Tamara.'

Maya realized that she was still under Shiv's spell, engulfed by a passionate desire to unite with him and become one soul. Shiv and she were tied together in an unbreakable bond that would last an eternity. She was shackled to Shiv. How was it that she could offer these words of comfort to the very person who had, knowingly or not, taken Shiv from her? Did she possess saintly powers? 'Mudita', as described in Buddhist literature—finding joy in another's happiness? Inscrutable indeed were the ways of the human mind!

Despite Maya's soothing words, Tamara could immediately sense that Maya still harboured feelings for Shiv; she realized that Maya's love ran deeper than she had ever imagined. It was a moment of revelation as she realized that it would be impossible to break these shackles; the chains would only get stronger and stronger over time and subsequently crush all three of them. They were no Prometheus or Heracles, or any other hero from Greek mythology to break free from their chains. There would be no respite from its destructive potential; it was destined to happen.

Tamara started to weep, hoping nobody would come barging in at that very moment. Brides were known to weep on the day they left their homes for their in-laws', not on their wedding day—and certainly not when the marriage was to a man who lived only a short walk away.

★

It was time for the *haldi* ceremony, the hour when the bride is lathered in turmeric—a ritual meant to purify her in preparation for union with her husband. For some, it symbolized the showering of love from parents and relatives, while for others, the turmeric appeared as an agent not just of purification but fairness—a hangover from ancient times. It also symbolized fertility and glowing health, and was considered the harbinger of peace and prosperity.

The day felt endless to Tamara, not just from sorrow and misery but more from a foreboding of what lay ahead, a feeling that struck her with ferocity and vengeance. Tamara tried her best not to expose her feelings. A bride should not cry on her wedding day but merely smile along, never mind if the smiles are forced. She had to smile, for the photographers, the guests, her husband, her in-laws, and for the life she was about to begin.

Tamara wondered how she was managing to smile. She was a strong girl, but she underestimated her strength! Was it not more natural for her to break down, weep inconsolably, to drown all her sorrows in a cathartic stream of tears? What was even stranger was how nobody had managed to gauge her angst! Were people truly so oblivious? Or were they just pretending? Surely, the rumours would have reached at least some of the guests by now. Perhaps she simply was a brilliant actor. In that case, maybe she should try her luck in Bollywood.

She had snatched away from her best friend the one person she was willing to sacrifice her life for, someone who had pervaded her heart and soul. And she was the only person who was privy to Maya's feelings. Tamara feared that her friend's future was dark and uncertain. But why were such thoughts crowding her mind now? Had not many others, through time, faced similar predicaments? Was Maya's situation unprecedented? Were all jilted lovers doomed? Did they not manage to survive the heartbreak and move on?

Tamara tried to console herself, clinging to the thought that Maya, naturally resilient, would find the strength to move on. Yet, that day, she had seen the future in Maya's eyes, and had heard it in her tremulous voice as she had tried to console her. Maya had been play-acting, but Tamara could see through the mask. She resolved to pull Maya back from the edge, but it appeared tricky. She would still try till the last moment.

The night before the wedding, Maya stayed with Tamara. Throughout the night, she woke repeatedly to the sound of Tamara crying in her sleep. She was whimpering, calling out for help. She seemed to be in a state of extreme disarray. Worried, Maya decided to wake Tamara's mother.

Creeping out to the porch where the women and children lay sprawled under the twinkling stars, Maya tiptoed towards Tamara's mother, who lay sleeping in one corner. 'Auntie, Auntie,' she whispered, trying her best not to rouse the others, which was no easy feat since they were all sleeping close to each other. Her soft voice did not wake Tamara's mother, who was exhausted, having worked hard through the day and was sleeping like a log. Maya, her desperation mounting, ultimately shook Auntie's shoulders, hoping to wake her up.

She was surprised that no one else stirred, sleeping as if they all had been drugged. *What would happen if there were to be a burglary or robbery?* Maya wondered. At long last, Tamara's mother moved, blinking open her tired eyes, but closed them again almost instantly.

'Auntie, Auntie,' Maya whispered again, the shaking now vigorous. Auntie finally managed to wake up, and stared at Maya.

'*Kya hua, beta?* (What happened, dear?)' she mumbled. Her bloodshot eyes conveyed a sense of shock and foreboding. She possibly expected the worst, recalling the news of her mother's death a few years back. She weighed the possibilities that could have prompted Maya to wake her at this odd hour. Glancing around in growing awareness, she asked, 'Is Tamara okay?'

Maya felt happy to see Auntie anxious for her daughter. Over the last few days, she had got the impression that Auntie had no feelings for Tamara and that she simply wished to complete her parental duty and get her married off, irrespective of the consequences. Maya gestured for her to follow. Luckily, everyone slept soundly, their snores sounding like a well-rehearsed orchestra.

They tiptoed, balancing delicately as though crossing stones in a stream, each step a small reminder of childhood games that momentarily transported Maya back to simpler, happier days. Suddenly, Maya felt an urge to return to her childhood days, the carefree days when there was only joy and peace around—

notwithstanding the tensions at home arising out of her father's autocratic and violent behaviour that persisted throughout her childhood. Despite the situation at home, she would almost instantly forget all her worries and tensions when she was in the playground.

When they reached the room, they found Tamara writhing in her sleep, as though struggling to free herself from invisible bonds. Her breath came in heavy gasps, body curled tightly. Maya immediately looked at Auntie, searching for a reaction, but there was none—or perhaps Auntie was masking her horror too well. As Tamara continued to whimper and shift, Maya turned back to Auntie, seeking some comfort or reassurance.

After a moment, Auntie spoke up, the words staying with Maya for a long time—words difficult to forget even over the years, words that summed up her helplessness. What surprised Maya even more was how she had managed to read her thoughts. 'Maya, you must think that I don't care about my daughter, but please shake that thought from your mind. A mother cares deeply for her daughter—perhaps even more than her son. Fathers may worry more for their sons, but we mothers know the pain of being daughters ourselves. We've been through all of this. Tamara at least goes to school, has much freedom, plays in the afternoons and participates in extra-curricular activities. I was not allowed any of this. My father married me off at the first opportunity.

'You may think I am cold-blooded, anxious to send off Tamara, but please understand that life would have been worse for her if not for this marriage. Tamara was not born with a silver spoon in her mouth; our family would not have been able to support her education longer—this was the best option for her. Please try to place yourself in my shoes.

'I know Shiv. He is a good boy. He will be kind to her and take care of her. I have seen how affectionate he is towards his sister. We are sure he would take care of Tamara also in the same way. He will grant her the freedom she enjoys at home. His mother is also a lovely lady, despite her drinking habits. She will never harm Tamara. He has a gentle heart, a rare quality in young men today. Poverty isn't everything in life, you know. Shiv's nature is what truly matters. If they ever face a desperate situation, he will feed her before feeding himself. She will be loved. That is why we took this decision; it was not an easy one. If I had opposed this marriage, Tamara would have been married off later to an old hag as many of your friends have been. As a friend, you should support her and encourage her. I am confident you will do so.'

She paused, then, after a long sigh, concluded, 'Tamara may not understand this now, but will realize it later as she grows more mature and level-headed. This marriage is the best thing I have done for my daughter!'

Maya felt a shiver run down her spine. The very name of Shiv and the manner in which Auntie had described his qualities sent her head reeling.

Auntie lay down beside Tamara and motioned for Maya to join them. There was enough room for the three of them. Maya wept silently through the night, her gaze shifting between Auntie's peaceful face and Tamara's troubled one. Maya hoped that Saria would appear, though she knew Saria never visited the homes of others.

Finally, exhaustion took hold, and Maya started feeling sleepy just as the ochre light touched the distant horizon, blending with the golden marigold to pierce through the dark remnants of night. Birds started chirping loudly and clearly, welcoming dawn.

Maya sincerely hoped that this new dawn, signalling the advent of an auspicious day, would carry blessings from the Almighty and turn the tide for them. She vowed that she would neither marry nor love anyone else. She would never forget Shiv; nobody would ever be able to take the memories of Shiv away from her After all, she had dedicated her heart to him long back. Shiv would continue to belong to her and not Tamara. Even if they never united in this life, there would be seven more lives in which their paths might cross. But as she drifted off, she wondered whether the same held true for Shiv, whether his love carried the same depth. *Boys are far more heartless,* she thought.

11

The irate *baraatis*, the worried *dulhanwalas*, the flowers, the garlands, the bamboos, the drapes, the dazzling dupattas and vibrant ghagras, overlapping chatters, the delicious food and spicy chaat, the chaos and clutter, children running helter-skelter, uproarious laughter, the jitters, the exhilaration, the dholaks, guests dressed in their best attire, the chants of the priest, the warmth of the fire, the firecrackers, the tense hosts, the groom astride his horse, the dancing and singing—these were some of the images of the wedding morning that stood out to Maya. They marked the culmination of truth—an inevitable, calamitous day. Shiv was marrying Tamara, a fact now indisputable.

'Tamara Weds Shiv', the marigolds proclaimed in both English and Hindi. It felt clumsy, the letters falling over one another, the petals wilting with a lack of freshness. The shabby arrangement felt like an insult to one of Maya's favourite blooms. But would it have made any difference if the display had been more creative and aesthetic?

Marigolds lay crushed on the floor, trampled by the wedding guests, who bustled about with gifts wrapped in brightly coloured paper. The wives leaned on their husbands as if they were crutches to support them, never mind that these same arms had probably beaten them a few hours or days back, leaving them black and blue. Young girls, some still toddling, darted about in ghagra cholis, without their dupattas, their carefree movements lending a different aura to the evening. Only a few years ago, Maya and Tamara themselves had frolicked in a similar manner.

Maya was in an introspective mood, with new revelations striking her every minute. As she thought about the peculiarities surrounding the wedding, she was not just stunned but disgusted by the guests' smiling faces as they devoured the delicious spread like gluttons. It dawned on her that the entire town was party to an unpardonable form of criminality unfolding brazenly before their eyes. A 14-year-old girl was being married off to a boy who was also not much older—both robbed of the carefree years that should have been dedicated to play, study and youthful pursuits.

It dawned on Maya that she could also be married off similarly, perhaps to someone worse. It could be next week, the following month or a few months later. The dread of someone other than Shiv touching her body crippled her mind. She felt brain-dead, paralysed from below the waist. She would escape. She would escape to some place outside Bhai's and Maa's reach. She had already started plotting her escape in the last few days, initially dismissing it as childish and immature, but now, it slowly seemed to be the only hope. She had initially refused to accept that Shiv was marrying Tamara, but the idea of her own marriage was even more preposterous.

Maya, having recently created her own email ID, was always on the lookout for promising career opportunities. A few days ago, she had stumbled upon an advertisement for a course in her inbox. Living in Ranikhet would render the possibility of getting married even more real, so it was better to escape sooner rather than later. Though enrolling in the course initially had felt like a remote possibility, the idea of leaving the stifling town increasingly began to consume her thoughts. She dreaded the prospect of being married off to an older man, perhaps a distant relative with substantial money in the bank, who would be able to 'support' her. She had heard countless incidents of girls being married off and sent to other villages, becoming victims of abuse and ill-treatment. Maya had also read about marital rape recently. She was, after all, growing up and at the threshold of adulthood, and with that came an awareness she could not escape.

She had decided her future course of action. She was going to leave for Mumbai as soon as Tamara was married. She had earlier not entertained such thoughts because of Shiv, but now with him out of the way, it seemed like the best possibility. She would escape both Shiv and marriage.

Maya had been tasked with helping Tamara get dressed up for the wedding. As she entered the room, she paused, taking in the sight before her. Tamara was nearly ready, her movements precise and confident as she finished dressing. Renowned for her skill at dressing others, Tamara had little trouble perfecting her own appearance. Her sari was draped flawlessly, and her hair and makeup were impeccable, exuding an air of effortless elegance.

Maya watched quietly, the familiarity of this moment tinged with an undercurrent of something she could not quite name. The room was suffused with a nervous energy that hovered between them, unspoken but palpable.

Tamara was dressed in a crisp white sari with a striking blood-red border, which was the norm in these parts. Tiny flowers adorned the fabric and shimmered with a faint golden sheen in the sunlight. Yet, she still wore the same emotionless expression, which now scared Maya. She genuinely wanted Tamara to look happy, bright and cheerful. Now that she was slightly more reconciled to the situation and had gotten over the initial shock, she wished Tamara would also overcome her sadness.

Auntie had attributed Tamara's discomposure to the jitters of an early marriage, but only Maya knew the true reason. The future felt scary and ominous to her. The thought of hurting Maya and not protesting the unjust marriage tore at her. Tamara had not expressed it to others, and Maya wished she would never do so. A selfish thought appeared—better that Tamara continue to bear the burden and have nightmares—but Maya immediately felt ashamed for even entertaining such an idea.

As Maya worked on putting the finishing touches, she placed a garland of tuberoses in Tamara's loosely tied bun, filling the air with their intoxicating scent. Maya fretted they might wither before the ceremony as there was still some time left. Tamara didn't react to Maya's presence and just stared ahead of her.

As they walked out of the room, Tamara squeezed Maya's hand, as if silently begging her to stop this wedding that had wreaked havoc on their lives. But what could Maya do? She was as powerless as Tamara. Her conversation with Auntie the previous night had left Maya conflicted; she found herself clinging to Auntie's reassurance that Tamara's marriage to Shiv was to avert a greater disaster. Not that she believed Auntie. After all, she was pretty perceptive and might have said it to console Maya.

'Thank you for this,' Tamara said, pointing at the black thread tied around her right ankle.

Maya looked at her, confused. 'What?'

Tamara looked at her, concerned for the first time that she might not be able to control her emotions; perhaps she would break the promise she had made to Maya and her mother of not displaying any negative emotion on the day of her wedding. 'You gave this to me last night,' she replied softly. 'Don't you remember? You said it would act as a talisman, protecting me from evil spirits and ill-wishers. You had made me promise to never take it off. Maya, I am promising you again. This will be my protector and keep your memories alive—wherever we may be 10, 20 or 30 years from now. It will remind me of you at all times and inspire me to lead a life of purity under your distant guidance.'

Tamara's concern deepened as she noticed Maya's strange expression. It had apparently slipped her mind. Tamara was disappointed, wondering if Maya had not presented it to her with sincerity and earnestness. She was also perplexed at Maya's memory loss—it was so unlike her. She continued to stare at

Maya, looking for clues, but Maya still displayed no semblance of recollection.

Tamara continued, attempting to jog her memory. 'Maya, you gave it to me and said that Saria, the angel who often visits you at night, had given it to you. I didn't believe you because neither do I believe in angels and fairies nor do I believe in talismans. I was reluctant, but you insisted I wear it and I didn't want to hurt you. You tied it with your own hands. I am surprised that this could slip your mind.'

Maya's expression darkened, shifting from confusion to a deeper fear. A flash of memory returned, but it was clouded by dread. She was scared for a different reason—the failure to distinguish between real and unreal. This had happened several times before, and Maya avoided giving free rein to her imagination; but this time, it appeared that she had gone against her grain. The sooner she could forget this, the better.

Maya's mind raced. *How could I not remember this? This is the sacred thread Maa gave me, something I carry around everywhere… I gave it to her and forgot about it, and then made up a story about Saria, which is patently false.*

Suddenly, a laugh escaped her, which was fake, and Tamara was sharp enough to see through the façade. Maya quickly tried to cover up her lapse of memory with a feigned nonchalance. 'Of course, I gave it to you. I was just pretending not to remember.'

Tamara remained unconvinced, her expression unambiguously conveying her scepticism.

'Now, hurry up, or Shiv will run away,' Maya quipped in an attempt at light-heartedness. She had meant to ease the tension, but Tamara knew better. Something was wrong. But now was not the time to dwell on it; she had a thousand other things to worry about.

Just then, Maya caught sight of Shiv standing at the doorstep, looking extraordinarily handsome in a cream-coloured kurta. Maya flinched—he would be Tamara's from that day onward. Her heart sank, but surprisingly, the pain felt less acute than yesterday. She couldn't quite explain why or how, but she whispered her teacher's words to herself: 'Time is the best healer.' She had always believed in it, and now it seemed time was acting faster than it usually did.

Proud of her composure, Maya stood tall, ensuring no tears escaped her kohl-smeared eyes. She walked alongside Tamara, gently holding her hand, as they made their way towards the lake. She did not want to make Tamara feel uncomfortable at this juncture. It was a moment of transition for her, and she needed support and comfort from her friends, parents and everyone who loved her. Maya could not let her friend down.

Shiv also looked simple, docile, humble and unassuming like always—a true reflection of his character. Although most residents of Ranikhet constantly demeaned him, Maya had long discovered his true nature—the day she first saw him at his shop, the days he came to drop his sister off at school, on the fateful Holi, the day he had saved Tamara and the little girl, and the day he had rescued Maya from sure drowning. Maya was aware of his affectionate self. She had witnessed it; she had felt it.

He stood there, a garland around his neck, looking much like he had the first day Maya had seen him. Some people's appearances never change, and Shiv was one of them. He barely looked up. His shyness was often mistaken for aloofness or arrogance. In Ranikhet, cynicism and gossip were rampant, and Shiv often bore the brunt of these harsh judgements. People said he never looked anyone straight in the eye. Maya's classmates also said so; even Bhai had made similar comments, subtly hinting at what he believed was Shiv's true nature.

But Maya saw beyond the rumours. She knew Shiv was concealing something deeper—he was hiding his emotions and feelings, just as she had tried to. Had she not blushed like a bride when Shiv had looked at her that day on the street, amidst the bustle of honking cars and folks gathering all over the place? Human beings are masters at the art of veiling genuine emotions—true love, true faith. But why? Why did society, the so-called civilized society they all were part of, not value truth? Why did it encourage people to hide the truth, to be fake in their behaviour? The upcoming marriage, orchestrated by the families, was one such deception. They were exuberant at having managed to complete a mission in life; the emotions of the bride and groom hardly mattered.

Cautiously, with measured steps, Tamara and Maya walked towards Shiv. He seemed slightly nervous as he looked up at Maya. She looked into his eyes. Had she spotted the tell-tale signs of tear? She tried her best to control her emotions—crying was the last thing she wanted to do. Her efforts were futile as a few drops escaped. The pain within her surged, and she found it increasingly difficult to contain it. She was, after all, a human being, just a 14-year-old girl grappling with her feelings.

She quickly picked up one end of her dupatta to wipe her tears, but Shiv had spotted them. He clenched his fist and dug his nails into his skin. Though the people of Ranikhet always found it difficult to read his expressions, Maya was perceptive. His feelings were palpable. Even the tiniest movement of his eyes and subtle gestures convinced Maya that Shiv was equally unhappy about this marriage but had to bow down for the sake of his family.

This was, however, not the day to complain. It was undoubtedly a poignant day, marked as a watershed, a milestone—a day when three individuals were stepping into adulthood. Adulthood for Maya and Tamara at 14! A day that would irrevocably alter their lives!

Maya grew weak inside for the first time that day, looking at Shiv and Tamara, who now sat on the mandap stools. She could not take it any more and rushed towards the bathroom. Shiv and Tamara exchanged a look; it was perhaps the first time they had looked into each other's eyes. Maya, on the other hand, wished that she could disappear. All the positivity she had meticulously cultivated, all her resolutions, evaporated into thin air. She now felt that the wedding should not be allowed to take place. She wished that everyone witnessing the event would vanish, because what was happening felt like a crime—a crime against humanity, a violation of fundamental rights. Did Tamara not deserve the freedom to choose her partner and decide when to marry?

The emotions Maya had buried deep inside were spouting from the recesses of her heart like lava from a long-dormant volcano. In the solitude of the bathroom, Maya wept, gasping for breath. She pressed her handkerchief against her mouth to muffle her sobs; she refused to let her helplessness, pathos and tragedy be seen by the world.

She cried for what seemed like an eternity. When she looked at her watch, she realized she had been there only for 10 minutes, though it had seemed like 10 hours. She stayed there for a while longer, calming her trembling and shivering body.

Meanwhile, Tamara's anxiety was evident and raised many eyebrows, but she did not seem to care. She had noticed Maya's long absence and decided to head to the bathroom. No one could deny that request—it was nature's call after all. By the time she barged into the bathroom, Maya had composed herself. Tamara held her hand and then hugged her. For the casual onlooker, it might have appeared as a customary hug, obligatory and rehearsed. But only Maya could gauge the sincerity and the earnestness with which Tamara had embraced her and led her back to the mandap. She made Maya sit next to her. It was time to get married.

Shiv watched them with a hint of a smile, recognizing their eternal bond. It was the most beautiful relationship one could have—a pure, unadulterated friendship untainted by material pursuits or selfishness, not tied by any familial bonds but by the eternal thread of love.

Looking at Tamara, Shiv asked her, 'Are you both okay?' It was a rhetorical question, not meant for a direct answer but rather an acknowledgement of the complex emotions swirling around them.

Maya wondered about Shiv's intent. Did he truly expect an answer? Was he that heartless? Or was he delusional? Or a naïve fool? Was he pretentious? What was he implying? Was he trying to hint that all was fine with him, and he expected them also to affirm that? Did he believe all relationships to be ephemeral? That one needed to move on and forget as soon as possible? Had he ever cared? Had he lost all his memories—of Holi, of the incidents by the lake? Had they not professed their love for each other? So, what if they had not spoken? Were words all in life?

Doubts started plaguing Maya's mind. Was it all play-acting—the gulaal, lifting her dupatta, holding her by the waist, the gentle dancing of his eyebrows and eyelashes? Tamara was a witness to them all. Was he a manipulator? If so, what did that mean for Tamara's future? Maya was not even sure now whether they had ever had a connection. Perhaps it was a one-sided connection, like Radha's mythical love for Krishna spoken of in scriptures.

Tamara wrestled with her own doubts. She struggled to reconcile the validity of her memories; she started believing that only the present had significance—memories of the past were all hogwash. She had to focus on the wedding that was taking place. Tamara felt delusional, hallucinating that Shiv was marrying Maya and not her, which is why he was so nonchalant and stoic.

Maya resolved to not allow her anguish to overwhelm her. She was, by nature, strong, and had to get on top of it. The only way to overcome this feeling was to forget about the past and move on with her life, building a new future. And for that, she needed to leave Ranikhet for good. Living with Shiv and Tamara around, as a married couple, would amount to a life peppered with suffering. As Shiv and Tamara took turns around the sacred fire for their *pheras*, Maya gently browsed her phone, the one she had acquired a year back, searching for opportunities in Mumbai.

Meanwhile, Tamara had stuck to her promise—the only time she had tears in her eyes was when her father did her *kanyadaan*—'donating' her to Shiv, to another family, shedding off all responsibilities. It was an event that had to be done because that was how it was ordained. Tamara felt like an inanimate object being given away, like a gold pendant or a laptop or a television. She recognized the societal expectations and the historical significance of such rituals, yet she also saw them as archaic and, perhaps, oppressive. She knew others might consider her disillusioned or irreverent, but she had reached an understanding of these traditions, seeing beyond the surface, while others often followed them unthinkingly.

As the wedding rituals ended, the labourers moved swiftly to dismantle the mandap, carting away the bamboo, flowers and decorations, and loading them on to a waiting truck, after meticulously counting the bulbs and tubes. They pranced all over the place, their once-white caps now beige, smeared by dust and sweat, as the supervisors shouted commands over the clatter. They marched like soldiers, stomping on the ground with their heavy boots and cracking jokes to make their work easier.

The scene resembled a war zone. To Maya's disgust, the flowers strewn on the floor were swept off with a broom. After all, the flowers had adorned the wedding ceremony and deserved more respect. Both Maya's and Tamara's hearts broke, but by now they were used to more disastrous heartbreaks.

Within half an hour, the mandap had been transformed into a dinner space, and the place looked beautiful. Destruction, it seemed, was a prerequisite for creating something beautiful. The floor had a red carpet, with mattresses running in three straight lines for guests to sit on. Each spot had a rattan placemat for plates. Buffet-style service was not popular in Ranikhet. The brass plates varied in size—some of them were from Tamara's house; Maya could identify those since she frequently had meals at her friend's house.

Tamara's parents were preoccupied with ensuring Shiv and his relatives were content, a responsibility bound to age-old customs. The baraatis, accustomed to preferential treatment, had their expectations firmly in place. Stories abounded of weddings that had teetered on the brink of collapse over trivial slights—a missing glass of lassi, warm juice, or the oversight of failing to greet an influential guest at the gate. Once, a wedding had even been called off, leaving the bride unwed and the family entangled in whispers for years.

Maya found herself wishing, if only for a moment, that such a disruption might happen today. It was a fleeting, rebellious thought that fizzled out quickly. The ceremony was already too far along, and that brief hope dissolved as reality settled in.

The sight of Shiv sitting next to Tamara plunged Maya once again into the depths of despondency. She had dreaded this from the very first day. Her world had been shattered into a million pieces, all within the span of a few days. She knew she would not be able to gather the fragments, although she resolved to brave the adversities and emerge stronger. As she was coaxed into sitting next to Tamara, Maya experienced brief blackouts. She could not concentrate on her food, flitting in and out of a blank world, an empty mind bereft of material thoughts. This was a solace she had consciously created because therein lay her only chance of not breaking down.

She was brought back to harsh reality by the chatter of an older woman seated behind her, the blaring music and the occasional murmur from Shiv, primarily in response to the caterer's request to try some new item or repeat a previous item. Tradition dictated that Shiv and Tamara ate from the same plate, but at Tamara's insistence, there was a separate plate for her. Though her mother had insisted that the custom be followed, Shiv did not mind breaking it, and Tamara was resolved to defy her mother. Did Tamara subconsciously believe that she did not belong to Shiv, or was it a mere act of rebellion? For a moment, Tamara felt happy that Shiv was, in many respects, modern. She planned on taking full advantage of that.

Shiv inspected Tamara's plate and then Maya's. Neither of them had eaten much. He looked at Maya; as their eyes met, Maya immediately looked away. She had to be strong. That look of his should not be allowed to affect her tonight. She had momentarily spotted the same loving expression. There was no change in his gaze; he still carried the same love for her, still adored her. His gaze was intense, conveying raw passion—a passion that could overwhelm any girl. Or so Maya thought. She glanced up to notice other eyes looking slyly at them. So word had spread after all! Nothing was a secret in Ranikhet, and what happened on Holi had been quite open and in front of a hundred pairs of eyes. But Maya still could not control herself when he looked at her.

Tamara didn't notice any of this; she was in her own world. She did not, in any way, feel attracted to Shiv; the marriage was just a transaction for her. The irony of life! Tamara was sitting next to Shiv while Maya, who genuinely loved Shiv, was relegated to the sidelines!

Then the unthinkable happened. Shiv raised his eyebrows, gesturing at Maya to eat, as if he knew she hadn't eaten anything since morning. Maya's heart skipped a beat. No, quite a few beats. She hadn't anticipated this situation even in her wildest dreams. He was the obstinate type, unbothered by what others felt—that she knew—but this was something even she, with her intense feelings, was unwilling to allow, especially out of consideration for Tamara, her best friend. She could not do that to her. What did he think he was doing?

Maya wondered what kind of relationship he expected them to have.

Does he know what he is doing?

What if someone notices the signals directed at me? After all, there were all indications that the topic was being discussed across the length and breadth of Ranikhet.

Does he have a pact with Tamara? Was the wedding just a façade to maintain appearances and keep their folks happy? Does Tamara have someone in her life—perhaps Ashok—someone she knew her parents would never accept? Did she agree to marry Shiv so that she could continue her relationship with her lover?

Maya soon realized, however, that these thoughts were far-fetched and outlandish. While it could happen in Delhi or Mumbai, such things were unthinkable in Ranikhet.

Does he still want to be with me after all this?

Is this marriage just a sham for him?

Can he not imagine life without me?

Maybe this is the effect of the shock he is experiencing.

Does he want to leave Tamara and move to a distant city? Is it fair to Tamara, unless she is also planning something similar?

No, no, no. This isn't happening. He is just being polite, and I am imagining things. After all, he, by nature, is a polite person.

Maya immediately looked down at her plate and realized that in her daze, she had eaten half of the food on her plate—the food she had had no desire to touch a few minutes ago because she had no appetite. She looked up once again and saw Shiv smiling at her.

Right then Tamara's mother appeared. She looked exhausted—it showed in her eyes—but also satisfied that the event had passed without incident. She was looking forward to a week of well-earned rest. The wedding preparations had taken a toll on her tender body. As Maya looked intently into her eyes, she noticed a hint of sadness, of misery. Despite her weariness, she was relentless in wearing a mask of strength, happiness and excitement, as she did every day.

Maya felt the need to apologize for waking her the previous night. In that moment, it had seemed like a life-and-death situation, but now it seemed frivolous. Her panic had been unwarranted and Auntie must have been exhausted and overburdened—not just physically due to hard work but mentally from dealing with a dejected Tamara.

Approaching her, Maya whispered, 'I'm sorry for disturbing you last night.'

The sentence was barely audible to Auntie, who loudly replied, 'Huh?'

Shiv looked up, wondering what this was all about. Maya, embarrassed by the sudden attention, tried to brush it off, but Auntie insisted. 'Beta, tell me. You said something about last night.'

Maya hesitated, keeping quiet as she saw Shiv and Tamara looking at her intently with inquisitive eyes. A few others nearby too appeared curious.

'Nothing, Auntie. I was just apologizing for waking you up last night,' Maya mumbled loud enough for Auntie to hear.

'Wake me up?' Auntie looked confused. 'Beta, when did you wake me up?'

'Never mind,' Maya said. 'Auntie, forget it.'

'Beta, I do not remember you waking me. I slept soundly and woke up early morning.'

Maya was perplexed by Auntie's response, and started questioning herself. *Auntie said she didn't wake up. How is that possible? I spoke to her and told her about how she was destroying Tamara's life. I showed her how Tamara was whimpering and tossing and turning. Why was she denying the incident? Does she not want Tamara and Shiv to know?*

Maya was sure she had woken Auntie and brought her to Tamara's room. *Auntie explained why she was marrying off Tamara. How could that be an illusion? We had a long chat; she explained everything rationally.*

Was it my imagination after all? Have I started hallucinating and imagining things due to all the recent stress? Or was I just dreaming, and the distinction between real and imaginary life got blurred?

How can a dream be so vivid?

Was I awake or sleeping last night? I have dreamt twice of Tamara's wedding, of Shiv talking to me by my bedside and of Saria visiting me. But this couldn't have been my imagination. It was real, wasn't it?

Maybe it didn't happen. Maybe it happened. But Auntie seems very sure that she didn't talk to me. Maybe she is pretending.

Is this a one-off incident?

Am I losing my marbles?

I need to leave this town before I completely lose my mind.

Maya had never been so perplexed or unsure of her actions before. She shut herself off but, after a while, noticed Shiv and Tamara staring at her. She glanced at her hand—it had bothered her the whole day; it had itched and ached, but she had not had the time to examine it. Looking down in annoyance, she found the tell-tale sign on her hand. When had she cut herself? Why had it not bled? How could the mark of a blade escape her attention for so long?

She wasn't shocked or flabbergasted by this, but merely surprised. Shiv was, however, furious at what she had done to herself. She saw it in his eyes.

His eyes begged her to be kind to herself.

His eyes begged her to take care of herself.

His eyes begged her to forgive him.

His eyes begged her to know that he still loved her, even if circumstances had led him to marry Tamara.

His eyes also told her that one thing she longed to hear—that he loved her and would continue loving her for eternity.

Part II

12

Perched on the windowsill, Maya watched the bustling street of Mumbai, captivated by the city's vibrant energy. It wasn't just the rush of pedestrians or the food stalls offering pav bhaji and vada pav, but the resilience of the people amidst the chaos. The worn walls, cramped living spaces and the mix of hope and hardship defined the city's allure.

In contrast to her peaceful home town of Ranikhet, where contentment came naturally, Mumbai's pace was relentless. Yet the pursuit of dreams—even for those unlikely to achieve them—was intoxicating. Maya admired the city's sense of community—strangers helping each other without judgement, something her small town lacked.

Though Maya often longed for the tranquillity of Ranikhet, she couldn't help but admire the unwavering spirit of Mumbai's youth. They seemed to find joy in the smallest moments, thriving in a city that never paused. But she sometimes wondered if their relentless pursuit of happiness came at the expense of true peace of mind. Ultimately, Maya realized that life in Mumbai was an open canvas, full of potential—ordinary or extraordinary, depending on how one chose to paint it.

As she watched the world go by, Maya noticed a trail of delicate silver dust meandering across her palms—a collection of particles gathered from the windowsill. She picked up a cloth and swiftly wiped away the residue—a well-practised ritual inherited from her mother that had firmly taken root within her. As her hands became pristine once more, her focus shifted to the intricate lifeline etched into her palm, wondering if its abrupt deviation hinted at the unexpected detours her life had taken. Although the astrologer's predictions had materialized with uncanny accuracy, a curiosity beckoned her to seek out the palmist she had seen earlier, seated on the sidewalk with his vibrant parrot.

Mumbai had transformed her in more ways than she had anticipated—not just in appearance or habits, but in her entire way of being. The city's influence was direct and relentless, leaving little room for her rural sensibilities to remain intact. Her attire, her stride, even her manner of speaking had evolved, subtly infused with the rhythm and customs of a place that changed everyone who lived within its bounds. The shift in her destiny mirrored the profound transformation in how she presented herself and engaged with the world. Mumbai, with its sharp lessons, had far exceeded her initial expectations.

She took a sip of her tea, her gaze drifting towards the distant horizon. There was no natural beauty to behold—only the urban wilderness that loomed before her. Her attention wasn't captured by any concrete objects but rather the void that stared back—a vacant expanse rarely found in Mumbai. Even amidst the bustling surroundings, she had developed a knack for finding these empty spaces—a skill acquired since moving to the city. Here, as a dreamer, she had to fabricate these voids as they were not readily available.

The ethereal nature of these spaces fascinated her, for in Ranikhet, she had never needed to invent solitude. There, she had possessed the power to envision and conjure events that had never occurred—a realm where she could imagine conversations with Shiv, relive the transformative day and night of his wedding, and envision the existence of Saria. Her imagination often ran wild, the scope for creative reverie boundless in her small town. Here, however, she had to carve out intangible spaces for herself.

Another change that had taken hold was her ability to stifle her thoughts—a skill she had honed through sombre self-discipline.

Engaging in introspection during her train voyage to Mumbai, she had traced the root of her anguish—at least in part—to her inclination to brood. Yet, she could not bear to relinquish her past. It remained an integral part of her being, regardless of her surroundings or her future endeavours. Those pangs would accompany her until her final moments, dissolving only with the flames of her cremation. What she had managed to teach her mind, however, was to halt its wanderings at the appropriate moment. Excessive contemplation led nowhere; it only added to her misery—a painful lesson derived from recent trials that she yearned to internalize. Besides, her long-term memory had rarely been exceptionally vivid.

Her abode possessed a quaint charm, offering her and her flatmates a sense of solace. Though cramped and suffocating during the day, once each flatmate gradually departed by 10 a.m., Maya could enjoy solitude and a diminished sense of claustrophobia. This respite lasted only for an hour, until she too had to leave for work. At night, they would engage in conversations until slumber overtook them. On nights when the ocean breeze persisted, sleep was a pleasant experience; on other nights, Maya would douse herself in water just before midnight—a survival tactic she had learnt from her flatmates.

Her flatmates were her lifeline in Mumbai, a bond that had been forged during their hostel days. Now all of them had means of income, enabling them to indulge in life's modest delights. Seeking financial aid from family was not always desirable, particularly for Maya, who had not set foot in Ranikhet for seven years.

Though Bhai and Maa visited her annually, she had not been in touch with Tamara since her departure. It had been challenging initially, but Maya had gotten used to it. After all, everyone moves on in life, as must have Tamara.

Lost in thought, Maya had not noticed her roommate, Zahra, slip into the room. Seeing Maya sitting on the windowsill with a cup of tea, Zahra poured herself one and joined her, looking out at the same cityscape but with a different perspective. Maya's eyes were fixed on the horizon, gazing at the blue sky, the occasional seabirds flapping their wings and the white clouds drifting past.

Maya's mind was preoccupied with the events leading up to the day she left Ranikhet. The windowsill was her place to relive those moments, hours and days during her brief hour before work and on Sundays. However, she also observed the happenings in the sky—a multitasking ability she had mastered with considerable effort.

Zahra knew what transpired in Maya's mind during those moments by the window. She was among the select few entrusted with Maya's story and was aware of the mountains of pain that lay buried in Maya—pain that had faded over time but refused to go away. Zahra never broached the topic unprompted, respecting Maya's private space. Friendship is profound when you are told without asking. Asking questions to draw out secrets was not the hallmark of a true friend—this was what Zahra sincerely believed in. The moment you asked, the relevance was lost.

It was Sunday, and most of Maya's flatmates were home. It was the only day of the week when Mumbai witnessed a palpable shift in the city's relentless rhythm. Youth drifted along aimlessly in groups, crowded tea shops bustled with debates on everything from Bollywood to cricket to politics, and urchins claimed stretches of road for makeshift games of cricket or football. At home, too, no one was in a hurry; there was no rush for the shower, for ablutions, to grab food and prepare the vital cups of tea, to catch a train or to reach work on time. The day would be filled with chatter and tittle-tattle, consumption of varied food items, and perhaps an outing in the afternoon. Those whose families were nearby took advantage of the day to visit home, while Maya and her flatmates, hailing from distant towns, couldn't afford that luxury. Not that Maya was dying to go to Ranikhet.

One of the rooms was occupied by an immaculately dressed and clean-shaven man, with impeccably brushed hair. He was tall, dark and handsome, but the irony was that he was unemployed. He had nowhere to go, but always appeared to be busy, walking out in a hurry every morning. Nobody asked him questions or ridiculed him. He had appeared for countless interviews, confident each time, but somehow always returned without an offer. His room was lined with all the self-help books available in the world, along with a few others on general knowledge. He was intelligent and had flair; why he could not secure employment remained a mystery to Maya and her flatmates.

What Maya admired most in him was his tenacity—his refusal to give up and his unwavering belief that he would crack an interview sooner rather than later. Others felt he was trying for the wrong jobs and needed to understand his strengths and weaknesses, but nobody had the heart to tell him that. Maya wanted to help him, but felt she might be misunderstood. His optimism encouraged her; she felt it was a quality to be emulated. She supported him by passing along job listings she'd come across in newspapers or magazines at her office or the ones she had noticed on local trains, station walls or the internet.

Aman was the son of a farmer who had refused to stay and work on the family farm, much to his father's disappointment. Not that his family held acres and acres of land, but they could afford a reasonably decent life. Aman was the epitome of an aspirational Indian, wanting to break out of their traditional mould and make it big, but unfortunately no company in Mumbai would accept him. Still, he didn't give up. His flatmates appreciated his determination and perseverance, though a tinge of sympathy coloured their admiration. It was Maya who had offered him a room in their flat, after securing Zahra's and Shama's consent, because Aman had no other place to stay.

Shama was a whirlwind of energy, her vivacious spirit

infectiously lifting everyone around her. Since Maya's arrival in Mumbai, both Shama and Zahra had been her pillars of support. They survived the vicissitudes of life in a metro city through their synergy, strong bond and willingness to lift each other up whenever required.

Aman, meanwhile, had been an unexpected blessing to their group. He was an excellent cook, and the three girls relished his dishes. He invariably cooked their Sunday meals, which were mostly *chole puri* with *boondi raita*, though he would often come up with novelties picked from cooking websites. Whatever the dish, his cooking was gobsmacking. He never resented being commissioned for items of their choice because he loved to cook and try out new recipes. Maya had once considered suggesting that he try his luck as a chef but desisted, thinking he might not appreciate the comment.

Maya was not a foodie, nor had she met anyone so fond of cooking. And that, too, a man. Watching Aman at work reminded her of how she had longed to enter the kitchen as a child, and how Maa would not allow her until Maya's persistent pleas wore the former down. She recalled her first attempt—the thrill of cooking, her initial excitement and then her fear when she had dropped a few grains of rice outside the pot, close to the fire. Her enthusiasm had waned with time as her prime motivation had been to provide some relief to her overworked mother. However, the sight of Aman cooking was somewhat intriguing—perhaps because she hailed from Ranikhet's male-dominated society where it was anathema for a male member to enter the kitchen.

Aman had satisfied her physical needs, enabling her, at times, to forget the memories of Shiv. She had not yet managed to erase them permanently, but even the brief interludes when he would not appear to trouble her were a relief. She would forever remain grateful to Aman for that. Most importantly, he had calmed her nerves; her nightmares reduced when she slept next to him, as did her urge to make that one last call to Shiv. Maya never looked at him primarily as a person who satisfied her sexual needs, but as someone to fall back on—a kind of buffer, someone who could be relied upon when she and the other girls had exhausted their resources and stamina. Her expectations from him were also minimal.

★

It was a typical Sunday.

Everyone was lazing around, waiting expectantly for Aman to concoct a delicacy. They all thought his dishes were far better than the food at the restaurants, including the upscale ones they visited on rare occasions. While lounging on the sofa, Shama called out for a cup of tea. Anyone else would have likely objected to her frequent requests. Aman was not their servant; he cooked not out of compulsion but because he loved to. However, Shama had a childlike charm, and everyone, including Aman, doted on her.

Aman looked at her with one of his gentle and sincere smiles, and called out while preparing the tea. 'I am honouring your request, Shama, but on one condition. You will have to help me apply for jobs after lunch.'

Shama hated staring at the laptop on a hot afternoon, particularly on a languid Sunday. She knew he would make the tea even if she refused, but she had a soft corner for him. A few months back, when she lost her job, she had sulked for days, broken down and slept through the days. She was so distraught that she could not even apply her mind to job applications. Maya and Zahira had encouraged her, but Aman had gone out of his way to offer her an out-of-the-box solution. He had motivated her to become an entrepreneur, which she now was, having achieved reasonable success in six months. She was passionate about her enterprise these days—a travel agency with unparalleled customer service. Her clientele was growing, primarily through word-of-mouth recommendations, although she was miles from achieving break even.

Shama tried to pass off the task to Maya and Zahra, but they refused to entertain her.

Zahra retorted, 'You are the one who asked for tea.' Maya, too, was blunt in her refusal.

As they waited, watching the Sunday morning television programmes, Maya had a sudden flash. She had glanced at the calendar that morning to calculate how many days were left until payday—she needed cash but did not want to borrow money from Zahra or Shama. They were sure to provide, but Maya was a girl with high self-esteem. The date had seemed highly familiar, but the significance had eluded her. It was now that she remembered; it was a day that was stuck inside the crevices of her memory— Shiv and Tamara's wedding anniversary. Another year had gone by. Seven years since that fateful day. She was astonished at how she had emerged unscathed that day. Passions that refused to die down even after seven years had been undoubtedly far more intense that day! Maya felt that she would perhaps have created mayhem during the wedding if it had been any other girl, but she had held back because it was Tamara, her best friend.

Maya had tried her best to close that chapter of her life, and for the most part she had succeeded, yet memories continued to haunt her, especially on days like this.

The electricity suddenly went off, and everything went silent— the television, the fans and even the faint hum of the tube light near the door. Fortunately, it was a breezy day, and it seemed better without the fan, which had been creaking so loudly it reminded Maya of an old aircraft propeller, ominously suggesting that it might come crashing down any moment. She was always scared that her head would get chopped off one day, while Shama went a step further, convinced the Devil possessed the fan.

'Maya, did you pay the electricity bill? It was your turn this month,' Shama ventured hesitantly. She hated speaking to Maya about monetary issues.

'Of course, I did! Don't you remember? I was sitting on the couch, Aman was cooking dinner and you sat beside me while I paid for it online, from my laptop.'

Shama was a bit ashamed for having asked the question. 'Now that you say it, it does ring a bell.'

Whenever there were power cuts, it seemed that the world had come to a standstill. The racket created by the fan was unbearable, and the silence and serenity that now dominated the surroundings provided a respite to the inhabitants, especially on breezy days when the heat and humidity were not stifling. It seemed that the dogs and cats had also quietened and the hawkers had stopped yelling. Even the sounds of the croaking crows were no longer audible.

Maya felt unsettled. Zahra could almost hear her mind racing like a car on a highway and her heart beating like drums during a jam session. Zahra, the only person there who knew a bit of her story, could sense each time Maya lapsed into silence. She could make out that Maya was not at peace mentally, and feel her agony and pain. Yet Zahra could not comment because others were unaware of Maya's past; she too would not have liked comments on a phase in her life that she was trying her best to eject from her memories.

'Let's go and see what's cooking,' Zahra said, trying to divert Maya's attention.

Maya replied, 'Don't bother; relax. Let me check,' and got up from the sofa.

Zahra did not push, but she and Shama exchanged a look with each other.

Maya returned after two minutes, laptop in hand, and sat down on the sofa. 'I paid the bill, sitting right here. I was having tea at the time. This was the coaster on the table that day. See, I can vividly paint the scene,' she insisted.

Zahra and Shama once again pierced one another with intense glances. Why was Maya repeating herself? They had not questioned or expressed any doubt about her earlier assertion. Had she really paid?

Maya was indeed a mysterious girl; it was challenging to identify what went on inside her mind. It was more baffling for Shama because she was unaware of her past. Even though Zahra knew, she thought Maya should have moved on by now; seven long years had passed. In the past, too, Maya's behaviour had, at times, been inconsistent and erratic. While Maya thought she was suffering from amnesia, this was not endorsed by the others. At times, Maya would withdraw into a cocoon that the girls called a 'black hole'. She would stop communicating for days on end and barely eat. Whenever she was at home, she would sleep through the day, sometimes skipping breakfast, lunch and even dinner. Zahra and Shama would be at a loss during those days, not knowing how to care for her.

Zahra walked into the old-fashioned tiny bathroom with its light blue tiles dotted with pink dandelions and pastel green leaves, the tobacco-stained brown sink, along with an Indian-style toilet with ripples meant to massage the feet while squatting. They lived in a minimalistic house because they could not afford anything better. It had taken Maya some time to get used this kind of housing situation. Their bathroom in Ranikhet was larger, though the styles were similar. She had been impressed when she had visited a friend's apartment in Mumbai, with its modern showers, a western-style toilet, bright tiles and clean drainage. She longed for the day she could afford a similar home and invite Maa and Bhai to stay for longer.

Maya opened the electricity board website on her laptop and noticed the bill hadn't been paid! Quietly, she paid the bill, feeling embarrassed. It wasn't the first time she had forgotten to pay it; her memory lapses were becoming more frequent. Forgetfulness was typical for all human beings but being unsure whether a bill had been paid or not could not be taken lightly. When confronted,

Maya would deny, argue, insist, and even scream at the top of her voice. Her flatmates tolerated her during those phases, but how long would they continue to do so? Her behaviour, at times, could be repulsive.

Maya would insist she had paid the bills, accepting her forgetfulness only when the next bill arrived, showing the pending amount. Zahra had once paid on Maya's behalf, not wanting it to reach Shama's ears because she might not have been so forgiving! It was not as if Maya was unwilling or wished to cheat them, but her memory lapses and her refusal to accept it was a result of her ego, which sometimes made her behaviour preposterous.

Maya went into the kitchen to help Aman. As he started caressing Maya's back gently and suggestively, it relaxed and even calmed her—there was magic in his touch—but it rarely aroused her. She had gone to bed with him only when she was desperate to shrug off the vestiges of Shiv's memories. Zahra noticed their interaction and smiled. She loved the fact that Aman was there for Maya. They were perfect together, made for each other.

Maya leaned on his chest while stirring the delicious red curry he had prepared. Every few minutes, he would bend forward to kiss her nape and earlobes, gently caressing her freshly shampooed, fragrant, jet-black hair. Aman was madly in love with Maya, aroused at the sight of her—he made it pretty obvious each time, often overdoing it. He seemingly could not exist without her. Zahra, however, knew Maya's feelings were more physical, which made her pity him.

Shama came in, squeaked and pushed Aman aside to hold Maya firmly by the shoulders. She then manoeuvred Maya out of the room, lifting her by her waist and seating her on the windowsill.

'Maya, you can do whatever you wish after he finishes cooking. I am famished, and Aman will never be able to focus as long as you are in there. Remember how he burned the rice last time?'

Maya recalled the day she had arrived in Mumbai; the first person she had encountered was Shama. Maya had entered her dormitory and noticed a girl with a baby face who radiated luminosity, sitting on the bed and diligently stitching her dress. They had developed an immediate bond, although Maya had been hesitant to repose complete trust in any individual after what she had experienced. However, their bond had deepened with time. Now, Maya could only hope that she would not be betrayed again. It was, after all, hope that keeps the human spirit going!

That afternoon, Maya found herself drifting between wakefulness and sleep, pondering endless questions.

What if Zahra had not covered for me with that electricity bill? How would Shama have reacted?

What if Aman hadn't fallen head over heels for me?

Do I love Aman?

What if we hadn't found each other? Would I have found someone else?

13

The sun shone mercilessly, casting its harsh rays across the city. There was no sign of respite, so the next best option was to spend the whole day inside the library. For college students, it's anything but a place to study; it's a place to enjoy the pleasures of air conditioning on a hot day, a place where young hearts meet, a few hearts break, some beat faster and crushes blossom into full-fledged affairs. It's where lovers become strangers, friends turn into sworn enemies, rebels turn into conformists, mockers get mocked and players get played. Of course, a few go there to study; for them, the library is a repository of knowledge and a storehouse of ideas.

College was where Maya first let her guard down because she felt she belonged there. She had fought with her family to attend a vocational course in Mumbai, eventually qualifying for college a few years later. The library was the only place she loved, the only place where she longed to be. Its silence was enticing, reminiscent of gentle streams on the outskirts of Ranikhet. She could almost hear the rushing water. The occasional noise of chatting students disturbed the silence but the librarian quickly intervened. The clatter of shoes stomping on the floor was often the only sound. The stillness in the air reminded her of Ranikhet and its gentle, laid-back life.

The library was also an abode of solace, peace, happiness and tranquillity—where Maya forgot life's woes and felt closest to her near and dear ones. Yet, amidst the tranquil surroundings, spasms of memories would hit—memories of Shiv, Tamara, the wedding night, Shiv dropping his sister at school, the visit to the astrologer, Saria, the day she fought with Bhai and made him jittery. But it was Shiv who kept appearing from the shadows, and even a fleeting thought of him would cause her heart to shed tears. He visited her in the library, caressed her, stroked her hair and back, stared at her with expressive eyes, consoled her and finally reassured her that he would be back—soon!

Mumbai was nothing like Ranikhet—different in appearance, people, weather, and attitudes. In Mumbai, no one cared for you, yet help was always available when you needed it. Ranikhet, on the other hand, was like one big family where everyone took care of each other, but when Maya needed help, no one had stepped forward. Zahra had once told her she should've asked for help, but Maya knew it wouldn't have mattered. Ranikhet was bound by tradition, and no one, not even her family, would have gone against it for fear of ostracism. In contrast, Mumbai was a city of rebels and iconoclasts, where Zahra and Shama had become her lifelines. She knew they would have fought for her because this city had no strict conventions. They shared their lives with each other, standing ready to defy the odds together.

After finishing college, Maya decided to retain her library membership because that was the only place that felt like home. She did go through a dozen crushes in this library, but they were not serious—just convenient distractions to help her wade through memories of Shiv. These crushes brought her closer to reality because life without a crush felt unreal to her—a perspective she had gained while sitting inside the library. Her heart didn't allow her to love anyone after Shiv, no matter how hard she tried.

Maya often deceived herself with tales of her fleeting crushes, filling her mind and the ears of her friends, who she doubted ever believed the stories. Zahra had an uncanny ability to see through people, to decipher fabrication, but she was polite enough not to bluntly confront Maya. Maya feared Zahra's perceptiveness; she could see the disbelief in Zahra's eyes, yet Zahra never mocked her. Instead, she pretended to believe Maya and even empathized with her.

It was one of those days when Maya felt the need to step away from the noise of her routine. Taking advantage of her pending leave days, she left the office slightly early and made her way to the library, a sanctuary where she could lose herself in the company of books and the quiet energy of readers around her. The proximity of both her office and the library was a rare blessing in a city like Mumbai, where most spent hours navigating crowded trains and buses.

As she settled into her favourite corner, Maya relished the brief escape, knowing that tomorrow would pull her back into the relentless pace of her work. This small reprieve was a reminder that moments of calm were as essential as the bustling days in the office—a balance she needed more than ever.

Maya's office was vibrant, quaint, cosy—different from the unsympathetic, stern, taciturn and strictly professional corporate world. They were a team of eight, working together in tandem and feeding off each other's energies. The company culture was open and transparent, free of the hierarchies that often stifled creativity.

She led the team in her boss's absence, as he was based in Pune. Her room was always open for anyone seeking advice, opinions or knowledge. There was a general atmosphere of happiness and joy that pervaded the office. Colleagues were willing to help, exchange views and guide one another when required. One was not reprimanded if they spent a few extra minutes at the coffee machine or the canteen, as long as they finished the assigned work on time. It was a place where she thoroughly enjoyed herself.

Maya's boss was a taskmaster, but a soft-hearted man. Though he worked with them remotely, he was always there to teach and inspire the team virtually, extracting the maximum effort from his junior colleagues. He understood the needs of the team members and rarely refused genuine requests for perks or time off—a combination of qualities challenging to find.

The entire team was driven by the thought of making a difference in their community. They worked as a cohesive unit, never in silos. They were a team of bloggers tackling real-life issues, highlighting them with a satirical touch. They always took the bull by the horns. Their organization was primarily dedicated to social causes, including but not limited to women's issues, aiming to create awareness and foster enlightened consciousness towards the day's burning issues. Their current project focused on developing a civic sense among the masses, encouraging them to perform their societal duties and become socially conscious and aware citizens.

Kanya, the youngest on the team, had a vigour that was unmatched. Hailing from Indore, the cleanest city in India, she was aghast at the stench and filth that marred Mumbai. It appalled her that the nation's commercial capital was so filthy. Her mission was to eradicate the dirt and squalor from the city, and her dedication inspired Maya.

'Why don't you people start keeping your city clean? Why not begin with your own houses?' was Kanya's common refrain. Explicit and brazenly straightforward, she was someone who could not sleep peacefully at night unless she had vociferously expressed her views on at least one topic close to her heart during the day.

Maya had decided to make Kanya the spokesperson for an upcoming conference—a decision their boss had approved.

She approached Kanya one morning. 'Why don't you represent us at the conference next week?'

The entire team started giggling. Conferences were not their cup of tea. Attendance was usually limited and the crowd was generally disinterested as they were forced to attend by their respective organizations. Most considered these a waste of time. Some came for networking, career opportunities or the free lunch. Kanya fell for the bait. She wanted to make her presence felt, even though she was a bit shaky.

'Maya, do you think I will be good as our company representative? After all, my experience is limited; I have never done public speaking,' Kanya said hesitantly.

Maya, however, was convinced that Kanya was the best choice for the session. 'Every individual, even the most experienced person, had a first exposure at some point, right, Kanya?"

The others scoffed; they were confident that Kanya was not the right choice and would goof up. But Maya was serious about sending Kanya, recognizing her passion and commitment. Throwing her into the deep end would be the best way to help her grow.

She asked Kanya to prepare a few talking points and deliver a mock presentation that afternoon. This would keep her quiet for a while. While Maya loved Kanya, she was also sick and tired of her constant blabbering. Kanya loved to talk, which made her a misfit among the more mature team members. The others worked quietly, focusing on their laptops and drafting their blogs. However, they lacked the passion that Maya valued deeply, although her own intensity had somewhat decreased with maturity. Kanya's heart was pure, and her commitment to the causes she espoused drew Maya to her.

Kanya reminded Maya of her last days at Ranikhet when she had loved Shiv with a passion that was hard to control and persisted even after so many years. Such reminders made Maya melancholic, and she would quietly sigh, muttering Shiv's name under her breath. It was difficult to brush the memories totally under the carpet, but she tried her best.

Maya would often wonder how long it would take for her to forget Shiv.

How long would his memories remain trapped in my soul? Was there no escape?

She needed but an excuse to start thinking about Shiv—the latest being Kanya, who was not even remotely connected to him. Maya thought it was Shiv who wanted to stay close to her heart, and there would be no respite for many more years—perhaps even till she breathed her last.

She had created a world where she, Shiv and Tamara lived together, attending college and visiting the library. As she indulged in her imagination, sitting in the library, she would select a new person and personify him as Shiv each day. She would steal glances at him while pretending to read her books. They imagined them swimming together in the local swimming pool and playing basketball, reaching the state and later national levels—all three of them. Shiv would pick Maya and Tamara from their workplaces and they would sit in a café, enjoying cold coffee and croissants. They would then return home together, a cosy place with air conditioners fitted in every room, marble flooring, and walls covered with paintings. In this parallel universe, there was scope for triangular relationships. But alas! Shiv could belong either to her or Tamara in reality.

Maya often wondered why Aman could not take Shiv's place. What did he lack that Shiv had? He was more educated than Shiv, perhaps even a tad more handsome and, above all, he expressed his love for Maya through actions, not just his eyes. Even Shama and Zahra proved to be far more empathetic towards her than Tamara had ever been, especially towards the end of her time in Ranikhet. Strange indeed was her mind that tethered her to Shiv, refusing to let go even after seven years.

The people Maya missed most were Bhai and Maa. Bhai was the only person other than Shiv she often called out in her sleep. She was sincerely waiting for the day she would have an apartment of her own, where she could ask Maa and Bhai to come and live with her. Bhai would quickly obtain employment in the city; by then, her contacts would have increased manyfold. Time would have erased her sad memories by then, and she would have forgotten Shiv. Perhaps.

The only thing she held against Bhai was his intense dislike of Shiv. But hadn't he been right after all? In the end, Shiv had shown himself to be spineless. Bhai's apprehension had been justified. Why had Shiv agreed to the marriage if not for the prospect of using Tamara as a way to climb the social ladder? That had been Bhai's concern from the beginning, and it had proved to be true.

Maya wondered why Shiv could not have used her as the ladder. Maya's family was better off than Tamara's. Had he sensed Bhai's dislike for him and concluded that the match would never materialize—that he was only chasing a chimera, a mirage?

Recovering from her reverie, Maya decided to focus on her work and return to the real world. The best action would be to take her team out for coffee, which would not only distract her from the memories triggered by the thought of Kanya's passion but also motivate the team.

Deciding to lighten the mood, Maya suggested, 'How about a field trip?' Dressed in a bright blue shirt neatly tucked into smart black trousers, with a hint of blush on her cheeks, she exuded a quiet authority that no one dared challenge. While she was a caring and flexible team leader, she was uncompromising when it came to deadlines.

'Meet you all at Let's Chat. Kanya and I will take one cab; I want to discuss the speech with Kanya on the way. The rest of you can take another.'

For Kanya, this was a moment of pride. She eagerly grabbed her writing pad and pen, ready to jot down every idea she could gather from Maya's insights

'Instead of taking notes, I suggest you sit back and look around. There are a million things to absorb around us. Look at the dirt on the road, the piled garbage and the people who overlook basic civic discipline,' Maya suggested as they rode along.

Kanya was so excited that Maya could feel her heart thumping and brain going into overdrive. She instantly put her writing pad inside her purse and looked out. Her naïveté baffled Maya, but she had also been naïve and unaware of such basic stuff once, so blaming Kanya was unfair. Maya knew that Kanya would do anything for her; so she decided to act as a leader and not pull her down. The only thing Maya did not like about Kanya was her desperate attempts to please the world, especially people who mattered. Maya planned to work on that, but decided to tackle one thing at a time.

Maya made it a point to ask the driver to stop the cab whenever she saw someone trying to cross the street. She did this especially for a young mother carrying a child in one arm and some grocery bags in the other. If she had not asked the cab to stop, others would not either. Pedestrians in a bustling city like Mumbai were often overlooked. Vehicles, especially in metro cities like Mumbai, were always in a rush and oblivious to the needs of pedestrians—those on foot got the least preference. Of course, there were zebra crossings where pedestrians were expected to cross the road, but they were few and far between. As someone who walked more often than travelling in four-wheelers, Maya understood the plight of those waiting to cross the road.

'Did you understand why I asked our cab to stop?' she asked Kanya.

Kanya nodded, a discernible look of admiration flashing in her eyes. This was the Maya Kanya admired.

As they entered the café, Maya noticed the other team members already seated, working on their laptops, not in the mood to waste a single minute, their dedication and commitment palpable.

The café's branding on a board by the door caught her eye:

Let's Chat

Not on our phones.
We want you to look at each other and talk.
So let's chat!

This motto appealed to Maya, and she often frequented the outlet because of it.

'Okay, everyone, we have come here to chat, not work! Shut your laptops, please,' Maya ordered with a grin.

A bunch of college kids were lounging around—some chatting, others on their phones, a few snuggling their partners, some eating and a handful studying. There were also some brokers and office-goers stealing a few moments of respite from work, while a few unemployed individuals brooded, hoping that fate would soon work in their favour.

Kanya with her usual outspoken energy, commented loudly, 'The people here display a lack of civic sense. Look—two people are sitting at a table meant for six, and one is at a table meant for four. This makes others hesitate to sit on the empty chairs because they desire privacy, so some walk out and the restaurant loses business. We should do something about it.'

She walked up to the lone person sitting at the four-seater and requested him to move to the single table nearby. He complied immediately. The entire group was shocked and Maya was impressed by Kanya's advocacy of civic sense and her assertiveness. She was reminded of the girl Kanya had been six months ago when she had arrived from Indore—shy and introverted. Mumbai had changed her so dramatically in such a short time! Maya sincerely felt that she needed to imbibe some of Kanya's qualities. There was also a feeling of pride because Kanya unequivocally and repeatedly declared Maya to be her role model.

The café had several high tables for those who liked to stand and work on their laptops while sipping coffee. It was refreshing to see small changes that could lead to a paradigm shift. It was, after all, a healthy practice. Unfortunately, no one occupied those standing slots; everyone, including her team, chose the comfortable cushioned seats instead.

As they all settled in, it was time for Maya to address the other team members. 'Didn't any of you feel you should have helped Kanya?'

The team members exchanged remorseful looks, feeling ashamed as they apologized profusely to Maya.

She decided to ease the situation. 'Never mind. Every minute is a learning opportunity. Do not repeat this in the future, whether we are here or somewhere else.'

The décor of the café was casual yet eclectic, with abstract art and psychedelic colours covering the walls and uniquely designed furniture making for pleasant sights for eyes fed up with the drab and monotonous banners and hoardings that dotted the Mumbai skyline. As a waiter approached them, the team ordered coffee and sandwiches. This was Maya's way of connecting with her team, and they loved these interactions. She loved her team and was empathetic to every member's needs, going out of her way to make them feel comfortable and motivated. They were like a little family.

Maya opened the discussion. 'I would like to cover the filth tobacco smokers and chewers create on the streets, spitting out betel juice and other disgusting things from their mouths. These actions do not only make the roads shabby but also unhygienic. People spit outside their houses to avoid dirtying their homes, showing little care for the environment around them. They feel that if their houses are clean, they are clean. They don't understand that they are part of a civic society and an unclean environment hurts everyone, including themselves. This myopic outlook harms all of us. We need to create awareness in society. Short-sightedness takes us five years back.'

One team member added, 'Traffic and road safety violators disgust me. I want to discuss how these little actions constantly put our lives at risk. Speed-breakers placed without warnings can cause accidents. I also want to speak up against rash driving and drunk driving. We all know how a film star's drunk driving cost the lives of poor homeless people sleeping on the pavement. I want to expose those who break the law and the officers who take bribes to let them off.'

Another chimed in, 'We should cover pure negligence of parents who do not teach their children basic manners and etiquette. They are not instilling civic sense in them or holding them accountable for their actions. The parents are often the violators; they try to act like heroes before their children. How will the child learn? I want to appeal directly to such people. Movies and advertisements have been failures; we must think of other ways.'

'The real problem is people in cars,' one member said, her frustration evident. 'They're the worst offenders, tossing out everything from cigarette butts to wrappers, food containers, even ice-cream cups and paper plates. It only takes a few seconds to find a bin, but they just don't care. This is something I want to tackle head-on.'

Maya was happy to see her team work together and ideate, but she was also aware that this was just a drop in the ocean. There were numerous things wrong with the city, but simultaneously, there were many things right in the city, including how individuals helped each other. The positive aspects also needed to be highlighted; when people are praised, they tend to be more open to criticism. Empathizing and reinforcing the positive sides of the story while highlighting the negatives was the best approach to adopt. This is how change takes place in society, slowly but steadily.

However, they were unanimous on one point—civic sense, like charity, began at home.

'Kanya, please jot these points down for the conference. Thanks to this small chat session, you have enough material. Please put your best foot forward and be eloquent yet brief. People are generally not in a mood for long presentations.'

With their boss from Pune expected to visit them in a week, Maya was feeling slightly tense. This would be her first encounter with him. She only hoped he was not visiting because of any adverse reports that may have reached him. There was no dearth of enemies. Maya desperately needed the job, and finding another job in this economy would be challenging, if not impossible.

Maybe he thinks that we aren't doing our jobs.

Maybe he wants to downsize. I will be the first target, being the highest-paid.

Maybe he thinks I am not competent, and plans to replace me with someone else.

In her heart of hearts, she knew she was worrying unnecessarily and that her thoughts were outlandish and bizarre. After all, only a few days back, the boss had sent her an email complimenting the latest edition of their blog. Brooding was second nature to Maya, especially after the bitter experiences during her last days at Ranikhet.

Maya managed to push aside her thoughts as the server brought the bill. Looking at her team's beaming faces, a soothing thought came to her mind: *No matter what happens, I will leave a legacy here, and I will continue to be the topic of discussion, even if they let me go.*

As she left the café with her team members, Maya suddenly felt blessed and on top of the world.

14

Maya stood draped in a soft pink sari adorned with white roses embroidered intricately across its length, paired with a halter blouse sequined with tiny crystals; the silver jhumkas dangling from her ears reflected the sun's golden rays. Her cheeks had turned red with fear and uncertainty. Something was brewing, and she was apprehensive of Mr Shah's upcoming visit. Her premonitions seldom proved wrong, and she only hoped this would be an exception. Although she had been with the organization for months, Mr Shah had never bothered to visit. They had spoken innumerable times on the phone but had never met in person.

Kanya was the first to arrive at the office after Maya. That was usually the case because they both lived close by. Maya had glanced at her reflection before leaving home, and again after reaching the office, and she was convinced that she looked like a paragon of beauty. She was dressed to the nines to welcome Mr Shah.

One look at Kanya's face, however, told her something was amiss. Kanya seemed to appraise her outfit with hesitation, so Maya asked her, 'Do you think I have overdone the jewellery? Maybe I should remove the jhumkas?'

Kanya immediately grabbed Maya's hand and stopped her from doing so. It surprised Maya. The movement seemed abrupt and impulsive. The grip of her hand was also a bit firm, which was not to Maya's liking. It smacked of nervousness. Kanya quickly composed herself and pulled back, commenting, 'If you take off the jhumkas, you will look dull. This is perfect. You look gorgeous, as always.'

Maya was unable to gauge Kanya's reaction. She appeared shaky and perhaps felt that Maya had not appreciated her interference. She had a crush on Maya and tried to keep it under control. Looking at Maya in the morning made her want to hold her tight and hug her—sometimes even kiss her—but she could never go down that road because Maya was, after all, her boss. Kanya consoled herself with the thought that it was not a romantic crush—she was just overawed in her presence and it was a manifestation of a deep fondness.

The office soon buzzed with banter as the team members arrived one by one. Happiness and vivacity pervaded the office every morning, followed by intense chatting for 15 minutes till they settled down to work after a mild admonition from Maya. She often prayed that they stayed as one team for years on end, if not till retirement.

Maya quietly went into the bathroom and sat down on the commode, stroking the nail marks on her thighs. She had dug into her skin last night till it bled profusely—her coping mechanism to divert herself from unpleasant thoughts. No portion of her body escaped these depredations. Of course, all pain ultimately led to thoughts of Shiv.

Shiv had inflicted more pain on her than she could bear. It was the pain of a lifetime. Strange were the ways of the human heart! She still loved him immensely; she often got up in the middle of the night, chanting his name under her breath. Zahra, who slept next to her, never woke up as she was a sound sleeper, though Maya sometimes wondered if she heard but pretended to sleep, giving Maya her private moment of vulnerability.

She struggled to understand love's innate irrationality. Should not her love for Shiv have disappeared the day she heard the sad news? Or perhaps later, on the day of his wedding? Like a computer program, love was strangely coded inside her brain.

Maya wasn't sure whether inflicting harm upon herself was

intended to punish Shiv or Tamara. Or was it just her way to stay calm and at peace with herself? Or to put her inner voice to sleep for a while and gain some respite from the unpleasant thoughts that kept whirling in her mind? Maya would deftly press a cotton pad to her wounds, cry into her pillows, hum a lullaby to herself and drift into bittersweet dreams. She only hoped that she would never commit something more serious, which would lead to irreversible damage.

Saria had started reappearing in the last two years. She had, as usual, grown with Maya, but Maya had nowadays stopped looking forward to her visits. She felt that Saria's philosophical thoughts were empty and hollow, mere attempts to console her—a futile attempt. Even if she were ever successful in permanently erasing the pain, it would not be due to Saria but through an exercise of self-will and determination. Or another shock in life would facilitate this, or—hopefully—a pleasant experience that may turn out to be a game changer. She was sceptical of the last option as she considered herself unlucky.

Still, she was grateful to Saria for not having abandoned her. Nor had Bhai and Maa done so, but Maya felt that they no longer missed her. Video calls were few and far between; Bhai had obtained a job at Ranikhet as a travel guide and worked long hours, but that should not have prevented him from calling her more often. Maa was becoming more and more distant and inscrutable with time. They visited her once a year, chatting with her for hours after she returned from work and on weekends, but somehow the connection seemed to be missing; after two weeks, Maa would invariably begin to long for home. Zahra had told her that it was natural for ageing people—they wished to stay close to their roots and lead independent lives.

The topic of Shiv never surfaced, although she looked forward to speak her mind with them. She found their reaction strange and even cruel, and refused to believe that they had not sensed or heard about her deep feelings for Shiv and the reason for her abrupt departure. Was not the announcement of her desire to move out immediately after Tamara's wedding indicative enough?

Maya snapped out of her thoughts, glancing at her watch. It was time for Mr Shah's arrival. She was sweating profusely, so she took some time to wipe off the sweat, clean herself and touch up her makeup.

When she entered the hall, she immediately spotted Mr Shah. He was tall, young, dynamic, dark and handsome. He had developed a paunch, which was somewhat unusual for his age. He was sitting on a chair, waiting for her. Her team members, including Kanya, were working on their laptops, not looking at him. *He must have asked them to focus on their work. But why is he not chatting with the team, praising their work, motivating and inspiring them?*

Mr Shah wore a crisp white linen shirt with beige cotton chino pants. He appeared somewhat slouchy and grumpy. *Must have gotten up early in the morning.* It was a four-hour drive from Pune to their office, and had likely taken its toll. He was tapping furiously on his phone; it was part of the culture of the western part of India. Everyone was in a hurry; time was money here. There was little time for leisure, nuances, introspection, and to sit and chat. Not once did he look up—Maya kept standing at the door, waiting for him to finish his bout of solid typing. She then proceeded towards her desk rather noisily, trying to draw his attention; the other members looked up but he still did not stir. Either his concentration was intense, or he was, for some reason, dissatisfied with her and wished to ignore her. This was speculation, of course.

Ultimately, he raised his eyes after five minutes. As soon as his gaze fell on Maya, he appeared mesmerized by her beauty—it was quite evident to her. His face lit up, and he stared at her for several seconds. The time Maya had taken to dress up in the morning, ignoring Zahra, Shama and Aman's teasing, had not gone to waste.

He walked up to Maya and greeted her with a firm handshake. 'I'm Ram,' he said with a smile that could perhaps break a thousand hearts. He was positively handsome, with lustrous skin and a deep voice. He could easily model for some glitzy advertisement. His eyes were mysterious, igniting Maya's imagination. Yet, for a brief moment, as their gazes met, she felt they were devious and slimy. She immediately brushed off the thought, attributing it to her cynicism that had developed over the last few years.

Maya felt that he belonged to a class of individuals who could, at first glance, steal the heart of every girl they met and then discard them the moment they encountered another. Maya felt safe in the thought that her heart was no longer hers—Shiv had long stolen it—so she had no reason to be concerned.

She glanced at her team—they were all gawking at him, drooling over his charm. *This was an ominous development*, Maya thought, though she did not understand why she felt that way.

'I'm Maya,' she finally murmured, flashing a coy smile. She made no move to ask him why he had chosen to visit their small blogging unit to demonstrate his organization's commitment to CSR—corporate social responsibility. Although he did routinely scroll through their blogs, complimenting or critiquing them and offering constructive suggestions, her apprehensions lingered, despite the promising beginning to their encounter.

Maya stared at Mumbai's skyline, which was visible through the glass panes. She noticed that the windowframe was speckled with rust, pigeon droppings and black soot. She cursed herself. The cleaner had not done his job sincerely despite being told to—she should have checked it herself before leaving the office the previous day.

Ram waved at her, realizing her mind had travelled far away. With a jolt, Maya came back, clearly embarrassed. 'I'm sure you are wondering why I'm here,' he said with an impish smile.

Maya kept quiet, partly because she did not know what to

reply and partly because she did not want to share her thoughts with him. Instead, she smiled hesitantly, her mind racing with anxiety that the visit's sole purpose was to fire her. Perhaps he had identified a cause more worthwhile to spend his CSR budget on, something that would give him more reach than civic amenities in Mumbai. In this case, the entire team would be fired. Maya felt sorry for Kanya and the other team members because they were a dedicated bunch.

Maybe he was planning to relocate her to the headquarters in Pune or some other city in India. He had offices across the country. This was an eventuality that scared her. She could not bear the thought of leaving Zahra, Shama, Aman and her entire team. Pune seemed like a better option than other cities because she would then be able to visit Mumbai on weekends. She had fallen in love with the city.

She couldn't help but note his interest in her. Ram clearly desired her, his lust evident, but Maya was confident he wouldn't risk ruining their professional relationship by acting on it, especially with strict workplace harassment policies in place.

To him, it was love at first sight, but for Maya, all she cared about was keeping her job. She loved her team, which felt like family, and the work itself was fulfilling. She would do whatever it took to maintain status quo—except compromise her integrity.

After a few minutes, Mr Shah asked Maya for the year's projected financial data—the figures they expected to earn, budgeted expenditure, and the net profit or loss for the unit. Maya had prepared well and he appreciated her meticulousness. He suggested certain superficial modifications and then closed the topic. It seemed he had already lost interest, his attention drifting elsewhere.

Maya introduced him to her team one by one, beaming with pride as each member passionately described their work. After meeting everyone, Ram expressed unqualified admiration, but

Maya noticed that he seemed particularly captivated whenever she spoke. She wondered if this was because he liked her work or for some other reason.

'Quite an impressive team you've put together, Ms Maya,' was his ultimate comment while sipping his fourth cup of coffee. He then stared out of the window at the mid-morning sun and the blue sky, only partially visible through the towering concrete structures. For 10 minutes, he sat silently, while Maya waited with bated breath for him to say something. Various thoughts crossed her mind, some a little too far-fetched.

She heaved a sigh of relief when he finally spoke. He wanted to rework the numbers, which struck her as odd since he had approved them just a few minutes ago. He could barely concentrate on his work that day, repeatedly forgetting the numbers and asking her to repeat the figures. He would return to the first line of the profit and loss statement once again after she thought it was all over.

Ram was now thinking about what he might do after work. Should he return to his hotel room and think about Maya until he fell asleep, dreaming of her? Should he ask her out after they finished work? It felt like she had somehow turned his world upside down.

Suddenly, his phone buzzed, jolting him back to reality. The screen flashed 'Wifey', accompanied by a picture of a beautiful smiling face. She was gorgeous. Pictures, of course, could be deceptive. Maya had seen quite a bit of this on social media. All one needed was a good photographer, a flashy camera and some expert editing. Perhaps her photograph was also similarly done. Or perhaps not.

Why were people these days so keen to impress others? Why were they so eager to communicate intimate details of their lives? Where they visited during the day, the social functions they attended, the food they ate, the people they met? Why did they assume that the world was interested in their personal lives? Was Maya wrong in her assessment?

While freedom of thought and action was an essential component of modern existence, Maya felt that social media often invaded people's personal lives. It often served as a weapon to initiate vitriolic attacks against those with differing views or for spreading gossip. This was not freedom of expression, in Maya's view. She was firmly against exposing her personal life to the scrutiny of others. She felt those who did so were anxious to keep up with societal expectations, engage in self-promotion and indulge in exhibitionism. Genuine compassion and rational discourse seemed increasingly rare.

These thoughts crowded her mind as she overheard Mr Shah speaking with his wife. Embarrassment washed over her as she listened to his intimate conversations, and she quietly moved away. After a while, Mr Shah stepped outside the room to continue his conversation, leaving Maya puzzled. *Had things gone south?* When he re-entered the room about 10 or 15 minutes later, he appeared pale. Immediately, his wife's picture flashed in Maya's mind: a woman holding a *belan* (rolling pin), with her sari's *pallu* (loose end of the sari) tucked into her waist. Maya couldn't help but smirk at the image, despite her efforts to control herself. Her reaction lightened the mood, prompting a smile from Mr Shah, though he was unsure Maya had smirked.

He flippantly remarked, 'Wife called. What to do! Can't live with them, can't live without them.'

Maya had no clue how to respond to his remark. However, the tension in the room eased to some extent. Maya discreetly gave a thumbs-up to her team, which shifted their expressions from concern to relief. Perhaps they had also feared the worst. Everyone had been concerned about the boss's visit. It was not normal for the chairman of a company to visit a small and young team of bloggers who were not integral to his main business but merely employed to create a façade of CSR.

Despite her reservations about his immediate attraction to her,

Maya saw Mr Shah as a fundamentally kind man, not heartless like those who fired employees without a second thought; he had earned her respect. She believed him to be polyamorous, prone to romantic dalliances but unlikely to cross serious lines.

Ram Shah had a history of infidelity, often blaming his behaviour on genetics and upbringing. Despite his rationalizations, he knew deep down it wasn't right. He even wrongfully suspected his devoted wife of cheating, refusing to let go of his baseless doubts and using them as a convenient excuse for his own actions.

He ordered a sumptuous lunch for the team and expressed his desire to hear their plans for the upcoming editions. They convened in the conference room to present their quarterly plans, which covered various aspects of basic amenities and how to instil civic sense among citizens. These plans had emerged from the discussions held at the café and were developed over the past week. He also wanted them to cover the state of the 'commons'—parks, transport, roads and the police force. It was a stimulating discussion, and they enjoyed every moment of it.

Kanya was the most enthusiastic of the lot, despite being the youngest. She was also the most nervous, which was reflected in her erratic behaviour. In her nervousness, she missed out on several of her achievements, which Maya covered for her. Mr Shah commended her leadership qualities, and though Maya was the designated team leader, she believed that all her team members should be appreciated—success should always be celebrated.

Maya also noticed how creative Mr Shah's ideas were and how promptly he grasped the issues at hand. It was a long but rewarding day.

As they began packing up, ready to go home, Mr Shah looked straight at Maya, although his comment was directed at the whole team. 'Your constant referring to me as "Mr Shah" makes me feel old. I would appreciate it if you called me Ram.'

Then he stepped closer to Maya, closer than she would have

liked, and spoke in a soft tone, 'This remark was mainly directed at you.' He flashed his trademark smile, a smile Maya and the others had witnessed countless times since the morning. Maya would have felt perfectly comfortable with the departing grin had he also not winked.

The team noticed the wink and exchanged glances. Kanya, in particular, seemed to dislike it the most; she did not want the boss flirting with her role model and guru. Maya was taken aback; she did not know how to respond. The image of his wife flashed in her mind again—holding a belan with the pallu of her sari tucked at her waist.

15

The next day, Maya chose to wear her trademark blue jeans and white shirt. Her hair fell in soft curls, cascading past her ears and shoulders and on to her back, bouncing with every step she took. The soft pink hue on her high cheekbones reminded her of Tamara on her wedding night. These days, while looking at herself in the mirror, Maya had started to believe that she was as good-looking as Tamara. Back in Ranikhet, she had rarely dressed up; her mother discouraged excessive ornamentation and flashy dresses, and Maya had also been not too interested in dressing up. Yet, after moving to Mumbai, she felt inclined to dress well.

There was also the belief she had nurtured that Shiv had fallen for Tamara because of her looks. Maya had earlier convinced herself that family pressure had pushed him into the marriage, but lately, she had begun to believe that she had been fooling and consoling herself. Perhaps Shiv had taken the initiative and made his mother propose the match to Tamara's family. Or maybe it was Shiv who had proposed to Tamara, which was sanctified by the family later on. She tried her best to dispel such thoughts, but they continued to haunt her.

As Maya stepped out of the bathroom, ready to head to the office, Aman noticed her. His gaze lingered, captivated, and he scooped her up by the waist, gently placing her on the bed. She smiled and kissed him passionately. He sat on the bed, adoring the gorgeous lady he was madly in love with, whispering to himself how lucky he was to be there with her at this moment.

Aman's behaviour, at times, was impulsive and decidedly

immature, but he was calm and collected when the situation demanded. Maya was not in love with him; she tried her best not to become emotionally involved as she had developed distrust for all men after her experience with Shiv, but Aman would not let her go; she sometimes felt she was the object of his carnal desires and lust.

He would become exceptionally amorous on some days. She had to go to work, which he did not, and Maya had a tough time extracting herself from his grasp. He behaved like it was the last day they would be meeting, and had to make the most of it. Aman was aware that she saw him as someone to take care of her physical needs, and nothing more—at least, not yet. He was like an anchor for her, someone who would make her temporarily forget Shiv. Yet, he did not seem to mind. Perhaps he was biding his time. He was still without a job and perhaps thought that Maya was waiting for him to secure one before making any commitment.

Aman had brought a semblance of order to Maya's life. She could finally feel, in some ways, like those couples she saw along Marine Drive or other haunts, huddled close, clinging to each other, oblivious to the surroundings. Without him, she would have broken down completely. He had brought not only normalcy to her life but also comfort and sanity—especially on the nights she felt the world was coming to an end. He had been instrumental in reducing the days she would dig into her thighs with her nails and when she would wake up in the dead of night, muttering and sometimes yelling Shiv's name. For this, Maya would forever remain grateful to Aman, even if they had to part one day, though she dreaded it. She tried her best to help him secure a job in Mumbai so that he would not have to return to his village.

A thought suddenly struck her—why not speak to Ram about him? But would not Ram demand a pound of flesh to provide Aman with employment?

After a round of hugging, kissing and groping, Maya begged Aman to release her as she would get late for work. This was the time the apartment would be overtaken by frenzy, everyone scrambling to reach their offices on time. Aman took charge of breakfast and rushed to the kitchen to boil eggs for the three women, who were walking in and out of their bathrooms or locking the rooms to finish dressing. At least one person would invariably forget to carry an important file, their tiffin box or purse. Shama sometimes even forgot to wear her shoes and only realized after reaching the station; Zahra would leave her dupatta or her umbrella behind, scrambling back after a few minutes, and Maya occasionally left behind her makeup bag—an essential component these days.

Aman had also brewed a pot of steaming masala chai, pouring it into stainless steel glasses and setting aside a half-full jug for refills. He was amazing!

Shama asked Aman, 'What do you think, Aman? Is it going to rain today?'

Being a farmer's son, Aman had an uncanny knack for predicting the weather. He would feel the humidity, look once or twice at the sky and predict whether it would rain, and most of the days, he was accurate.

Mumbai rains were notorious—they could turn the city ugly on the days it poured heavily, making it indistinguishable from its surrounding seas, the sewers overflowing with muck. In contrast, on other days, it was a pleasant experience. The moist breeze would remove all traces of desolate feelings, and Maya would walk to her office to enjoy the cool weather. She always packed a spare set of clothes, preparing herself for an unexpected drenching. Autos were exposed on both sides, and it would be difficult to ward off the streams of water. Cabs were expensive, but on certain days she had no choice but to flag one down.

In her previous job, Maya had occasionally acted irresponsibly, wandering off to Worli Seafront or Juhu Beach, indulging in vada pav and coffee, sometimes even taking the train to Marine Drive or the Gateway of India to soak in the sea breeze. However, now that she was a team leader, she had developed a sense of dedication and rarely skipped work.

Aman leaned out of the window and looked at Mumbai's cloudless, polluted and dingy sky. It was a gloomy day, with no clouds on the horizon. Aman had this habit of pretending to think deeply whenever the girls asked for his verdict on any issue, and this was no exception. Finally, he declared, 'Looks like it will rain. You might laugh at me because it is a clear day, but do not forget that I am a visionary; my vision reaches where no one else's does, right into the future—near or far. A farmer's son can boast of insights regarding nature's peculiar ways. It is my verdict that it will rain. So, Shama, I suggest you stuff your brown bag with the pink umbrella you purchased from the market recently.'

As Shama gaped at him, Maya chuckled. 'Shama, can't you see? He probably read the weather report on Instagram this morning. He isn't a visionary, but a phoney guy, a con man. Never trust him!'

Zahra, normally an extrovert, found solace in her early morning ritual of masala tea and quiet reflection while the city slept. These calm moments brought her a sense of peace and served as a healing moment for hidden scars. Though Maya suspected Zahra's depth, she respected her friend's discretion.

That morning, while reading the newspaper, Zahra sparked a conversation about 'Snow Globe Moments'—memories one wished to preserve forever. As they each shared, Maya's mind drifted back to a poignant moment with Shiv, filled with longing and regret. Despite Aman's affection for her, her heart remained tethered to Shiv, the ghost of her past.

Shama, preferring to keep her thoughts private, lightened the mood with a funny story, shifting the atmosphere. However, Maya's sadness was palpable, though she chose to focus on the future, feeling relieved about her work situation as she prepared to leave.

She thanked Zahra for the meaningful discussion and rushed out, her vibrant energy evident as she departed.

★

The office was empty when Maya arrived. Despite the morning's distractions, she had still managed to reach early. The traffic, for some reason, had been light. She had a few more minutes until everyone arrived. She liked to organize herself before the others came in, to gather her thoughts and focus on what had to be done that day. These few minutes were like a lull before a storm. Then she read her WhatsApp messages. The one on top said that Ram was still in Mumbai and would be joining them later. *What is wrong with him? Why is he spending so much time with a team that is on the fringe of his business interests?*

Maya decided to jot down a few points to discuss with Ram. She had planned to do so the previous day but it had slipped her mind. Slowly, everyone started trickling in, the chatter increasing in both volume and intensity. Soon, the coffee delivery arrived, and she ordered an extra-large flask to keep them fuelled through the day's work.

The team was buoyed by their interaction with Ram the previous day. His approval of their proposals had sparked excitement, and some even believed he'd developed a genuine fondness for them. Cheekily, Kanya suggested she knew why he had approved their plans, prompting laughter all around.

'We needn't worry about Mr Shah; he is in our pockets.' Everyone cheered, their decibel levels loud enough to bring the house down. Maya wondered if Kanya's statement had any underlying implication, but she did not want to spend much time thinking about it.

They all turned towards Maya and looked at her pointedly—Maya appeared to be clueless as always. She gave them an innocuous look and wondered why they were staring at her. *Did they notice*

Ram flirting with me? Of course, they did; they are not dumb fools.

'He was drooling all over you, Maya Ma'am. He couldn't keep his eyes off you,' Kanya let it slip, and Maya felt her cheeks turning red. The team cheered on like hooligans, as if it was a moment of triumph for them.

Another team member remarked, 'It's good that we have our office in order, but even if it weren't, he would not have noticed it. He was too engrossed in staring at Maya Ma'am; his eyes were only on her and only for her.'

Maya now felt distinctly uncomfortable and self-conscious, but it was time to behave like a boss. She gave a mild smile and responded, 'You girls are watching too many Ranbir Kapoor movies these days; Bollywood romance is getting to your heads. Come on, shake it off.'

She paused until the laughter had settled before adding, 'Now, let's return to some real work. I came across an excellent concept this morning—my flatmate spotted it in today's newspaper. It's called a "Snow Globe Moment"—a moment in our lives that remains entrapped within us, refusing to go away. When we relive it, we forget all about the world, our environment and our surroundings. We remain engrossed in thoughts of that moment—a moment to treasure and cherish.

'Let this be the topic for our forthcoming issue. We need to digress a bit; our blog is getting a bit hackneyed and clichéd. Of course, we need to relate it to civic sense, but indirectly. This will generate a buzz and grow our readership. It will help us to reach our target for the month, and sponsors will not hesitate to dish out more money.'

She noticed the team was enthused and charged by her words. They were no longer in the mood for quips, their faces bright, and she could sense that some were already deep in thought.

Just then, their attention shifted to the door, and there was Ram. He had a cheerful smile on his face, and his teeth shone like pearls. *Rich kids know how to carry themselves.* Maya was surprised by his casual attire. He was wearing a T-shirt, jeans and sneakers. *Something was amiss. Something was the matter.* She gave him a formal smile and requested him to join them. She hadn't expected him so early.

★

The morning was productive for Maya; she learnt a lot from Ram. Though she'd known him as a finance expert, she was surprised by his command over marketing. Maya was also interested in the subject but had yet to get the opportunity to learn it, so she was glad for Ram's guidance.

She was captivated; he had swayed her.

She had been with Aman for a year, but there were very few common topics between them; she considered him a friend and a person who could satisfy her in bed. Maya hated to admit it, but she knew she could never love him. She was even willing to go to bed with someone else, and though that would be cheating on Aman, she did not feel any remorse at the thought.

Absently, as she picked at her food, Maya caught herself reflecting on what pulled her towards Ram. Was it his personality? His wealth? Or was it his knowledge? She could not find any answer and felt embarrassed by her thoughts.

I have my values, she reminded herself, *morals nurtured by Ranikhet, by my mother, Bhai, my teachers in school. I should not deviate from them.* However, she also sensed that she was teetering on the edge of another disaster that would pull her into a dark and bottomless abyss.

It was at this moment that Ram came and sat right next to her. His charisma and aura dragged her towards him, though she desperately tried to pull herself back. He was sitting so close that she could smell the perfume on his body. She tried to ignore it but the scent lingered. Then it hit her—it wasn't perfume. She had smelled it before—on the day of Holi and while drowning in the lake.

It was Shiv sitting next to her.

Maya realized her mind was playing games with her. But as much as she tried to dispel the notion, it kept returning to her spasmodically. She desisted from thinking; her mind was aware that it was Ram and not Shiv, but her heart, which had yearned for Shiv for so many years, dragged her towards believing she had finally found another Shiv. Aman had never invoked such a feeling in her.

Is this just a mechanism for the mind to cope with the trauma of separation from a soulmate? Maya had no clue. All she understood was that she was in danger, and that Ram was married.

She had to get away from him.

Just as she steeled herself, Kanya broke the silence. 'Hey, how about a party tomorrow night?' The question was directed at Ram.

Ram's eyes light up, 'Sure, why not?'

Maya fixated on her bowl of rice as if it were a scientific invention she was working on and had no time for small talk. She was oblivious to the two pairs of eyes focused on her. She felt cornered and desperately wanted to say no, but her heart leapt with joy. Her heart and brain were fighting, but without waiting for the verdict, her lips blurted out, 'Yes.'

It was the beginning of the end for her, and she knew it.

As Kanya dashed off to announce the plan, Maya sat frozen under Ram's gaze. She couldn't bear his smell any more, but felt paralysed; she could not bear to command her legs to move away from the man.

She was in seventh heaven! She had found her Shiv!

That evening, when she entered home, Maya saw Aman roaming around the house. Guilt stabbed at her; she felt bad for even thinking about being with Ram. *Aman has been with me through thick and thin; he has done so much for me, adored me and loved me. Getting swayed by someone just because he reminds me of Shiv and smells like Shiv is just not right. It is downright immoral.*

Maya made up her mind; Ram's charm would not consume her.

Zahra, seeing the turmoil on Maya's face, cautioned, 'Don't do it!'

Her words took Maya by surprise. *Did Zahra possess psychic powers?* She had suspected it all along, and was now convinced. She meekly replied, 'You are a psychic—a freakishly intuitive person in the making. We are your guinea pigs.'

Zahra smiled but repeated, 'Don't do it. It will destroy you!'

Maya heeded her warning, but how Zahra could gauge her feelings escaped her. Zahra only knew fragments of her story, bits and pieces. She only knew that Maya had loved someone who had married someone else. That's it.

16

Ram had planned the night meticulously, arranging for everyone to meet at the nightclub at 9 p.m.

A WhatsApp group named 'Nightclub' had been created for the occasion. Maya's team was busy discussing the details of their dresses and accessories. While Maya loved dressing up, she disliked their obsession with it. Of course, this was a special occasion for them, for they rarely had the opportunity to visit expensive nightclubs, and wanted to make the most of it. It struck Maya that it had been ages since she had attended a formal party; the last one had been perhaps three years ago. However, she was concerned that this party may not turn out to be a formal one. She had yet to understand Ram fully.

Maya reached the nightclub around 8.30 p.m. She hated being late. Punctuality was a habit she had imbibed from her student days, thanks to Maa and Bhai, who used to push her out of the house to ensure she was never late. She could recall only a handful of instances when she had been late for school. As she paced in front of the club, she noticed the vendors hawking smuggled goods on the sidewalk. She picked up a few favourite cosmetics, which were available at unbelievably low prices, and also grabbed a copy of *Vogue*, which she had always wanted to read but never knew where to find.

Entering the club at exactly 9 p.m., she took in the thumping music and spotted a few individuals already on the dance floor. Ram had reserved a table for the team, and after ordering a drink, she sat in silence, sipping it slowly. Despite her years in Mumbai, she hadn't developed a strong taste for alcohol, preferring the bhang they used to enjoy on Holi back in Ranikhet.

Maya glanced at her phone—it was 9.15 p.m., and Ram was yet to arrive, so she went through the WhatsApp messages. A few members had almost reached, while some had just left home. She made a mental note to tell them that punctuality was important even at parties, but decided not to mention it that night, as it might dampen the team's enjoyment. She scrolled through Instagram, but grew bored after a while, watching the same repetitive content. *How do people find the energy to post the same things day after day? Do they not get bored?*

By 9.30 p.m., she was annoyed, more at Ram than the others. As the seniormost member and the host, he should have been punctual. Just as she was considering leaving the club, she spotted Ram. He wore a pair of black jeans, an orange T-shirt and fancy sneakers that gleamed even in the dimly lit room. One look at him, and Maya couldn't take her eyes off. Her heart skipped a few beats. *No!* She had to control herself; she could not make it too apparent. Whenever Shiv's thoughts crossed her mind, she would try to visualize Aman's face. He was so sincere and dedicated; she hated the thought of causing him any misery.

She sincerely hoped that the others would turn up soon. What had happened to Kanya? She was usually so punctual at the office! The last thing Maya wanted was to be alone, within the confines of a nightclub, with a man her heart craved but her mind wished to avoid. She sincerely tried to stop the chattering in her brain and was partially successful.

It's going to be a long night.

Ram walked towards her, waving. He called out something, but it was inaudible in the cacophony of the nightclub. Maya was good at lip-reading, but the dim lighting made it difficult. As he got closer, she caught a whiff of the cologne he had generously sprayed on himself. It was an expensive one, likely picked up on his recent trip to France, which he'd mentioned in the morning, where he had been accompanied by his wife.

Then, it happened again—Shiv was standing in front of her. How could she overcome this delusion that kept overwhelming her mind? There was no similarity between the two. Shiv hailed from a low-income family—a struggling young man from the rugged heart of Ranikhet. He was hardly flashy and could not speak a sentence of English without grammatical mistakes. He wore simple clothes and would never have sprayed fancy perfume on himself, not even on his wedding.

How could the sight of Ram invoke memories of Shiv? Mysterious were the ways of the heart and mind.

Ram's smile broke through her reverie. 'What are you drinking?' he asked, his grin lighting up the space. He then apologized for being late; he had gotten caught up in a conversation with his wife.

Why does he keep mentioning her? Maya was certain she had never hinted at having fallen for him. On the contrary, she was always taking extra care to keep a greater-than-necessary distance. If anything, she'd done her best to maintain a professional boundary.

He continued, 'She is the nagging type and never gives me my space. I sometimes feel suffocated, Maya.'

This was just too much. I have to act. NOW.

'In my case, it's the reverse. I've got a friend like that—Aman. I am sure he will ring me 10 times tonight, asking if I am safe, what I am doing, what's the music like, and so on.'

Her words hung in the air, met by a heavy silence. She immediately regretted her somewhat impulsive mention of Aman. It hadn't been the right moment, not when the night was supposed to be one of carefree fun. How could she be so heartless? She then tried to rationalize—it was Ram's fault; he was constantly hinting at his fascination, if not weakness, for her, and trying to charm her. Even the others had noticed it. She could be wrong, but could the entire team have misread his actions?

The chatter in her mind returned. Ram was now looking at his phone, and Shiv crept back into Maya's thoughts. He would always remain an enigma. She had not spent more than two hours with him—15 minutes on Holi, 15 minutes on the evening he had rescued Tamara, 20 minutes on the night he had rescued her, and an hour on his wedding night. They had never even been alone together, except in her imagination. How could he occupy such a significant part of her mind? *How could the sight of Ram, so different from him in all aspects, remind me of Shiv? How? How could those two hours define my life forever? Shiv will forever be my love and the reason for my doom.*

Her thoughts drifted to her brother's cautions, the astrologer's cryptic words, and her own unheeded instincts. Bhai had always tried to steer her away from Shiv, and now it seemed his concern had been justified. She recalled that early morning car ride in the dim light, the unsettling gleam in the goat's eyes that had struck her as an omen. Had Bhai taken the sadhu's warnings seriously? Was that why he had been so vigilant, always trying to keep her from passing by Shiv's shop? He had sensed her growing fondness—she hadn't hidden it well, and Bhai was perceptive. Yet, even his watchful eye couldn't alter what was to come. No one, not even she, could have foreseen how quickly she would be swept into an infatuation so intense, so consuming, with someone she barely knew.

Maya was immersed in her thoughts, but Ram decided to talk to her anyway, finding the silence between them awkward. The problem was that every time he spoke, he moved closer to her, both physically and metaphorically, to be heard over the loud music. As he leaned towards her to make himself heard, he reminded her of Shiv. Maya soon fell into a trance, loving the moments when he was close.

She found herself wishing Ram would speak more, as it brought him closer. She began hating the brief interludes in which he would keep quiet. There was no rational explanation for what she was feeling. Ram was also enjoying the situation, now that he had managed to break the ice and draw her to himself—a girl he was both enamoured and fascinated with. It had been a long time since he had managed to captivate a girl.

Ram was determined to make conversation, and even small talk proved to be fine. 'This place is amazing. Have you ever been here before?' His conversation lacked finesse—after all, how many talents could one man possess? Maya was far superior—she had the uncanny knack of steering the conversation in a direction she wished. She carried on with the conversation, but her mind was preoccupied with Ram's sweet scent and memories of Shiv.

Just when an awkward silence had settled between them again, Kanya walked in—a godsend, Maya's saviour. She wore a golden halter dress with Swarovski heels—a bold look that few could pull off, but on Kanya, it worked. She looked stunning.

The rest of the team began to arrive in batches. Some started dancing immediately, while others chatted, enjoying their drinks. A few drank alcohol, while others preferred mocktails. Maya was surprised to hear many hidden facts about her team members as they started opening up, sharing certain aspects of their personal lives she had not bothered to ask about before. She cursed herself for being so formal at work. She only knew Kanya well, but with the rest, she was just beginning to connect. And what better setting than a nightclub.

Ram appeared to be enjoying every moment of the evening. He soon ventured on to the dance floor, not bothering to invite anyone to join him, perhaps shy. His focus seemed to have shifted from Maya, and she was thankful. After all, he managed an industrial conglomerate and knew how to carry himself; as a leader, he had to motivate the team. Maya concluded that Ram was aware of his responsibilities, and she appreciated it—the last thing she wanted was to get involved with a married man and, at that, a prominent face in society. The complexities would be too tough to handle.

But then came the million-dollar question she had dreaded all along; the moment she had hoped would never come that night—an offer she knew would be tough to refuse. 'Will you dance with me?'

Maya knew the dangers of being too close to Ram—the outcome would be disastrous, if not fatal. Yet, she also wanted to bridge the gap. Conflicted, she finally muttered, 'Absolutely,' and walked towards the dance floor, gently led by him.

They danced close to each other. The moment was indescribable. Maya was soon in a frenzied state, a state of bliss, euphoria, perhaps jouissance, but she held herself back, surprised at her incredible self-control. Ram danced with the rest of the team also, calling them to the dance floor one by one. He was discreet and knew how to be tactful, having been educated in private schools and growing up in a family that had taught him the dos and don'ts of social behaviour.

The night wore on as they all danced to Bollywood and Hollywood tunes. There wasn't a single person who did not groove to the DJ's beats. Some perhaps just swayed along to the music, but they were all on the dance floor. It was a night to remember. Maya let her hair down and allowed herself to let go of her inhibitions. She was surprised at how she could bring herself back from the brink when things threatened to spiral out of control.

It was a tough job, but her mindfulness saved the night for her. But had it truly saved her?

★

Ram, the perfect gentleman, had arranged cars for everyone. Mumbai was a safe place for girls, unlike many other cities. They could return alone even at three in the morning without feeling unsafe. But his gesture was appreciated; it was an elementary courtesy expected of a man of his standing. Despite his constant sarcastic comments about his wife, Ram embodied propriety.

They were all half drunk by the time they began piling into the cars. Suddenly, Maya felt Ram's hands clasping hers, ostensibly to help her steady her gait. In that moment, with her inhibitions loosened by alcohol and the rush of dopamine, she believed she was enjoying the connection, and the decisions she was making were for the best. She was also scared that her views would change the next morning.

As his rugged fingers entangled hers, she convinced herself she had no choice. She felt nothing untoward in holding his hand to steady herself. It was but a small gesture—a person holding another person's hand. As they scrambled into the cars, Kanya's eyes fixated on Maya; her admiration for Maya seemed to vanish, evaporate and wither away. This was not the Maya she knew, not the Maya she adored, respected and looked up to. Like any other flirt on the road, Maya seemed naked, stripped of all her qualities. Kanya did not want that to happen; she wanted this moment to be considered an illusion, a mirage seen through the haze of drunkenness. And it was not just the holding of hands; it was the way Maya looked at Ram, how she was visibly expressing her passion for the man, and how she seemed to have escaped into a dream world of her own.

Maya stared at Ram with drowsy eyes. He held a cigarette in his mouth, but no smoke escaped his lips. Kanya was angry; she wanted to approach him and hurt him. To her, it seemed he was toying with Maya's future, and would hurt her emotionally. Kanya was young but had seen many such men. They would never leave their wives, afraid of societal consequences, of getting beaten up by their family members or being at the receiving end of scorn from friends. Girls like Maya were dispensable to men like Ram—meant to be enjoyed and then discarded like the seed of a mango after the fruit had been devoured. It was a pity that Maya had fallen into this trap. Kanya resolved to try her best to counsel her, but she doubted whether she would succeed. It was a tricky position she found herself in.

For Maya, Ram embodied Shiv. Shiv had once held her hand while smearing her with gulaal on Holi, the same hands had saved her from sure drowning. Her heart wanted to believe this connection, and she felt compelled to obey its dictates.

Ram had reserved a car for himself and Maya, pretending that his hotel was close to her residence, but the truth was far from that. He took her to his hotel room, and Maya walked in boldly, in a daze and unable to comprehend that her second downfall was awaiting her in the plush suite of the upscale hotel.

Ram, aware of her drunken state, wanted to keep his conscience clean. He wanted things to happen between them when Maya was in a conscious state; he reasoned that taking advantage of her drunkenness would be unfair. Even demons have some semblance of a conscience, and the remnants of his conscience created a cacophony in his mind.

He offered her water and some antidotes to help her sober up while turning on some music. Maya was dancing to Shiv's tune; the music played was orchestrated by Shiv—the lyrics were his, the rendition was his. She pined for his golden touch. Shiv was not just playing music for her, he was also inspiring her to dance, to display her prowess. She desperately wanted to slip into bed, but continued to dance because even in that state, she was conscious of her worth; she wanted Ram to make the first move. He had not brought her to the hotel room to discuss business plans, and he better ask her for whatever he had dragged her there for. He, too, needed her.

The room was small, with one queen-sized bed and a view of the Mumbai skyline, the city that never slept. The streets shimmered below with the headlights of cars as revellers returned home. There was a time for everything, and this was the time for passion and lust—the passion that sparked the flames of eternal joy and bliss. This moment was an opportunity, and she intended to seize it.

Our karma is to keep moving forward, regardless of the circumstances; the past is barricaded, like a maze of concertina wire. We navigate our lives like rats in a labyrinth, choosing paths without knowing if they lead to cheese or poison. Predators pursue their prey with focus, but humans often stumble along blindly. Perhaps it's not our fault; how can we know if it is heaven or hell that awaits us at the end? Only the wise understand, while most simply ride on, urging their horses in any direction, oblivious to the consequences that lie ahead.

The colours in the room were dark and faded in places. Maya found it odd that an expensive hotel would be so ill maintained. Five-star hotels typically enforced strict policies on whom one could bring to the room, and the chances of encountering a known person were always there. The hotel staff would also know who Ram was, and Maya knew how gossipy people could be, even in a liberal city like Mumbai.

She started feeling dizzy and rushed to the tiny windowless bathroom, where she heaved until there was nothing left in her stomach. Ram stared at her with a concerned look. Would the night turn out differently than he had hoped? He didn't help her; he didn't seem to care. As she knelt on the cool tiles, Maya was reminded of Bhai; whenever she was unwell, he would stand by her, sleep in the room with her, pat her and offer her medicines. Aman was similar. Possibly Shiv would have also done the same, but she couldn't be sure of that. At that moment, she wondered whether Ram was, by nature, insensitive, or was it merely the effect of alcohol.

Maya worried that as the alcohol began to leave her system, so too would her only excuse—that this was just a drunken night, that she was not in her senses and the alcohol had dulled her consciousness. She could still convince herself that she was not cheating on Aman. Anxious, she started pinning her nails into her thighs, making them bleed, yet she felt not an ounce of pain; her mind and body had become immune to it.

The bathroom had a glass partition that allowed anyone in the room to see the person inside in all their glory. Modern couples seemed to enjoy watching each other shower and perform their ablutions. This was the first time Maya had been in such a room; she had heard of it from Shama, who had stayed in a five-star hotel during a training session in Delhi. Maya, however, abhorred the concept. The flamboyance of the rich struck her as not just weird but toxic, especially given her upbringing, far removed from the excesses of Mumbai—both literally and metaphorically.

Why would anyone in their sane mind design a bathroom door out of glass, exposing it to the room outside?

Does everyone not deserve privacy, a space to themselves? If nowhere else, at least in the bathroom?

Where is the element of suspense if everything is bared?

What pleasure would one derive from observing their partner in the bathroom?

Does every individual not deserve an identity of their own?

If everything is out there for all to watch, where is the anticipation? What is there to look forward to? Another partner? Another fling?

She found the entire concept perverse.

As sanity returned to her, Maya walked out of the bathroom, smelling of vomit. Ram took her hand and led her to a chair, the passion in his eyes replaced by pure, unadulterated lust. The scant respect he had for her as an individual had evaporated, leaving only desire. Ram perched himself on the edge of the bed and leaned towards the table. He had prepared lines of white powder on it; there were traces of the powder on his nose too.

He grabbed Maya by her hair and gently pushed her head towards the table. This was her first sniff of cocaine. She followed him obediently, like his slave, bent over and inhaled. She had no idea what she was in for. Immediately, her head started spinning and her body felt as light as a feather—it felt like it did not exist at all. It was like a dream she had once had under the tree on Tamara's wedding day, where she had imagined herself as a skeleton, half her body consumed by a beast.

Maya began to dance without any music. She felt a hand on her waist—the same hand that had held her before. She heard Ram murmur, 'I wanted to kill the hesitation in your mind about whether you should do it. Debates only create stress, and this one gives you clarity.'

She once again saw Shiv as Ram pulled her closer. When he kissed her passionately, she reciprocated without any hesitation. Time, she felt, was the worst enemy of humanity—one did not know what would happen if one allowed it to fly past. Soon they were biting, kissing and holding each other tight as if they were long-lost lovers, separated and reunited by fate. The pain from his bites was sweet, and she longed for more. She urged him to bite every part of her body and wanted him to leave his mark on her—a sign of possession.

Ram was also under the influence of drugs, and succumbed to her every desire. He, too, was her slave, as she was his. She asked him to caress her, beat her, hold her high, fling her on the bed and allow her to suck his penis. She called him Shiv, but he didn't seem to mind. After all, what's in a name? To him, she was also someone else.

They were both victims of broken hearts and shattered promises, an ideal duo swimming in their oceans of sorrow. In their minds, they could justify breaking the hearts of those who stayed with them because others had already broken theirs.

★

Maya woke up to bright light piercing through the windows. She tucked her face into the pillow to protect it from the harsh and dry rays. She had no idea of the time. She touched her thighs and looked at the dried blood on her naked legs. She could not remember whether she had scratched herself or if Ram had done it. She looked around the room and outside; now, the sun seemed dull.

She quickly grabbed her phone and realized it was afternoon. There was a barrage of missed calls waiting for her—Zahra, Shama, Aman, her team members.

She brought herself back to her senses, hurriedly typed 'I'm okay, will call back after a few meetings' to her flatmates, and rushed to shower. As the hot water touched her body, she recalled the events of the night vividly. And just then, her whole world came crashing down. She understood why she had allowed herself to be dragged along. It was not Ram who had dragged her; it had been Shiv. And a small part of her still believed that Ram was the incarnation of Shiv.

She shook her head and felt a heavy thumping between her forehead and the back of her head. She thought that the water from the shower would wash away her pain, that it would erase the horror she carried within herself, and melt the heavy burden she carried wherever she went. The water was getting hotter and hotter, and she stood under the scalding spray until it burned her skin, jolting her out of her numbness. She realized she'd been standing there too long—she was losing her sense of time; for the first time, she felt scared for herself.

But who could she tell this to? Two names flashed—Zahra and Kanya. No, they would moralize, not sympathize with her, and blame her for dragging herself into the morass; they would admonish her. No one knew her; no one understood her. Not Maa, not Bhai, not Tamara, not Shiv, not Kanya, not Zahra. Perhaps Aman? But how would she tell him all that had happened?

How can I blame them? Do I understand myself? Especially after what happened last night?

She cried in the shower for what seemed like an eternity. Finally, she dried herself, put on her clothes and walked out of that hotel, ashamed of herself, not bothering to look at the prying eyes staring at her. As she hailed an auto and sat in it, thoughts engulfed her.

What if I had not gone to the party?

What if I had left early, as everyone had been late?

What if Kanya, the most militant in the team, had insisted that I get into their car? Would Ram have been able to resist Kanya's decision?

What if Ram didn't remind me of Shiv?

What if I had taken Aman to the party?

What if I had refused to sniff the powder? Would Ram have forced me?

What if Kanya, in all her innocence, had not asked for the party in the first place?

What if? What if?

17

Strange indeed are the manifestations of love! Not long ago, she had despised Ram with her heart and soul, seeing him as the embodiment of villainy. But as the auto made its way towards her home, her feelings transformed. She convinced herself that she loved Ram, rationalizing that what he had done the previous night was a mere expression of love—nothing more, nothing less. Twisted as it seemed, she managed to persuade her body, mind and soul that Ram was the Shiv she lacked in her life. She was prepared to go to any length to ensure she did not lose him. Despite any obstacles on the way, and there might be insults, travails and anguish, she would endure and cling to her source of sustenance—a hope for a life of companionship and love.

This was her hope to live a whole life. She needed to love someone and be loved in return. It did not matter that Ram was already married and cheating on his wife, and that he could possibly cheat on her just as easily in the future. The poor soul could not understand that a life built on the harm of others would lead only to emptiness. Life needs to move forward, but Maya was regressing into the memories of a person she should have left behind long ago, replaying her past like a video of a decades-old cricket match.

She chose to stay silent and bear the weight of her choices—a sacrifice that still haunted her. Backing down was not an option. Life, she believed, was about seizing opportunities and confronting challenges head-on. Though she knew impulsive decisions often led to regret born of poor judgement, she chose to push that reality aside. After all, decisions always carried a degree of risk and uncertainty, sometimes hinging on sheer luck. She understood that circumstances beyond anyone's control could shape outcomes and that wise individuals accepted these risks, making peace with the consequences. If a choice backfired, luck was often blamed, and sympathy, rather than blame, was extended to those who bore the fallout. Life's decisions could rarely be labelled as simply right or wrong; more often, they were moulded by the unpredictability of fate.

But hers was not a calculated risk; it was rooted in emotion, disconnected from reason or rationality.

The questions she'd had at the start of this journey gave way to new ones:

Do I love Ram or Shiv?

Is Ram invested in me or does he consider this a one- or two-night stand?

Am I fully aware of the consequences of getting involved with a married man? And if I am, am I prepared to face them?

Would Ma and Bhai accept it?

How will I break the news to them?

Would Zahra and Shama continue to maintain relations with me?

What would happen to Aman? Would he irretrievably break down? Does Aman truly love me, or is it something less?

She soon dismissed these thoughts as inconsequential to her decision. These would get sorted out with time. What mattered now was that she had got her Shiv. She could not obtain the first one, but the Almighty had tested her resilience and she had passed all the examinations, so He had rewarded her resilience with a new embodiment of love.

Was that not what the astrologer told her? She vividly remembered his words: 'You were born to live fully, to embrace both the glories and the agonies of existence. But to attain this ultimate bliss, you will have to traverse the seas, experience volcanic eruptions, and endure tempests and rough earthquakes. You were not born to live an ordinary life; angst will be a constant companion in your journey. You will have to follow your heart, take risks in life and suffer pain. Once you start following your heart, there is no looking back.'

The sadhu had proven that he was not an ordinary man—he had the divine touch! Now, she had to follow her heart through volcanic eruptions, tempests, floods and earthquakes.

Her clothes were tattered. She had her credit card on her and she could purchase a new dress, but decided not to. This was her life, and she did not wish to hide anything from anyone. She decided to go home; Zahra and Shama would have left for work by now. If they had been concerned about her and had not left in the morning, her text message would have calmed their nerves. And why should they be concerned? Zahra had Kanya's details; they had met once at a café and exchanged numbers. She would have learnt from her that Maya and Ram had left together. Although he had said he would drop her off at home, neither Kanya nor the other team members were fools.

As she walked into her apartment, Maya felt ashamed and guilty for the first time. The apartment was quiet and peaceful; no one seemed to be home—*Aman must have gone for an interview or to the library to study*, she thought. She threw herself on Aman's bed and was soon asleep—the effect of the cocaine was yet to wane.

In her dream, she was standing on top of a mountain. *Was it Ranikhet or somewhere else? The hills seemed unfamiliar, and where were the snow-capped peaks?* Her clothes were tattered, her hands dirty with sand and soot. She stood on one leg, trying to imitate Lord Shiva. She had a stick in one hand, and her face was blackened and unrecognizable. She was unconcerned that her clothes resembled rags; she was desperately trying to maintain her balance on one leg. That was the posture in which she could replicate the Lord, and she was serious about it. The longer she could stand, the closer she could get to her God. It was not too difficult; she had been, after all, a distinguished sports personality in school.

The sun was burning brightly, and it was hot. She stood there for days and nights, under the sun and starry skies. She stayed in that position in summer and winter, until it started snowing heavily. She persisted through the blizzards; she refused to back down. She wished to unite with the Lord, whom she worshipped with total devotion. But she also felt lonely, wishing she had a companion who would stand with her to support her or at least provide her company. Someone who would hold her if she ever lost her balance, someone whose body warmth would heal her bruised feet, which had turned cold from standing for months. Someone she belonged to, who belonged to her in turn. It had to be someone who would communicate this to her through whispers. Someone whose warm breath would calm her nerves and soothe her.

Maya woke up late in the night to find Aman sleeping next to her, unruffled, careless and nonchalant. She envied his sound sleep and sincerely wished she could, too, sleep as deeply. But they were different—he had no worries or hang-ups. He was unconcerned about his repeated failures at interviews. His family's farmland was sufficient to feed him and his family without needing him to secure a job. Maya wondered if he genuinely loved her because if he did, would he not pine to possess her? How could he sleep so soundly after she had spent the previous night elsewhere?

Most nights were terrifying for her. The nights she enjoyed deep and unhindered sleep were few and far between. That night, she wanted to sleep peacefully, but her mind refused to; it kept working overtime. She sat up on the bed. There was an excruciating pain in her thighs; the cuts were fresh, and visible even in the faint light that peeped in through the windows. She must have done it while sleeping and dreaming about Lord Shiva. She considered applying medicine but was scared about waking Aman; she was in no mood to start a conversation at this hour, and he would have lots of questions.

Maya once again started to ponder. Her mind told her she was heading for disaster, but as usual, her heart clung to a different truth. The road to disaster was her only way to everlasting peace. It was the only way left for her, the one she believed would finally redeem her years of pain and suffering.

The fact that she had hurt herself in her sleep left her uncertain about whether she should feel good or bad about it. But the realization that she had attained the power to harm herself while unconscious made her feel possessed—not by demons, but by her gods. A bizarre thought indeed but nonetheless, she stuck to it. It was a secret she had hidden from herself for so many years. The irony was that it didn't bother her; on the contrary, it pleased her. It was just a way of life, a self-correcting mechanism to cope with life's adversities and setbacks. The secret had come out in the open and rather than rejecting it, her mind had accepted it, embracing the harm to her body as just another part of life's rhythm.

Maya noticed Aman tossing in his sleep and suddenly felt pity for him. She had no intention of hurting him any more, and it was her responsibility to explain her change of heart to him so that he did not feel offended. She would disclose her past to him and explain that she had found her Shiv, whom she had not found in him. She liked Aman—she had nothing against him nor was anything lacking in him, but it was a feeling that she could not explain rationally.

Her instincts urged her to wake him and spill everything weighing on her heart, but she held back. *Not now!* It was not in her nature to let emotions take over uncontrollably, so she kept her thoughts clear and composed. In her relentless pursuit of Shiv, she had lost herself entirely. What had once been an obsession had now manifested into a tangible problem, culminating in infidelity.

A persistent fear of catastrophe gnawed at her, yet she remained ensnared by her unfulfilled desires, captive to her own longing.

She could hear the faint call of the birds. It was almost morning now. She sat on the edge of the bed, staring at the pale ochre glow of the sun, the blackness of the skies clearing slowly but surely. It was just another morning for most of the residents of Mumbai, but not for her. A battle was raging within her—to follow the brain and stop the hunt for a love forbidden by society, by ethics and by a sense of justice. Yet, she decided to follow her heart, which resonated with Shiv. It was an obsession consuming her sanity. Her heart had always been her weakness, and it usually emerged victorious in the battles against her brain. This, too, was no exception. It carried her to unknown destinations, to torture her mind. It repeatedly gave her the worst advice, yet she followed it. She had abandoned her family, home town, and near and dear ones for someone she had barely even spoken to. Her insanity was narcissistic and simultaneously masochistic—a unity of opposites!

She was once again being manipulated to go down the road leading to a fictional future that, in all probability, would never come true!

Her rapid gasping and irregular breathing led to incessant digging into her inner thighs, reopening old wounds and creating fresh ones. Tiptoeing into the bathroom, she tended to them with some antibiotic ointment. Fortunately, the tube was visible in the semi-darkness and she did not need to turn on the light. It struck her that the ointment had gotten over just the day before, and she had forgotten to buy a replacement. But this tube was packed to the brim! Only Aman could have purchased one on seeing the empty tube!

Aman was sweet, sensitive and an actual human being. He was a man of few words, but one who loved serving others selflessly. He never reprimanded or even asked Maya about the wounds, which he must have noticed the nights they slept together, the nights they had sex. He had remembered to purchase the tube and had kept it on the bathroom counter when Maya herself had forgotten about it!

The thought of betraying this man crushed her. Maya broke down, covering her mouth with her hand lest the sound of her cries woke Aman up. The only way she could cope with this was to dig her nails into her thighs, so she did it again! The skin ripped open and blood oozed out, trickling down her legs. This was the most she had ever hurt herself!

She stayed inside the bathroom for half an hour. When she walked out, her eyes were swollen and her hair was in disarray. The sun was prominent on the horizon, its rays reflecting off the windowpanes and striking her eyes directly. Her cheeks were still wet with tears, a mix of intense misery and pain, and they were quickly drying, leaving patches across her face.

Aman was already awake and preparing tea for all of them in the kitchen. She wondered why he had not knocked on the bathroom door. Aman's feelings for her were as deep as hers were for Shiv. What she was about to do to him was perhaps worse than what Shiv had done to her because, while her love had remained unexpressed, Aman had expressed his love in no uncertain terms before.

Just then, Zahra came out of her room and saw Maya standing, looking distraught and unsure. It was almost time for her to start dressing for work, but Zahra was not sure whether Maya intended to go to work. The shock was palpable in her expression. Zahra had intended to haul her over coals regarding the previous night, but morning was not the opportune time for that. She would do it in the evening. Instead, she cautiously approached Maya and said, 'Good morning. Is something bothering you?'

Maya just looked at Zahra without blinking, and then turned

towards the kitchen where Aman was preparing breakfast. She halted for a moment, unsure of herself. Zahra wanted to alert Maya, make her see reason and pull her back from whatever destructive path she was on, but she could not find the right words. Maya looked like someone who was about to willingly jump into a fire, and Zahra knew that it would be challenging to save her from it. She resolved to keep trying, as she felt responsible towards her.

When the dark clouds block the sun's rays, flowers refuse to bloom, roots dry up, birds forget to chirp, and the sea gets rough; no force on earth can prevent a calamity. When an earthquake strikes or storms blow, it is beyond the capabilities of the human race to prevent the impending Armageddon. One can predict the doom but cannot stop it from engulfing humanity. It struck Zahra that human beings were indeed helpless before the forces of nature.

Zahra wanted to approach Maya to nurse her wounds and pat her. All human beings are tactile, and a simple touch could work wonders, but she was unsure how Maya would take it. After all, Maya's personality had altered over the last few days and she was not the Maya they knew. Wounds and blood patches dotted her body, but Maya perhaps did not feel the pain—maybe she had transcended it. Zahra's grandfather, a freedom fighter who had endured enormous torture at the hands of the colonial police, had once told her about pain that manifested as pleasure. If Zahra snatched away the pain from her, it would be construed as taking away her pleasure, and Maya would resent it.

Yet, Zahra persisted. She walked towards Maya in baby steps, piercing her with her looks. When she was close enough, she whispered just three words into her ear, 'Don't, Maya, don't.'

Maya replied, 'This is the last chance I'm giving myself, Zahra. I need one more go at redemption. Please accept me; try to understand my predicament.'

She conveyed a look of helplessness, beseeching Zahra through her eyes to support her and provide strength. She was one of her few friends, and no one else would support her if she let her down. Zahra was like a pillar for her, an anchor, a prop to help her stand on her legs. Zahra could see that Maya had embarked on a path of self-destruction.

Aman was humming in the kitchen as he worked. Maya approached him, turned off the stove and broke down, sobbing inconsolably. Intuitive as he was, he, too, had sensed an impending disaster. He hugged her tight and shed tears without asking her why. He had known that this love was not meant to last. From day one he had realized that someone else was lurking in her mind, and she would perhaps never be able to set herself free of him. Who this man was, he had no clue, nor had he ever bothered to ask. It was too personal, too private; it would only disturb her. But he would continue to love her. He would cherish the memories, recall the sweet moments they had spent together, and savour the sweet smell that emanated from her body.

When he opened his mouth, it was to state something profound, words that would haunt Maya till her last day. 'The first thing about love, Maya, is that we know how to fall in love, but rarely how to fall out of it. This is the nature of love, and it is everlasting; I will keep loving you.'

They held each other close, tears streaming as they clung to one another. Just then, Zahra entered the kitchen and witnessed love in its purest form—untouched by the harshness of life. She realized that Maya's love for Aman was deeper than the fleeting connection she had shared with the man from the other night. To Maya, perhaps Ram was nothing more than a reflection of Shiv, an image she had crafted in her mind. Maya would never truly love Ram, and that was the allure—the echo of Shiv she sought in him, a yearning she could never quite fulfil.

Love appears calm on the surface, yet beneath it, chaos brews. It follows no laws and is random. Experts have called it by many monikers, but at its core, love is simply the heart's call to connect, to possess another. You could call it enchantment, passion, obsession or mania, but what ultimately lies in a name? It is the essentials that count. It is erratic, unreasonable and illogical, but that is what love is meant to be, after all. It numbs the mind, floods it with dopamine and creates pleasure, which is all that truly matters!

But who is anyone to judge or explain love, a word that defies definition because it is unique to every individual? What love means to one person may not hold true for another. The outsider may wonder what drew X to Y, but they would never find a clear explanation—because if they did, it would no longer be love. One thing is clear: love creates an indefinable sensation, calmness, peace of mind and pleasure; if it doesn't, it is not worth pursuing. Love is obsessive and illusory. It propels one into a parallel universe—a metaverse, to borrow from modern terminology. It fools one into thinking that they are winning when they are actually losing.

Zahra joined the embrace, butting her way inside a small gap between the two, and sobbed uncontrollably. Though she was not directly connected to their shared feelings, she felt a deep sense of involvement. By nature, Zahra was the epitome of calm and tranquillity, non-interfering, but sensed that someone was piercing a knife into Maya's stomach and felt like a silent witness.

Just then, Shama came out of her room, ready to depart for work, but the sounds of three people sobbing in the kitchen was not a situation she could walk away from without investigating. She did not know what to say when she saw them crying profusely, but she, too, couldn't control herself and started weeping. She had no idea of the reason, but they were all her close friends, and since they were crying, she could not bring herself to remain aloof. It wasn't a conscious decision to commiserate; the tears came spontaneously, for the sight was simply too excruciating. She hugged them tightly and drew them as one mass towards herself.

In the process, Maya lost control and fell flat on the floor. As she clambered up, Aman brought her a glass of water; she drank it and joked, 'Is this poison?'

As they all laughed, Aman hugged her tightly once again.

Here is a truly noble soul, Maya thought. And so did Zahra and Shama.

Shama had by now understood what was happening; she had anticipated the break-up long ago—sixth sense had told her that their paths were not interconnected. She decided to lighten the atmosphere. 'So, Aman, Maya, from now on, you need not keep your love under wraps any more!'

They all joined in the laughter, and Zahra spotted the beauty in Shama's tears, which were yet to dry up.

Aman hugged the three of them, engulfing them in his long, protective arms. He sheltered them under an umbrella like a guardian, although he was only a couple of years older. A year back, he had walked into the apartment when they had been looking for a fourth partner. They had asked for a day to decide since they had been searching for a girl. Zahra and Shama had opposed, but Maya had insisted. Over time, he had transformed himself from a burden to a solid rock.

Shama wiped her tears and remarked, 'From today, Aman becomes a couch potato, and we become the couch! And no one can sleep on the couch without Aman's permission; it belongs to the potato! Is that clear?'

The rest did not understand what she meant and dismissed it as a silly joke. Shama was known for such antics, most of which fell flat, but at that moment, it was exactly what they had needed. The atmosphere had become too heavy, too loaded. Jokes can, at times, manage to bury emotions, and Shama was good at that.

Aman looked at Maya for a fleeting second, and once again, he took her heart away, embarrassing her with pain, but she did not wish to divert her emotions; she had no place for Aman in it. Hearts are not capacious after all; they have space for only one at a time.

18

Maya fumbled back into her room, wanting to escape, and banged her head against the wall. It was dark, and she couldn't see, but the voices were becoming louder, the footsteps approaching and receding, and the light flickering between bright and dim. It was like a live play—a theatre with the sets and props meticulously arranged in a long room leading to an alley. The sound crescendoed, and the director frantically waved his hands from the sidelines. The next moment, she heard the strains of raucous music, loud chatter, bangs on metal and joyous screams. She was confused—was it a play or was it a party?

She was reminded of their parties at Ranikhet. They had started the day Maya and her friends were promoted from Class 7 to Class 8. There was a strict ban on partying imposed by Maa and Bhai—they felt parties epitomized a decadent culture and were not meant for decent girls. However, they relented when the results were announced and Maya stood first, scoring full marks in mathematics and science. Bhai was the person who had relented first, the more pliable and flexible of the two.

Their parties were all-girls gatherings and without intoxicants—not that they were pining for it. However, once Tamara's boyfriend, Ashok, had joined. The party took place at Tamara's home, where the outhouse was tucked in an obscure corner—a dilapidated structure with a forest behind it. Tamara had instructed Ashok to come in through the forest, but he had decided to act brave and enter through the main gate. Her father had spotted him.

The party was called off immediately. Tamara faced punishment and was forbidden to meet Ashok, ultimately leading to a painful break-up, more so for Ashok than Tamara. She was also upset but got over it fast. She had reasoned that it was not her fault—she had instructed Ashok to sneak in through the forest!

As Maya lay in bed, these faint memories crept into her mind. *Why did Ranikhet always have to appear in my dreams?* Thankfully, Shiv's face was not visible that day, as it only led to pain. Of course, his presence at such parties was unthinkable. He was a pariah for the girls. Not only did he not go to school, but he was also rude and a recluse of sorts... But not to Maya, who had lacked the courage to accept it openly, to holler about it before her friends and others in Ranikhet. Perhaps if she had gathered the courage, things would have shaped differently. If only...

She banged her head against the wall again. This time it was different—it was not accidental—she consciously walked towards it, like a speeding car careening into the walls of a cul-de-sac. It was a car with malfunctioning brakes, heading for certain destruction. She could feel the loss of control over her body; her brakes were malfunctioning. She desperately tried to slow down because she knew the collision would be disastrous.

At the nick of the moment, someone pulled her back. She turned round. Who else could it be? Shiv, her saviour, with his uncanny knack for appearing from nowhere. But his face was blurred and unrecognizable, and so was his physique. The person was tall and handsome. Was it Shiv? Or someone else? She only wished someone would switch on a powerful torchlight and shine it directly on him, revealing his face and features.

She wished to hold him tight, hug him, nestle in his arms and look intently into his expressive eyes. She longed for him to embrace her back, kiss her cheeks, gently rub his face against hers, and caress her on her neck with his long, soft fingers. She felt dizzy, struck by vertigo. She closed her eyes and was scared that if he let her go, she would fall down. The world changed around her; the birds chirped, the sky turned an azure blue and the storm clouds disappeared.

Then she heard his voice. It was a whisper. 'Maya, don't ever leave me, okay?'

As if *she* had deserted him, as if *he* had not married Tamara—it was he who had not bothered to respect her feelings.

'Why did you leave Ranikhet?'

He was right; she had left Ranikhet and not returned in seven years. Yet, she had never considered that the boy she had left behind was not an unattached Shiv but someone already bound to another.

It was so typical for girls to blame themselves for all the misfortunes that came their way. It is a state of mind, a cognitive process to cope with misery. Blaming others only results in stress; blaming oneself removes rancour and hate. It calms down the emotions, the negative behaviours and the angst. Maya had used it quite successfully for many years now.

However, it ultimately resulted in more misery, and she had not quite grasped the fact that this habit led to bouts of depressive behaviour that woke her up in the night, when she would mutter softly and scratch her body till blood oozed from her pores.

Shiv said, 'Come here, I'll help you.'

Maya realized that she had instinctively moved away from him, her back pressed against the wall while he stood at a distance. This sense of retreat had become familiar, starting after a vivid dream of him that had been abruptly interrupted by Bhai knocking on her door, presuming that she had overslept. When she woke up from her trance-like state, Bhai had walked away. Later, at dinner, he had asked if she was all right, noting that it was unusual for her to sleep so long in the afternoon. She had merely shaken her head, prompting him to observe her intently.

Memories interspersed with imagination. Memories that were genuine, that corresponded to reality, while the dreams dwelt on an unreal world. A curious concoction of reality and surrealism!

With all her concentration, she looked intently at Shiv. Then she looked around to spot another person, and she had no difficulty recognizing him.

It was Ram. Why did he have to come and disrupt her intimate moments with Shiv? *Why?* But her behaviour was indeed strange. Although she resented his presence, she grabbed him tighter than she had held Shiv.

'Do not try the cocaine again, do not get addicted; it is harmful,' she heard Shiv say.

'But it reduces pain, which is important for me.'

'Never mind; there are several ways to reduce pain, Maya.'

She hated the after-effects—the semi-conscious state she had experienced since snorting it two days back. But she had also loved the experience—the feeling of inhabiting a separate universe, one populated by herself, Shiv, and his avatar, Ram. It was a blissful escape from the populated planet, insulated from the hustle and bustle.

And then she felt she was flying, like a bird, soaring high above. Then, she was a butterfly flitting along the hillside, descending the slopes. And the next moment, it was a feeling of cheer, of everlasting happiness, of liberation from earthly bondage and all thoughts of the self, of shedding her ego and merging into the vastness of the cosmos. Her life had finally ended, and now she could be reborn. The thought made her stomach sink, making her fling herself back to the planet; she was not yet prepared to leave the trappings of her familiar surroundings.

When she awoke, she found herself in a strange-looking bedroom. She had not realized that she had been hallucinating. A tender, gentle hand caressed her head—it felt like her mother's cracked hands were putting her to sleep. She was stroking her forehead and singing lullabies. Maya had been a problem child during her infant days; her mother had once told her that sending her to bed required Herculean effort. It was a common belief that stroking an infant's forehead removed the thoughts of their previous life, thoughts that persisted well after they had been born into their new lives.

It was Ram who appeared again. And Maya transcended all the ill feelings, starting to love Ram once more. After all, he was such a gentleman, a rarity in such times.

In her delusion, she even blessed him, as if she were a *sanyasi* who had descended from the mountaintops. Shiv had, in the meantime, vanished. Ram cleaned her face with a damp cloth, keeping Maya guessing why he had to do it. Was it covered with sweat, tears, soot or blood? She desperately tried to peer at the towel, but nothing was visible, adding to the mystery.

He smiled and kissed her cheek. She felt he was caring and affectionate, willing to sacrifice his life for her sake. She heard him utter, 'Sleep well. You are at a different level right now—you are now on a trip, and need rest and sleep.'

Her face carried the foul smell of rancid vomit, a reflux from the pits of her stomach. She also felt it in her mouth. She was disgusted at herself, but all she could do was curl up in a foetal position. She wrapped herself with a bedcover and a quilt, even though it was a hot Mumbai afternoon.

Ram switched off the lights and left the room, leaving her alone in the darkness. She soon fell into a deep sleep, free from nightmares or bitter dreams.

She slept soundly for 24 hours—that is what Zahra and Shama later told her. She had lost track of time. She woke up the next day with a severe headache. Slowly climbing out of bed, she felt every part of her body in disarray and croaking like a chair meant to be thrown away because it had reached the end of its life cycle. Each step was painful, but she managed to lumber towards the bathroom. The pain that she had inflicted upon herself had started hurting. She realized she was a total mess and would take time to recover.

She cried for some time. It was a unique kind of grief that engulfed her, not the familiar one arising from losing a job, a near and dear one, or a setback in the stock market. It was an indefinable kind of grief, where the sufferer did not know why she was grieving.

19

It had been six months since Maya resigned from her job. She hadn't earned a single penny and was dependent on Ram.

Tamara had called her a month ago—the first time since Maya had left Ranikhet. They had indulged in small talk; she had not asked Tamara about Shiv, nor had Tamara brought up the topic. Maya did not tell Tamara about losing her job.

Zahra and Shama used to drop in occasionally, but had stopped about a month ago. When they did drop by, they seemed so disinterested and aloof that Maya wished they'd stay away. She did not want them to perform duties towards her or shower her with pity. She was in any case suffering from self-pity, and there was no place for pity from others. She had not asked them about Aman's whereabouts; she presumed he would be in agony for her, and did not want to hear about it because it would only add to her misery.

Her body was dying for alcohol and cocaine, but both had been denied to her, leaving her in intense pain—an intolerable kind of pain.

Ram had been extraordinarily good to her, which left her wondering. He had rented an apartment for her, and dropped by once a week, claiming he was running a project in Mumbai. She wished he would spend the night, but he never did. He always departed for his hotel after putting her to sleep. He had taken care of her basic needs; there were attendants and maidservants at her beck and call—one for cleaning, one for cooking, one for taking care of her personal needs, which included massages to soothe her aching muscles and lull her to sleep—rare moments of extreme comfort when she could disconnect from reality.

Every morning and night, two injections stung her skin, but they also put her to sleep, where dreams and hallucinations were constant companions. A doctor came every alternate day to check her blood pressure and heart rate, and Maya wondered why. Ram had told her that she was under treatment for some ailment, but he refused to divulge the specifics. He promised that she would recover soon if she followed the doctor's advice. Maya did not have the heart to disobey him or ask too many questions.

All her contacts had been erased from her phone save for her mother's, brother's, Zahra's and Shama's numbers. She had been told this was per the doctor's orders and essential for a swift recovery. Often, she felt the urge to go out and mingle with the other residents, but her attendant reminded her that she wouldn't be allowed outside for several more months. She would stand by the window, watching the others, noticing how they, too, seemed distant and withdrawn.

Maya often dreamt of her surroundings in Ranikhet, which reminded her of her carefree life there. Not that her time there had been without its share of ups and downs, but she longed to return to those days. Bhai and Maa called once a week, and it was strange how her phone would ring immediately after her dreams. She found this coincidence curious, but she was not in the mood to dwell on supernatural explanations; her reality was overwhelming enough. Needless to say, they were not told about the loss of her job and or her current state.

Tamara and her other friends appeared regularly in her dreams, and Maya relived the days they spent swimming in the lake and relaxing on the banks, discussing varied topics. They gossiped, studied, played, pulled each other's legs and celebrated the changing seasons—the onset of winter, spring and the first blossoming of flowers.

At other times, she found herself at the beach, struggling against tumultuous waves that sprayed her with salty water, playing with dolphins and fish that mysteriously appeared every time she landed there. She would write Shiv's name in the shifting sands, only for the waves or the wind to wash it away. She prayed that Shiv would appear once again in her life.

Her past life came in flashes—memories long buried but now forced to the surface by the drugs coursing through her. Every obscure detail seemed to rise into her mind—Bhai hurting his leg, the auntie next door passing away suddenly, her father at his violent worst, the day they visited the astrologer in the creepy caves, the afternoon she ran away from home after fighting with Bhai, Pinky Auntie's bizarre story about her father-in-law, the jewels she'd stolen from her aunt, her first visit to the golf course, the storms that devastated Ranikhet, the swings on the banyan tree, the first snowfall, the long treks up the mountains, her mother's bitter experience with the sadhu, the tiger they had seen at Corbett on one of the few holidays their father had taken them on, and, of course, Shiv. The desire to possess him, the intense passion, had increased multifold. He appeared in so many forms: sometimes as gods, sometimes as their earthly avatars, and sometimes as Majnu, the archetype of the lover.

For the first time, she felt she had embarked on her ultimate journey.

The evening spent with Tamara beneath the banyan tree, her wedding night, the day of Holi when Shiv had picked up her dupatta, and the time he had saved her from drowning were milestones in her life. Tamara and Shiv's wedding night was never singular; it fragmented into countless visions on countless nights. She relived the wedding as though Tamara married Shiv over and over, and each time, without exception Maya wept.

The nightmarish dream of her as a formless spirit devoured by wild animals was a regular occurrence. Saria had also started visiting her every night. She was her best consolation in the harsh life she had to endure. But, strangely, she had stopped growing and was still a little child. Maya once asked her why, and her answer had been elusive—'You've stopped growing, Maya.' Maya initially did not understand what Saria meant, but comprehension dawned later. Yes, Maya was still a quintessential child, unable to see beyond Shiv at the vast world outside—in her dreams, hallucinations and thoughts.

Her life had transformed, but her world remained static. Call it obsession; call it fixation. The fact remained that she was stuck with Shiv. It was not love, not by any stretch of the imagination. She had witnessed her friends fall in love, but those were everyday affairs. Some led to fruition, some to break-ups. It took time to grow out of an affair, but only very few people could not move on. She remembered the face of Ashok, madly in love with Tamara, who had moved on. And she was certain Aman had also moved on. Otherwise, he would have come at least once to meet her. Did he finally secure a job? She was curious, but had forgotten to ask Zahra or Shama during their last visit. Now, of course, both had forsaken her. She still had their numbers but was in no mood to get in touch. And what guarantee was there that they would take her call?

At times, Maya found herself questioning how the Almighty could be so unfeeling. Her mother and Bhai, along with others, seemed oblivious to the depth of her emotions. Even Tamara hadn't understood her struggles, and Maya had come to see her as heartless, convinced of it now more than ever.

Maya had turned her teenage love into a liability, a jinx for life. She either deserved Shiv or a closure, an erasure of sorts—anything in between felt like a cruel trick, keeping her tethered to an illusion. She wondered at which point a simple love had turned into an obsession. After all, Radha had not turned obsessive, and she, too, had taken it in her stride when Krishna married Rukmini. Loneliness brought distress to her; Maya was at the end of her tether—a drug addict, an alcoholic, a recluse, a total mess—waiting for her last days, which she sensed were not far off.

Love can become a demon or, worse, an ugly dragon spewing poison into the soul.

At other times, she wondered whether it was at all love. It was perhaps something else—maybe a psychologist could guide her. There were too many improbabilities—she had never conversed with Shiv on a one-to-one basis, and he had touched her only once; he had lifted her dupatta, but that was elementary courtesy, and anyone in his place would have done so. On the day of Holi, there were so many others who had smeared colour on her—men and women from all age groups, including middle-aged ladies and old people. Coming to think of it, was he to blame? Had he ever communicated his love? He had merely stared at her. She was reasonably beautiful, although not stunningly so. So many people on the road stared at her, even on the streets and beaches of Mumbai. Could she blame them also for betraying her? Then why did she blame Shiv?

She had gone and destroyed herself for a love that never was. Maya often wondered whether she was unique in this respect—a case study for those who studied human behaviour and the intricacies of the human mind.

Did she regret it? Not for a second. Even now, she could rebuild her life if she wished to. All she had to do was to visit a psychiatrist. There were many in Mumbai. Ram would indeed bear the cost, and she, too, had some savings of her own. As for her addiction, Zahra had told her of rehabilitation centres and had even volunteered to take her there. It was not for nothing that she had forsaken her; Maya had indeed behaved strangely. Had Zahra not warned her many times?

Maya embraced her solitude, savouring every moment of loneliness while secretly yearning for Shiv's presence in both joy and sorrow. Despite feeling trapped within the confines of her apartment, she made no attempt to break free of the chains that bound her. Sometimes, simply imagining his existence brought her immense pleasure, filling her with enthusiasm throughout the day until the next dose of her medication, which plunged her back into the depths of her depressive nightmares.

She began to understand that it wasn't Shiv she loved, not really; it was rather the idea of him. She found solace in thoughts of him, conjuring vivid images and indulging in fantasies where he visited and sat beside her. She couldn't help but wonder if his charm would dissipate when she saw him in the flesh again. This sparked a serendipitous thought: could this be the cure she longed for? Should she return to Ranikhet for a few days and spend precious hours with him, hoping to find healing and restoration for herself?

She had read a book about a girl named Sheela that Zahra had gifted her on her birthday. Sheela hallucinated about going to bed with a boy she had seen in the library. The doctor had advised her to try and have sex with him, just once. She had approached him, he had obliged her, and she was miraculously cured of her obsession. Should she also proceed on similar lines? Maya did give it a serious thought but also realized that she lacked the gumption and the energy to go to Ranikhet.

Perhaps she never had wanted Shiv; maybe she just wished to obsess about him, pine for him and yearn for his presence. And that was all there was to it! Her unfinished love story had no beginning and, hence, no end, and it would only end with her life, cremated with her, unknown to the rest of humanity. Or chase her to her afterlife, if there was one!

She was reminded of what the astrologer had said. 'You will experience utmost contentment and ecstasy but also endure the peak of heartache. And all that will come your way in the name of Love. If you wish to live your life to the fullest, you will follow your heart, but if you decide to do so and suffer pain, there is no way back.'

She was doomed from the very beginning, like Shakespeare's tragic heroes.

The sadhu's words kept ringing in Maya's mind. She was reminded of those prophetic words at odd moments, sometimes in the mornings, sometimes in the afternoons and mostly at night in her dreams. That was her destiny. Could a human being alter their destiny? Her fate proclaimed it was not possible.

Maya felt a deep internal turmoil as she grappled with the overwhelming circumstances of her life. It was like a piece of herself had grown monstrous, overshadowing everything else and dictating her path. She couldn't deny the charted course laid out before her, and it seemed there was no escape from its grasp. The weight of inevitability pressed upon her, and with each step she took, she became increasingly aware that she was descending down a treacherous and slippery slope.

Attributing her situation to fate and determinism offered little solace. Maya knew that believing her life was predetermined did nothing to alleviate the torment brewing within her. She couldn't shake off what Bhai had told her a few days after their visit to the astrologer's cave. He had insisted that one could change their destiny, but that required a strong mind and unwavering willpower—qualities she believed she lacked.

Amidst Maya's internal turmoil, there were numerous voices of dissent. Zahra stood as a vocal naysayer, who had expressed her disapproval of Maya's path, warning her of the potential consequences. Maya's encounter with Ram when she climbed into his car had not gone unnoticed by Kanya either. She also had tried to convey her disapproval through her suggestive looks, but Maya had chosen to ignore them.

These conflicting influences in her life only served to intensify Maya's internal struggle. Doubts plagued her, causing her to question her own judgement and her choices. She grappled with the desire to take control of her fate and break free from the supposed shackles of her circumstances. However, the seemingly insurmountable challenges ahead and her own perceived weaknesses made the path forward appear daunting and uncertain.

Maya stood at a crossroads, torn between the yearning for autonomy and the fear of the unknown. She knew deep down that the path she had embarked upon had its perils, but the allure of change and the possibility of shaping her own destiny beckoned to her. She would need to find the strength within herself to confront her doubts, face the consequences of her choices, and ultimately determine her own fate.

Only Aman had accepted whatever happened between them as fate, acknowledging that their paths had only ever been parallel lines. He had clearly mentioned it that morning. He had known all through that their fate would never meet and had prepared himself accordingly. Had he not heard the drums of destiny?

The very thought of her life being in her hands had become a source of misery. Attributing her predicament to fate provided solace, and why did she have to recall what Bhai or Zahra had said? *Why? Why?*

The grass spread before her, forming a clear path, much like how rivers flow according to their banks, bound to their courses. Even planes in the sky follow predetermined routes, guided by flight plans. Paths are not random; they are intentionally created. Even birds, in their grand migrations, follow routes passed down through instinct. Maya saw herself as no different—locked within her path, stepping where countless steps had already worn down the grass, shaping a trail through sheer repetition. She had accepted this route without challenge, tethered to it by her faith in destiny.

Could one change the course of their life? The answer, regrettably, seemed to be a resounding 'no'. This thought, albeit disheartening, became her solace and sanctuary. While one could argue for the possibility in theory, the mind had to be willing to traverse uncharted territory, to divert from the established path.

However, her mind had never perceived the necessity to alter its course, nor had it harboured the desire to do so. She attributed this unwavering adherence to what she called destiny, a force that guided human beings to create their paths and ignore the existence of alternative routes.

A vivid memory broke through, resurfacing from the bustling streets of Mumbai. Amidst a frustrating traffic jam, she had proposed to the taxi driver an alternate route to avoid the congestion. It was a gentle admonishment, aware that the suggested route was notorious for its snarls. To her surprise, the taxi driver responded candidly, confessing that he had forgotten about the existence of the alternative path. Force of habit had guided him down the well-trodden road, convincing him that any other route might also be plagued by congestion, even though it was unlikely. The revelation of the taxi driver's musings on life's broader implications had struck her as profound and thought-provoking. Truly, the ways in which the human mind operated were enigmatic and intricate.

In the intricate tapestry of existence, paths are crafted by humans, often unintentionally overlooking the possibility of alternative routes. They become ingrained, etched deep into the consciousness, leaving little room for exploration. It is a reminder of the human tendency to conform to familiar patterns, even when those patterns hinder progress or fulfilment. The mind, capable of profound philosophizing, remains a testament to the perplexing nature of human cognition and its relationship with the paths we tread.

We treat the path we are determined to take as sacrosanct, attributing it to destiny, rationalizing and making excuses that are often weak. Sometimes we might step back or take a sidestep, or stay motionless—content in a kind of passive existence, as if remaining stuck is better than daring to tread a new path that is clearly visible to us but is unfamiliar!

Perhaps that uncharted path is the only route to salvation.

Love consumes everyone. It is both a blessing and a curse, manifesting in various forms. Some of these forms, however, are not true love but mere illusions, traps to lure the hapless victim. We have the capacity to understand the peculiar nature of this feeling and take preventive measures, yet we rarely choose the path to enlightenment. We leave that to great souls—the saints, the sadhus and the chosen few who descend on this earth to proffer us advice. And most of us, unfortunately, do not listen to them.

Maya reluctantly roused herself from a fitful slumber, her surroundings thick with afternoon silence. The cook was on leave, the cleaning woman had completed her tasks and departed, and her attendant had gone down the road to procure provisions. Maya knew her attendant likely engaged in lively conversations with her friends whenever she left the house. The attendant had been cautious about leaving Maya alone in the past, but it seemed she was growing more confident about Maya's progress. And indeed, Maya herself had been experiencing some improvements lately—the intensity of her pain had diminished, and the frequency of her hallucinations had slightly waned.

With great effort, Maya stumbled towards the bathroom. Every step was a struggle, her legs trembling under her weakened frame, and her vision blurring. As she settled on the toilet seat, her gaze fixated upon her bruised thighs, as if seeing them for the first time. It was unusual for her not to feel the excruciating pain, despite having inflicted severe harm upon herself. The entirety of her being seemed to bear the weight of bruises; some resembled burn marks that had previously gone unnoticed. Soft sobs escaped her lips, but no one was there to witness her despair. The tears welled up from deep inside, a poignant reminder of her profound self-inflicted torment. She remained oblivious to the true nature of her actions, as her grip on reality had slipped away in the past. It was only recently that she had begun to regain some semblance of control over her emotions and find some measure of stability.

As the tears streamed down, she asked herself a tricky question. *Did I do this to myself, or did Ram do this to me?*

She did not know the answer. A series of questions followed.

What if Ram hadn't come into my life? Would I have slowly forgotten Shiv? After all, the intensity had subsided with time, though it still simmered beneath the surface, a dormant volcano occasionally spilling lava.

Was Ram the trigger who rekindled my obsession with Shiv?

Was Ram an avatar of Shiv? Or were both avatars of Lord Shiva?

Was my subconscious mind on a suicidal mission, determined to pull me into the abyss?

Could the astrologer's prediction have been just a prognosis? Or was the man a cunning sadist who enjoyed destroying others' lives? Is the prediction the cause of my misery?

And then the inevitable—*Does Shiv think of me the way I think of him? Is he also walking down a similar path? But that would have affected Tamara, and she sounded happy during our last conversation.*

Did Tamara realize that not marrying Shiv would destroy me? She had indicated it on the wedding day, but did she mean it?

Am I just a masochist who derives pleasure from hurting myself? Or are Shiv and Tamara sadists?

Is this a game the universe is playing on me?

Is this all real?

Maya had already destroyed herself once for a love that never existed. She wondered why she was making the same mistake again.

Why would Ram leave his wife for me? People like him fear societal judgement; they worry about gossip and its effect on their business and reputation. They prefer to keep their lovers hidden away in comfort, visiting them occasionally bearing gifts and seeking fleeting pleasure. I will never receive the recognition, dignity or rightful place I long for.

Why couldn't I see this simple truth?

20

The floors were wet and slippery, coated in a thin layer of soapy water. With each step, the woman struggled to maintain her balance. Her brain felt muddled, her thoughts clouded as though she were walking through a fog. Tears streamed down her cheeks, mingling with the dampness already covering her face.

As she looked at herself in the mirror, she couldn't help but notice the toll her circumstances had taken on her physical appearance. Her once vibrant and youthful face was now marred with bruises and burns, each a testament to her challenges. Her hair, once luscious and full, had grown limp and unkempt. She even noticed a few grey strands, further indicating her deteriorating condition. She looked as though she'd aged years overnight.

Summoning every ounce of strength, she attempted to navigate the treacherous path from the bathroom to the veranda. It was a constant battle to maintain her footing on the slippery surface.

Although the cleaning lady took great care to ensure the house remained spotless, the task seemed never-ending. A deep-cleaning team also visited the house to scrub every corner thoroughly. This level of maintenance was often associated with the rich and famous who spared no expense in keeping their homes immaculate.

For her, such extensive cleaning was reserved for specific occasions, such as before leasing out a property or settling into a new home. Deep cleaners were a luxury she couldn't afford on a regular basis. Instead, she relied on her own efforts to keep the house clean, even though it seemed an uphill battle against the relentless dirt and grime that accumulated over time.

Despite her exhaustion and the visible toll it had taken on her, she knew she had to persevere. The slippery floors, the constant cleaning and the physical strain were just a small part of the challenges she faced. Deep down, she clung to the hope that one day her circumstances would improve, and she would find respite from the demanding and relentless task of maintaining her home.

Ram had always taken perfect care of her, going above and beyond what anyone could reasonably expect. It left her bewildered, searching for answers. After all, wasn't Ram the one responsible for her current predicament? Hadn't he used her body to fulfil his own desires? She wondered if he was trying to atone for his actions, compensating for a guilt he never acknowledged.

Despite her attempts to make sense of it all, she remained dazed, unable to find a satisfactory explanation. The questions swirled in her mind, but no answers emerged. The enigma of Ram's actions lingered, casting a shadow over their relationship.

The chatter outside grew louder, disrupting her thoughts. This level of noise was unusual for the time of day. She strained to catch snippets of conversation, trying to make sense of the voices that seemed to float in through the window, but they sounded distant and muffled, as though echoing from a different dimension. She wondered if her mind was playing tricks on her, distorting reality even further.

Looking out of the window, she noticed a sign across the street. The words written in bold letters caught her attention: 'Sunday Special, Hot Jalebis'. It was indeed a Sunday. The mention of jalebis reminded her of the delicacies back home—the gulgula and luqaimat she used to relish. Memories of the carefree days spent in Ranikhet flooded her mind, evoking a sense of nostalgia. Those were moments to cherish, days filled with both joy and sorrow, where the world felt genuine and vibrant.

Comparing her current existence to those precious memories, Maya couldn't help but feel a stark contrast. Everything seemed distorted and detached from reality in this surreal world she now inhabited. Even in bustling Mumbai, she had found solace before meeting Ram, despite the nightmares that plagued her. During the day, she would immerse herself in her work, leading a team, fostering innovation and motivating others. Vibrant street food like pav bhaji and chaat brought her joy during those stolen moments when she would sneak away from the office—she had been an active participant in the real world, feeling a genuine connection to the people and experiences around her.

But now, everything seemed repetitive, devoid of meaning. Time had lost its significance, blurring into an endless cycle of indistinguishable moments. Maya's mind felt fuzzy, as if engulfed in a hazy fog. She struggled to grasp the passing days, losing track of the week, date and even hours. Each passing moment merged with the previous one, as though she were trapped in a daze that had started the day she moved into this apartment.

Maya longed for the vibrant colours of real life, the unpredictable twists and turns, and the freedom to explore the world beyond the confines of her mind. She yearned for the authenticity of genuine experiences. As she stood there, gazing out of the window, her heart ached to return to the life she once knew, where every day held the potential for happiness and heartache.

The biting wind found its way through her thin kurta. She had neglected to dry herself off, and the resulting chill sent shivers down her spine. Desperately, she turned around and spotted her jacket nearby. The colonial-style building, with its remnants of the British era, though worn and dilapidated from the outside, contrasted with the plush interiors Ram had painstakingly curated. He had deceived her, claiming he had purchased it as a guest house, a refuge for as long as she needed. Later, she discovered it was all a façade, but that revelation was a tale for another time.

The French windows framed with fragile iron rods resembled cages. She snatched her jacket and hastily draped it over her milky-white kurta, desperate to shield herself from the chilly wind. As she thought about her reflection in the mirror, she couldn't help but feel out of place, a stranger to herself.

Downstairs, a chorus of laughter erupted from a group of women. The aroma of freshly fried jalebis emanating from oversized pans had lured a crowd of residents to the lawn. The courtyard was a picture of neglect, with unkempt shrubs surrounding the forlorn trees, and the once vibrant yellow paint on the buildings now peeling under the relentless assault of salt-laden air. Despite the jovial atmosphere, the sight was undeniably disheartening. Maya sensed the artificiality of the laughter—a feeble attempt to mask their worries. A few stray dogs wagged their tails in anticipation, yearning for a share of the jalebis.

The women wore nightgowns that barely grazed the ground, perhaps a precautionary measure to avoid stumbling and falling. Or was it a trend that had eluded Maya during her six-month-long detachment from the world? Some of the ladies, in their knee-length kurtas, salwars and dupattas, painted a contrasting picture against the sea of nightgowns.

There was one thing, however, in common—each wore a wristband with numbers on them. It appeared so familiar, yet Maya took a few minutes to recall. Looking down at her hand, she noticed the same band. Her name was emblazoned with an ID number printed beside it. She could not remember how she came to wear it; her memory was hazy. She was puzzled. Where was she? And then it struck her like an epiphany. She was in a rehabilitation centre. She could now read the letters prominently displayed on the notice board: Atma Nirbhar Mandir.

Maya rushed out of her room and ran down the stairs, two at a time. The hot jalebis were available for everyone, and no payment was required. She glanced at the cloudless, pollution-free, azure blue sky. The skies in Mumbai were not so clear. She then realized she was nestled in a village, perhaps close to the city.

EPILOGUE

Someone touched her shoulder lightly, and Shiv's warm presence broke through the fog of her thoughts. It took a moment for her to recognize him, and tears filled her eyes as she grappled with disbelief. Was this truly Shiv, or merely a figment of her imagination? Questions swirled in her mind, amplifying her confusion. How had he arrived here? What was she even doing in this place?

Her mother had always told her to pinch herself to distinguish reality from dreams. She braved the sting and reached out to touch him, feeling Shiv's warmth under her touch—a wave of overwhelming reality. This was no mirage. Desperation flooded her as she explored the contours of his arms and face, yet words eluded her, tangled in an unyielding knot that stifled her voice.

Despite the chaos in her mind, joy surged within her. It felt as if her deepest wish had been granted, as if Shiv's presence signified the universe's kindness. Impulsively, she kissed his hands and embraced him, her heart swelling with emotion. Words were insufficient; all that mattered was that she was with Shiv, and she intended to treasure every moment of this miraculous reunion.

Shiv held her close as she cried in his arms.

★

After locking Maya in his flat, Ram had visited her shared apartment once. He had informed Zahra and Shama of her condition and recommended a rehabilitation centre for her drug addiction. With Aman away for a few days, they hurriedly admitted her, with

Ram covering the costs. The centre offered single-accommodation apartments for treatment, with the option of visiting the common space whenever Maya wished. Despite the expense, Ram insisted on paying in full, possibly to protect himself if her situation was ever exposed.

Zahra and Shama had helped Maya settle in, even escorting her to a small gathering on the lawn on her first day. Ram had insisted she remain out of the public eye, citing the doctor's advice. As they sat outside, Maya, in a haze, had noticed a man staring at her intently. He had claimed to know her, but Zahra and Shama dismissed him as just another creep, instructing Maya's attendant to keep him away. They could never have imagined who he truly was.

Shiv and Tamara had separated a year earlier. He had heard Maya was in Mumbai but had been unable to gather any details from Bhai or Maa. He searched tirelessly, often dismissed as a fool by others, ultimately finding work at the rehabilitation centre. He never gave up hope. The moment Maya walked in, he had recognized her instantly, though she was in no state to recognize him. Zahra and Shama had turned him away, and the attendant had warned him they would file a complaint if he persisted.

For six months, Shiv worked without a break, determined to be involved in Maya's recovery. He managed to obtain her contact information but was too fearful to call. The doctor had declared Maya free of addiction after a month, allowing her to leave the centre. Ram had vanished from her life that day.

Each day was a new beginning for Maya.

She and Shiv married at a registry office, without any religious formalities, surrounded by Bhai, Maa and Shiv's family. Shiv's mother had overcome her alcoholism and now lived with them. They had sold their house in Ranikhet, wishing to avoid the stigma of divorce. Bhai became Shiv's close friend, and over time, Maa also warmed to Shiv.

Maya reconnected with Zahra, who had been hesitant to

visit her during her recovery. She forgave Zahra for her absence, understanding the stigma surrounding addiction. Aman had returned to his village after struggling to find work in Mumbai, and now owned a small food processing unit. Maya had called him once; he had been supportive, never giving her grief about her choices.

Though Maya had lost contact with her team members after Ram's interference, she spotted Kanya one day at a café. Maya had hesitated to approach, knowing the hurt she had caused. To her surprise, Kanya walked over, her exuberance drawing everyone's attention. Kanya had heard about Maya's journey from Zahra, and had longed to see her again.

Ram called once, but Maya firmly told him not to contact her again, threatening to expose his actions if he ever dared to. He reminded her of his financial support, but she brushed it aside.

The climax came when Tamara called one morning. She shared the news of her second marriage and expressed her happiness for Maya and Shiv's union.

It's been five years since that jalebi-filled afternoon in the garden.

Life moves on.